NO WAY OUT

Nestor didn't shoot. He wasn't going to kill me right there. This he told me as he pulled me up to my feet by my hair and forced me into the hallway. This was the part of the movie where I would have been shouting for the victim to kick and scream rather than go silently into the apartment. It always seems like a good idea, until the bad guy's fingers are laced into your hair and his gun is jammed into the small of your back. At that point, it looked like obeying him was the smartest move. Still didn't think it would help much.

Losing hope is so easy, so painless, in some ways such a relief. As soon as the door was closed behind me, I knew I was going to die....

For Charlie,
Hope you like it.

Steven

THE
CONCRETE
MAZE

STEVEN TORRES

LEISURE BOOKS NEW YORK CITY

This book is for Damaris,
my rose, my dawn, my ocean wave.

A LEISURE BOOK®

August 2007

Published by

Dorchester Publishing Co., Inc.
200 Madison Avenue
New York, NY 10016

ISBN-10: 0-8439-5969-X
ISBN-13: 978-0-8439-5969-7

Visit us on the web at www.dorchesterpub.com.

THE
CONCRETE
MAZE

DAY ONE

Night

Luis Ramos, my uncle, left Puerto Rico when the U.S. Army took him out of a college classroom and sent him to boot camp and from there to Vietnam. In Vietnam, he came under fire a half-dozen times, once in a real firefight that lasted an entire day. He had medals, a knife wound and two bullet wounds. During his tour, he killed a man who was standing only three feet away, shooting him in the face. He shot another man, a VC soldier sitting in a tree. Others he might have killed or possibly didn't; he fired his weapon when fired upon or when told to, usually at some tree line or some clump of grass that an officer thought was particularly offensive. With his comrades he once burned a small village of empty huts. He says there was no one in the village when they got there, and though they searched for hours, they found no hidden weapons, no hidden anything. An hour's walk back toward base, a

1

grenade landed in the line somewhere behind him killing one and wounding two. That was one of the times he was told to fire into a group of trees; he's sure that at least one tree died.

After Vietnam, Tio Luis, the one who always gave me a dollar when I visited and who put a ten dollar bill in each of my birthday and Christmas cards even after I turned twenty, went back to Puerto Rico. That lasted six months. He never finished his degree. He moved to New York City, worked as a building super, then as a building manager, and made good money. He went on hunting trips every fall. He even took me twice. He was good at it, as the wall in his living room could attest. It was heavy with all sorts of mounted animals or their heads. He was a man's man if ever there was one—fixing his own car, the boilers of the buildings he managed, and my bicycle when I was seven. He removed drug dealers from one of his buildings with a baseball bat.

Now he was in my mother's dining room, his hands on my shoulders, looking me in the eyes as directly as I would let him, and crying.

I had been playing video games in my apartment; it's my only vice. That and Twinkies. My mother opened the door at the top of the stairs (without knocking) and called down for me. I paused the game and went up.

Tio Luis walked up to me as soon as I entered, wiping his eyes. He embraced me, then held me out at arm's length.

"She's gone," he said, and I knew exactly who he was talking about without him having to say more.

His wife, Titi Clarita, was the only other woman in his life, and she was at the dining room table, trying to smile at me though tears had run her mascara down to her chin.

His daughter Jasmine, my cousin, had turned thirteen a few months earlier; I had gone to her birthday party. She had started giving all the troubles that teenagers give—staying out late, talking back, cigarettes in her jacket pocket that were being held for a friend whose name she couldn't remember, and coming home with alcohol on her breath more than once. All of this from a girl who was struggling to reach five feet in height.

"What happened?" I asked. I was sure I knew the general outline of the story before he even opened his mouth.

"I dropped her off at the skate ring this afternoon. When I went to pick her up, she wasn't there."

There was no point in trying to correct his pronunciation of "skating rink." It was nine in the evening. The Skate Key, as the place was called, would be open until midnight or more. It catered to the teens of the Bronx, and was usually as full as the fire codes allowed on a Friday night.

"Do you want to go over there?" I asked. Of course he wanted to go over if he hadn't been there already. It turned out that he had, but he wanted me to give it a try. First, he said, he wanted to tell me all about what had already been done to find Jasmine. I ushered him out of the house. I knew what had been done without him having to tell me. He had gone to the skating rink to pick her up, waited a while, gone

3

in, looked for her, asked the manager or the ticket salesperson or one of the two security guards whether they had seen her, and been told a flat no. Then he had called one of her friends. All this Tio Luis told me, but there wasn't a step of it that wasn't familiar to me already. I had never learned how to skate, but I had a lot of cousins and several of them had pulled the exact same stunt; usually they were hanging out with friends. One of them was found in a pizzeria two blocks away; one had been brought home by police because she had tried to get onto a city bus through the back door, evading the fare; no doubt Jasmine was watching a movie at a friend's house or was maybe on a park bench in some dark corner necking.

Why go to the Skate Key? To the teens there, Tio Luis was just an old dude with hassles for them. I was a young dude with hassles, so they might give me a minute more of their attention than they had given him.

Tio Luis parked about a block from the Skate Key; it was about as close as one could get with Tio Luis's ten-year-old Cadillac—stylish when he got it, now just big. I told him to wait in the car, but he insisted on going with me, bleary eyed as he was.

"You got to pay," one of the security guards said as we went in. The music was so loud, he had to shout, and we still had to have him repeat himself. Tio Luis started to dig in his pockets, but I put a hand on his arm to stop him.

"We're looking for a girl," I said, and pulled out a picture Tio Luis had given me in the car. The guard rolled his eyes. He probably hadn't heard me, but he waved us in. Chances were that parents with photos were a daily nuisance at the Skate Key.

I started by showing the photo to a cluster of kids close to Jasmine's age. None of them knew her and they certainly didn't want to know me.

"Please," my uncle said to one of the girls. He was on the verge of tears, and she turned her back on him to avoid laughing in his face.

The next group of kids had one boy who said he had seen Jasmine. His girlfriend wanted to know why he noticed her out of all the people in the place. He shrugged.

"She left with some guy," he said. Then he and the rest of his group went onto the skating floor.

"Some guy," Tio Luis said. "Who?"

The boy shrugged again and was on his way. I held Tio Luis back from trying to get on the skating rink.

Another group hadn't seen her and clearly wanted to be left alone. We were turning from them when the Skate Key manager came up from behind us and put a hand on my shoulder. He had a security guard with him.

"Gentlemen," he said. Nothing else, just "gentlemen." Apparently, that's code for "Get the hell out."

I held up the photo. The manager, a man of about forty with a goatee and a ponytail, rolled his eyes behind tinted glasses.

"I've never seen her," he said.

"Then maybe we should keep asking," I said.

More eye rolling. The manager—STU, said the

name patch on his gray shirt—took the photo from my hand and gave it a hard look. He wanted to know her. He wanted to be able to say exactly when she arrived and when she left and with whom and to where. None of this out of kindness or sympathy but because he wanted some way to get us out of there without the trouble of police. Not that he would call them; that would be stupid, but that we might call them. No better way to clear out the Skate Key on a Friday night than to have the police asking questions on our behalf.

"I really haven't seen her," Stu said after a half minute.

"But I dropped her off at three," my uncle said. "In the afternoon," he added to clarify matters.

Stu took a look around his establishment. There were probably three hundred kids or more. Among them, there were a few dozen men who were a bit older than the rest of the crowd. Perverts who wanted to see teen girls in tight jeans fall on their asses.

"I don't know what to tell you," Stu said. "Ask your questions, but try not to disturb the kids too much. We don't want to have a problem."

He meant that he didn't want to have the security guards escort us out.

We showed the photo to a few other groups, but no one, even those who took the time to look us in the eye, could do more than say she had been there and that now she wasn't.

Back in the Cadillac, Tio Luis wanted to know what the next step was. I told him to drive me to the house of the friend Jasmine had gone to the Skate Key with. She had claimed on the phone that she had left early and didn't know where Jasmine went. In person, she might have more information.

"And if she doesn't?" Tio Luis asked.

"She will," I promised.

He turned on the car and was crying again. I looked out the passenger window. It was hard seeing him so broken up.

There are reasons for my uncle's tears. It isn't just that his daughter is missing. That is bad, but since she was only late by two hours or so, it hadn't reached tragedy yet. The problem, I think, was that Jasmine was missing in New York City. For many older Puerto Ricans, New York is a great place to make money but a terrible place to raise children. Too much crime, not enough shame. *Sin verguenzas*. Children were too quickly corrupted, a process which, in the old country, took longer.

This was probably true back when Tio Luis was young, but in 1992, things had changed. Big cities in PR were as bad as any in the states. Maybe the moral fiber of the entire world was being ripped, torn, soiled. That wouldn't have helped Tio Luis shedding his tears at the wheel of his car.

Jasmine's friend, Clarissa, lived in an apartment building in the Morris Park area of the Bronx. The neighborhood was supposed to be one of the better ones in the borough, but there were three young men sharing a forty-ounce beer on the steps in front.

"Yo," one of them said as I picked my way up the

stairs. The tone told me that he wanted trouble, desired it as though trouble would be the perfect way to wash down the beer, or to start a night of fun.

I kept walking, pulled on the door, found it was locked. There was a panel of intercom buttons. Someone would have to buzz me in. I pushed three or four at random.

"You know him?" one guy asked another. They were standing, the bottle of beer was being held defensively, away from me, to make sure it didn't get hurt no matter what else happened.

"I'm Tony's friend," I said. I smiled. Smiles defuse a lot of bad situations. It seemed to make these guys angry.

"Tony who?" the "Yo" guy asked. "There ain't no Tony here." He was young, black, thin, and tall. He wore a Knicks jersey and jeans, and his face told me he was angry though it didn't say anything about why.

"The chubby one," I said. Finally, someone buzzed the door open, and I went in. I could hear the intercom crackle with a "Who?" as the door closed behind me.

I headed straight down the hall, found the elevator, and jabbed for it to open. My last look out the glass front doors saw the three guys settling back down to drinking, Yo-man still staring at me.

Clarissa lived on the fourth floor. It was a little past ten. It would have been bad to disturb a sleeping family. No chance they would want to help if I got them out of bed. The TV was blaring through the apartment door, so I rang the bell. After a minute and a second ring, Clarissa opened the door partway; the chain was still on.

She had no idea who I was. Her sweatshirt told me her name in a large script font. Clarissa was thirteen and would one day be beautiful. She smiled openly though she wore braces.

"Clarissa," I asked.

She didn't answer me. It was clear I wasn't Publishers Clearing House; I also wasn't flashing a badge.

"I'm Jasmine's cousin, Marc. We need to know where she is."

Clarissa's smile turned into a deer-in-the-headlights look.

"I don't know where she is," she said. I believed her that far.

"Okay, but who was she with?"

"Me."

"She was with a guy . . ."

"Carlos?"

"Okay," I said. "Carlos who?"

"I don't know his name. Just Carlos. He lives in Manhattan."

"Where?"

"He comes in the Two train," Clarissa said. I could tell she was trying to be helpful at least to a point. Telling me about the #2 train didn't do much. It's the closest one to the Skate Key and anyone coming by train would have taken it eventually though it might have required a series of transfers. Finding a Carlos in Manhattan was like finding a Bob in Kansas.

"What does he look like?" I asked. I could hear the scrape of a chair being moved and slippered footsteps coming.

Clarissa shrugged.

"Tall? Short? Twenty? Fifteen?"

"Who's that at the door, Clarissa?" A mother's voice from a few feet behind her.

"Twenty," Clarissa said. "Your height, thinner. Fade. A cut in the eyebrow," she said, making a slicing motion with her fingernail through her own right eyebrow.

"Dominican, Puerto Rican?" I asked. Clarissa's mother stepped up right behind her.

"Who are you?" she asked.

"I'm Marc, Jasmine's cousin," I said. I was hoping this would open the door for me to get in at least a couple more questions.

"And what do you want here?" the mother continued. She wasn't happy, maybe five seconds from slamming the door.

"Jasmine is missing, and I—"

"That's your problem," the mother said and *slam* went the door.

"*Boricua*," Clarissa said through the door. Boricua, a Puerto Rican term meaning "Puerto Rican."

"Dark skin or light?" I asked the door, but there was no answer. The TV got louder still.

At the front door again, the three guys were waiting for me, standing at the bottom of the steps. Mr.

Yo was standing at the center, the other two guys leaning on the railings on either side of the stairs. Mr. Yo had an empty beer bottle in hand, the one they had been sharing. Another forty-ounce bottle was at the lips of the guy on my right.

"What you got to say now?" Mr. Yo said. He held the beer bottle back as though it were a secret weapon he was going to spring on me at just the right time. Standing three steps above him, I did what came to mind. I kicked out with my right foot and caught him right in the groin. He doubled over; I came down a step and gave him a hard shove to one side. His head hit the ground first, and I felt sorry for him for a second. I looked to his friends. They hadn't moved an inch. Apparently they were not those kind of friends.

I hadn't kicked him that hard, but Mr. Yo didn't want to get back up, so I walked toward the Cadillac. I moved as fast as I could without breaking into a run. I was hoping Tio Luis had the car on already so we could peel out. I didn't look back though I would have loved to have known if one of the guys was going to throw the empty bottle at me, or make a run at my back, or aim a gun.

Tio Luis was rubbing his eyes when I got in the car. He hadn't noticed the little tussle. He turned on the car and made sure I put on my seat belt.

"Move the car," I said.

"Where are we going now?" he asked.

"Out of here."

He pulled out onto the street. I took a look back

11

once we were moving. Mr. Yo was getting up under his own power. The other two were sharing the bottle. None of them were looking in my direction.

Stu with the ponytail at the Skate Key had no idea who my twenty-year-old Puerto Rican Carlos from Manhattan was. So he said, anyway. The guard at the door as we were leaving, the same guy who had tried to make us pay our first time there, did know.

"Carlos Valle," he said. "He's a bad dude. Lives on 135th or 136th in Manhattan. Maybe on Broadway. Something like that. Not too far from City College." I had graduated from City College so I knew the neighborhood.

"What makes him a bad dude?" I asked.

"Drugs. Maybe. I'm not too sure. He got the wrong friends, I can tell you that. Gang people. You don't want to mess with him."

"You know what building he lives in?"

The security guard squinted, searching his brain.

"I know he goes to Tato's grocery store. He has to live near it. About a year ago, I saw him give this little boy a beat down. Stomped him. They had to pull him off. That boy was about ten years old."

"What did the boy do?"

"Didn't see that part, but what's the difference?" the guard asked.

"Light skin or dark?" I asked.

"Pretty light. Short hair. I don't live in his neighborhood anymore, but he comes around here every few weeks."

"Any car?"

"That I don't know about. When he comes here, he takes the train."

"Gun?"

"Never saw him with one, but . . ."

I didn't really have any more questions about Carlos Valle.

"Did you see what time they left?"

The guard shook his head.

Tio Luis and I started to walk away; the guard called me back.

"Every time he's here, he picks up a different girl," he said in a whisper. This could be good or bad news. If Carlos got tired of girls and let them go every week or so, then Jasmine would be back. But what if Carlos was putting these girls to work? Prostitutes, maybe, or drug mules? Carlos might be leaving with different girls, but the guard didn't say what happened to them. It seemed that the guard had separated me from Tio Luis to give me this bit. I figured he thought bad things happened to them.

"What do you think we should do now?" Tio Luis asked when we were back out on the street.

"I think we go to that neighborhood, see if we can get a little more information."

"Maybe we'll see her," Tio Luis said. He had hope written all over his face. There was no more crying. He could see an end to this hunt. I wasn't so sure. Carlos Valle might have taken her to his house or a friend's house or any place in between. He might have drugged her, raped her, or killed her. Or left her at a bus stop with a token. I didn't see them roaming the streets of upper Manhattan, hand in hand, searching for a late-night slice of pizza.

My uncle phoned his wife at home. Jasmine hadn't called or come in. No news from anywhere. It was about eleven at night.

In the area of City College there are several businesses that are open late. I asked Tio Luis to take me to Tato's grocery store on 136th and St. Nicholas. Tato's store, like many in the area, had a counter space surrounded by thick Plexiglas. A spring shut door let Tato, or whoever was behind the counter, out easily, but it couldn't be kicked open. There was a little portion of counter where the Plexiglas is layered to let customers place their goods and the money to pay. Tato could reach around the Plexiglas on his side, bag the groceries, and pass back change. A thief could run out with an item or two, but the beers were in the back, and getting to the cash register was near impossible.

I went in and put a Pepsi and a pack of Twinkies on the counter with the money for them. Tato bagged them while talking on a mobile phone. I stayed where I was until he nodded to me; that was his sign that he wanted to know what else I wanted.

"Phone book," I said. He thought about it a moment as though there might be some trick behind my request. He handed me a ratty copy.

I quickly looked for Carlos Valle in Manhattan; none in the neighborhood. One about twenty blocks north, another fifteen blocks south. I handed the book back; Tato was done with his call.

"Do you know Carlos Valle?" I asked.

Tato put the book away and turned back to me.

"I don't talk about customers," he said.

"Do you know where he lives?"

"What did I just say?"

"How about this girl?" I showed the photo. Tato looked through the Plexiglas.

"Never saw her." There was no reason to think he was lying.

I surveyed the pedestrian traffic on St. Nicholas. It was fairly light at near midnight, not more than twenty people in sight.

"Anything?" Tio Luis asked.

"He comes to this store. The owner hasn't seen Jasmine."

"Is he sure?"

I ignored the question.

"How much money do you have on you?"

Tio Luis pulled out a tiny wad of small bills, singles, fives, a twenty mixed in.

"I can get more," he said. "There's a bank we passed a block up."

We went. There were two homeless men waiting to hassle people as they came out with fists full of cash. I waited outside and Tio Luis got out six hundred. It was what the ATM allowed.

"Spare change for a veteran?" one of the homeless guys asked. He was young.

"Veteran of the drug war?" I asked. He smiled.

"That's right, my man."

The other homeless guy sat on the pavement. He was pretty much out of it.

"Ten dollars for a little information."

The veteran scratched his beard. He was a black man, his beard thick and knotting.

"What's the information?" he asked.

"We're looking for Carlos Valle, young guy, twenty, Puerto Rican . . ."

"I know him," the veteran said. He was keeping his voice down and the look on his face told me to do the same thing. I did.

"Well?" I said.

He looked at his partner who looked to be asleep already.

"Listen," he said. "If I tell you about this guy, I got to move, you understand? You're not the police or you would have pulled his file. Hell, if you was police, you'd know all about him. He's got one of those warning labels on him. 'The Surgeon General says Carlos'll kill you,' like that."

In saying all of this, the veteran had been leading us away from his partner in a slow amble.

"Twenty dollars," he said. "And I'll give you his building address."

Tio Luis was digging into his pocket again. I stopped him.

"Thirty and you take us there," I said.

He scratched his beard some more.

"He'll kill me if he finds out," the veteran said.

"Forty," I said.

"I'll still be dead."

"Look," Tio Luis said. He held out the photo of Jasmine. "She's my daughter, and I'm looking for her."

"Aw man, I knew it was something like that. Forget it. I don't know anything. I was just hoping you guys would slip me a little cash." He started to walk back to his post at the bank door.

"Fifty," I said. "Just point out the building from the corner. If we find his name on the intercom panel, you get your money and we'll drop you off anywhere you want."

"Drop me off?" he said like it was the dumbest thing he had ever heard.

"If you want to get out of here."

"How about you give me half now, I tell you the address here, and you come back and pay me the rest when you check it out?"

Tio Luis got out twenty-five, handed it over, and we got our address. There were two mothers and two children on the stoop. The mothers were young and Latina, maybe in their midtwenties. The children were each nearing ten years of age, I guessed.

"Carlos Valle lives here?" I asked.

"Who?" one of the mothers asked. This fake hearing disability was the first step to shutting us out completely. No one wanted trouble with Carlos. Except for this woman's son.

"Carlos, ma," he told her. "Carlos is on the third floor. 3C."

His mother reached out across the steps, grabbed him by his ear and yanked hard, pulling him to her. When he opened his mouth to complain, she shut it for him with a backhand slap. Dr. Spock would not have approved.

"3C?" I said.

"We don't know nothing." This came from both mothers.

"Have you seen her?" Tio Luis said, again with the photo. "She's my daughter."

Neither woman looked at the photograph.

"Mister, you should have kept her inside," one of them said. She got up, which was the cue for all of them to get inside.

The front door closed behind them and though it was made of glass, just like in Clarissa's building, someone would have to buzz us in. C.VALLE had a button. 3C like the boy said. I didn't think pushing that button would get us very far. Tio Luis tried it anyway. Nothing. A minute later, as we were standing on the steps trying to think what the next move should be, a tenant came out and we went in.

The building was only five stories high and had no elevator. The stairs had a faint odor of urine, which is better than the strong odor of some of the other buildings in the area. There was graffiti on the walls that had obviously been there for a while, a sign that whoever ran the building didn't much care. The door to apartment 3C looked like all the others—painted a shiny mud-brown and with a peephole, but the brown was painted onto sheet metal instead of wood. This said one thing to me— drugs. Drugs told me guns and people willing to use them. Tio Luis banged on it with his fist. When no one answered, he banged again and again. Someone from down the hall opened his door a crack and looked at us.

"Take a hint," he said. He looked like he had been sleeping.

"Have you seen him tonight," Tio Luis asked.

"No. But if he doesn't answer, he's not there, no?"

Tio Luis pulled out the picture again.

"Have you seen—?"

The man shut his door and the lock sounded loudly through the hallway.

"What do we do now?" Tio Luis asked.

They had left the skating rink hours earlier and would have been there if they hadn't made any stops. They had detoured. Where they were or when they'd be back was impossible to tell. But eventually he would return, and she might still be with him. There were a few options open to us. It looked like we had the right apartment. We could wait as long as it took, we could come back in the morning, or we could call the police and have them wait. I took too long in answering.

"We should go to the police," Tio Luis said.

"That's not going to help," I told him.

There was more behind what I said than just cynicism. Police don't look for teenagers who are missing just a few hours. They would tell us to go home and come back when it's been twenty-four hours. I explained this.

"But she's been kidnapped," my uncle said.

"She went willingly."

There was no fun in saying this to Tio Luis. He didn't need a devil's advocate—thoughts of evil already filled his mind.

19

"Then what?" Tio Luis asked.

I knew he wasn't going to go for the option where we leave and return refreshed in the morning, but I threw it out there. It was the sane thing to do, I think, but parents are not sane that way.

Tio Luis seemed to think about it for a moment, though I knew it had been rejected as soon as it came off my lips.

"We'll wait here," Tio Luis said.

We arranged that I would wait right in front of 3C while my uncle went out to pay the homeless man the rest of what was owed him.

"What if this Carlos guy has a gun?" I asked.

"If he shows you a gun, you back down, say you're sorry, say you'll never bother him again. Then we go to the police and they have a reason to arrest him—brandishing." The only time my uncle had ever had a scrape with the law was for that exact charge. The police showed up, found the proper license and permit, warned him, and left. That was long ago. New York City was a lot tougher on gun violations now.

It sounded like a good enough plan. Of course, Carlos may not have been in the mood to brandish. He might be in the mood to just start shooting. That's why some people buy guns in the first place.

My uncle came back after about twenty minutes of searching for the veteran. He didn't find him.

"He's probably out looking for a hit," I said.

"Probably," was my uncle's answer. I looked at him and there certainly wasn't any concern for what might have happened to the veteran on his face. His thoughts were for Jasmine and himself. As I sat on the hallway floor next to him, I thought about this. I understood that for his daughter he was willing to sacrifice the homeless man who had helped us and probably every other homeless man in the world. Tio Luis—soldier, hunter, man's man—was, for the first time in my thinking, a dangerous man. Dangerous to the veteran, dangerous to Carlos Valle, and dangerous to me.

We took turns going to a bathroom in an all-night grocery store after Tato's had closed at two A.M. We had to pay for the privilege, but the fee was small and the need was great. Neither Tio Luis nor I were comfortable with the idea of going in the street or in an alley.

"Only bums and dogs do their necessities in the street," Tio Luis said. It was something my mother had told me as a child, and I wondered who had taught it to whom.

We spent an hour at a time saying nothing, just looking at the ceiling or counting the tiny black-and-white tiles that made patterns of interlocking boxes on the floor. When my wristwatch beeped each hour, we looked at each other and smiled, maybe said something. Nothing much about our chances of walking out of the building with Jasmine in tow. Nothing at all about what Jasmine might be doing or what might be happening to her.

At six in the morning, there was still no sign of Carlos or Jasmine. A man came down the stairs in jogging clothes, looked at us seated on the hallway floor, and kept going. Probably thought we were homeless. Worse, he might have thought we were early morning customers for Carlos.

"What do you want to do now?" I asked. Most likely Tio Luis could see nothing wrong with continuing the vigil. We'd already gone all night; might as well stay all day, too. He surprised me.

"Let's go home," he said.

Tio Luis dropped me off at home. At his house, Titi Clarita would still be whining like a wounded animal. I suppose a missing child feels exactly like that: a pain in the most basic part of the soul.

My mother informed me that Titi Clarita had called a dozen of Jasmine's friends. No results. Nobody had heard from her, seen her, knew who Carlos Valle was, or could give any idea where Jasmine might have gone after leaving the Skate Key. My mother's report was probably an almost word-for-word repeat of Titi Clarita's conversations, but I could only hear a little of what she had to say. My bed was calling me, and it spoke louder.

I had just fallen into a deep, soundless sleep when I was woken up again.

DAY TWO

Morning

I had been in bed for about ninety minutes. The sleep was dreamless but not enough. Tio Luis had been in his house even less time, and could not have even seen his bed with his wife needing comfort and with so much to say between them. But he was back at my door and ready for more hours on the search.

"He's a drug dealer," Tio Luis said. "He can't just take a day of vacation. He has customers that need their morning fix."

It made sense, but then for Tio Luis, anything would have made sense if it gave him the slightest hope of getting Jasmine back. He gassed up the car and made the drive into Manhattan again. I rode with the window down and my arm out in the breeze. Tio Luis, on a summer day, had on an army jacket, not his from the war, but a winter one he had bought at some thrift shop. The last name on the chest pocket was Ruiz. This scared me. A coat on in the summer meant you're sick or you were carrying something. I had no doubt Tio Luis had a handgun—as a building manager who had to collect rents and with his veteran background, it would not have been that difficult. He also had at least five rifles and shotguns. Plenty of ammunition. Only God and Tio Luis could be sure what was in the trunk. It was going to stay that way.

I had worked five months clerking in a law firm, but I knew enough not to dig for answers I didn't really want to know. If he told me we were going to execute Carlos, I'd still have to ride in the car, I'd still have to help; I was family. Best not to think about it.

We parked a block from the apartment building. Tio Luis didn't head for the trunk when we got out; I took that as a good sign.

He strode purposefully, his head high, his shoulders back like he knew he was going to be coming back to the car in a few minutes with his daughter, hand in hand, smiling.

We got into the building easily enough; a lady was coming out with her baby stroller, and we held the door for her. Tio Luis helped her get the thing down the front stairs, and we went in. Same urine smell; a little sunlight coming through dirty stairwell windows. No doubt a stronger sun would have raised a greater smell.

We banged on 3C. To my surprise, there was a shuffle. Someone came to the peephole and saw me; Uncle Luis stood a few feet to my right. His hand, I noticed, was behind him.

"What you want?" someone shouted through the door.

"What do you think I want?" I answered back. I held a twenty up in front of my face. I'd never visited a drug den before, but I imagined one didn't go off naming purchase items in the hallway.

The lock came undone; the door opened a crack, the chain was still up, and the biggest man I'd ever seen up close looked down at me. He was wearing a pair of khaki shorts, nothing else. He certainly wasn't Carlos.

"Do I know you?" he asked. The words sounded like a threat.

"Is Carlos there?"

"I asked if I know you." The hand that had been behind the door was visible now, and it had a gun, a big one, but dwarfed by the hand that held it.

"You don't know me," I said. Living in the Bronx, I'd seen guns before. They just weren't usually aimed at me. My heart was beating about as hard as it could. Any harder, and I would not be able to talk.

"You don't know me. My name is Marc. I'm looking for Jasmine."

"I thought you wanted Carlos."

"I want Jasmine. They told me she was with Carlos."

"Who said that?"

By this time, after all this back-and-forth, I figured out the game that was being played.

"Forget it," I said. I turned away and headed for the stairs.

"Yo, don't just walk away," the giant said. He pulled the door against its chain and put his gun hand out as though he was going to shoot to stop me. I kept walking.

"Hey," the man said. Tio Luis looked lost, but he went down the stairs.

"What's the matter?" he asked one floor down.

"Let's get out to the street," I said. "He was just buying time."

When we got to the street there was nothing to say that Jasmine or Carlos or both had been on the block, but I was sure of it.

"We missed them," I said.

"Who?"

"Carlos or Jasmine or both."

"What do you mean, 'we missed them'?"

"That guy up there with the gun," I said. "You think he was talking with me back and forth just to pass the time of day? If he was serious, he would have sent me to hell in two seconds. He knew we were coming. He knew what we were looking for and he was stalling."

Tio Luis looked up and down the street for the least sign of commotion. I suppose he was hoping someone would give him a sign of where his daughter had gone.

"Let's go," I said.

"Where?"

"Anywhere where we're not just standing on the sidewalk looking at each other."

We headed back toward the car. After a few yards, I looked up to the third floor of the building.

There was the giant, at an open window with bars in front, smiling at us.

I was a little bothered that when Carlos's friend or partner pulled out a gun and aimed it at me, then put his gun hand out into the hallway, getting it closer to me, Tio Luis did nothing. I didn't doubt he could have pulled out a gun of his own, but he didn't even twitch. I saw him out of the corner of my eye, and he was clearly waiting for me to draw out some useful information, and it wouldn't have mattered how I got it—if I paid for it with blood, he would thank me at my funeral.

In the car, I put my head back.

"Do you have a gun?" I asked.

Tio Luis paused a moment before his answer.

"It wouldn't help to get into a shoot-out back there," he said.

He was probably right. A shoot-out would have made me defenseless and put me in the middle. I don't at all think that was what he was thinking, but it would have been a waste of time to make an issue of it. I closed my eyes. From where we were, we could see anyone approaching the building. Tio Luis told me I could go to sleep if I wanted; he would watch out for Jasmine. I took him up on his offer.

Jasmine was a good girl whose breasts and hips had started to develop in the past few months and this gave her new rights and responsibilities. With a figure came the duty to watch it or flaunt it. Womanhood requires the woman's vigilance. This all came to Jasmine before she was ready. Had she been ready, there'd be no Carlos in her life.

Yet, for all the evidence that she was unprepared for her new position as an endowed young woman, she was smart. She had great grades in school. She liked her algebra class. She had just started listening to classical music. She followed science news, telling me stories by phone about new discoveries among the stars and planets. There was a hope that she might go to college and finish and be the first in her family to do that. Who could tell what the limits to her abilities and potential were? She might one day be Doctor Jasmine Ramos.

Beauty, brains, and didn't she have a good soul? Hadn't she insisted on bringing home a stray dog just a year ago? Or was it a cat? Didn't she go to Mass and confession? Didn't she cry for the pains of people she had never met—sufferers in Ethiopia and children picking through the garbage heaps of São Paolo?

These were my thoughts while the sun rose and Tio Luis kept watch on the building and the street. Carlos himself interrupted my thinking.

"You guys been in my shit," he said. I opened my eyes and there he was squatting at my side, staring in my face from inches away. Short hair, light skin, twenty years old. Necklace with his name in a gold plate. "I don't know you, and you sure as hell don't know me. Step off, or there's gonna be problems, I guarantee you."

He sounded tough. I'm sure my face registered no emotion. It never does when I've just woken up.

But I knew he could make the problems he promised. If not him, then his friend in 3C.

Tio Luis reached into his jacket. The move made Carlos nervous, and he stood up and to one side, reaching at the waistband at the small of his back. Tio Luis pulled out his photo of Jasmine; Carlos pulled out a revolver.

"I want her back," Tio Luis said. Carlos lowered his gun. I wasn't at that moment positive that was the safest thing for him to do.

"I don't have her. Look at me. Where do you think I have her? Want to check my pockets?"

Small as she was, she could not have been in Carlos's pockets.

"Where is she?" Tio Luis asked. He sounded calm and I wondered if the calm came from the fact that Carlos would have to shoot through me to get at him.

Carlos smiled.

"She's all right," he said.

"Where?"

Without putting his gun back in hiding, Carlos started to walk away.

"Where is she?" Tio Luis yelled at his back.

"I'll tell her to call you," Carlos said, turning to us for the second it took to say, "She'll call if she wants to."

With that taunt, I thought Tio Luis was going to lose it. I was ready to grab him if he tried to get out of the car. As he got close to his building, Carlos finally put away his gun and did a light jog up the steps, using his keys to get in. I craned my neck to look up at the window of the apartment. The giant was sitting at the window still, gun in hand.

"Yeah, I saw him too," Tio Luis said. He put the car in gear and drove.

At Tio Luis's house, Titi Clarita was still crying. She wouldn't stop until Jasmine was home. This, I guess, was her job. It was past noon when we got there. She had made another round of calls to Jasmine's friends, spoke to some parents, shared the information she had, got nowhere.

We knew Carlos was as bad as advertised. He knew where Jasmine was, but didn't have her at the moment. Maybe she was with a friend of his. What were the options, Titi Clarita wanted to know. I could only think of two—follow Carlos around every hour of the day or get the police involved. Maybe the brandishing charge would help; plenty of that to accuse people of.

We had lunch. Titi Clarita needed something to do to relieve her stress, and she was a great cook. Then we left for the precinct in Carlos's neighborhood.

Like most precincts in the city, the 36th was overworked and the building showed it. On the street outside, squad cars and the personal cars of the officers were parked in no order; inside was official drab. The flyers and memos posted on the bulletin board in the reception area overlapped each other. There were several others at the front desk including one man who had been arrested and was escorted by two uniformed officers. It took fifteen minutes for the reception desk officer to get to us. Tio Luis did the speaking; after a minute, the officer raised his hand to stop him. He looked at me.

"What's your story?" he asked.

"Moral support," I said.

"Ah. Moral support takes a seat," he said, pointing to a row of plastic chairs beneath the bulletin board. From the seat I took, I heard only one or two words of what Tio Luis had to say. The officer pulled out a form, started filling it out, picked up a phone, called someone. A few minutes later, Tio Luis escorted Titi Clarita to the plastic seats with me.

"I'm going with the police," he said. "Identify the giant." He left with two uniformed officers; Titi Clarita and I consoled each other. As we waited, another of the seats was taken by a young man who talked to me about how the older generation, by which he meant his father, could not be taught all the laws of New York City, especially those concerning cockfights. He was waiting to hear about his father, who was being held for arraignment. "Why is cockfighting illegal?" he asked. "We eat chickens anyway." I didn't have an answer for him. In fact, I didn't have a single word for him, but that didn't stop him.

Tio Luis came back with the uniformed officers, went to the front desk with them, waited as they made a call, then, after a few words, waved Titi Clarita and I over.

"We're going to see a detective," he said in a whisper. "About Jasmine."

"What about the brandishing," I asked.

"They weren't there."

We went upstairs to a big office room with about eight desks; our officer guide brought us to one desk and told us to wait. We did while he went back downstairs.

The detective—M. HAMILTON, a nameplate told us—wasn't there and we wound up waiting five minutes with the eyes of several other detectives and officers on us. Probably thought M. Hamilton's Bic pens weren't safe.

"What can I do for you?"

The phrase was appropriate, but the voice was tired and clearly would have preferred if we said there was nothing to be done. M. Hamilton—we were never given a first name—was in his fifties, overweight, and with hair slicked back and shiny. He wore suspenders and a shoulder holster and he smelled of cigars. Tio Luis looked at me before starting. M. Hamilton saw the look Tio Luis gave, a look that said he didn't think M. Hamilton was up to the job of finding Jasmine, or any other job. The detective jabbed a finger at my uncle.

"Anyone want to fill me in on the details?"

Tio Luis explained everything quickly and clearly, starting with going to pick up Jasmine the night before.

"Did you report her missing last night?" the detective asked.

"I thought I had to wait twenty-four hours," Tio Luis said.

"Is that a no?"

"I did not report her."

Tio Luis told that we had figured out who was last seen with her and where he lived and all about the brandishing issue and how that had been dealt with up to that time.

In all of this, M. Hamilton had not taken any notes. He fiddled with a pencil, but never put it to paper.

"So what you're telling me is that the brandishing thing is being worked, right?"

"The officer said he would be going back over there before the shift ended," Tio Luis answered.

The detective thought a minute, scratched his scalp, then sat up in his seat, pencil hovering over a notepad.

"Now what's the address of this skating place?" he said. Tio Luis gave it. M. Hamilton threw his pencil in the air and let it fall onto the desktop.

"People. This is a Bronx matter. In case you didn't notice, when you crossed the bridge, you came into Manhattan. Go to your local precinct, and get them to help you," he said. He leaned over his desk as though he were about to set himself to doing some real work now that enough of his time had been wasted. Titi Clarita could not take his indifference.

"Look. Mister. We need your help. Our daughter is missing. We know the name of the man who took her. We know his address. We did half of your work for you. We need you now to go in and get her for us. We need you to talk to him. We . . ."

M. Hamilton wasn't having it.

"You people," he said. It was a statement, not the start of one. "You people. You think you did half the work? Get out of here and do the rest. You got his address? What do you need me for?"

"You have the badge and the gun," I said. I wasn't as calm as I would have liked to have been, but I never did like bullies. My aunt and uncle were over a barrel and M. Hamilton was trying to stuff them both in.

"That's right I got a badge and a gun. And if I was going to use them to track down every Puerto Rican girl who's going out with a drug dealer, I'd never catch any real criminals. Now you people just go on over to see this Carlos guy. Or better yet, go back to the Bronx and wait for her; she'll come back to you in a few months with a little Pablito."

For a split second, I had the thought of clearing M. Hamilton's desk off onto the floor, nameplate and all. It would have been a dramatic flourish, but a terrible thing to have to admit to my cell mate in Rikers. The moment passed with Titi Clarita pulling at my arm. She was a whipped dog. Tio Luis was even more whipped. Of all the things they had expected, incompetence or indifference were the worst. They certainly never thought that M. Hamilton would actively dislike them just for the accidents of birth like skin color and ethnicity. We walked out, but as soon as I got to the hallway, I turned back.

"M. Hamilton," I called out. This got the attention of the squad room. "You can't tell good people from bad, and you would rather help a drug dealer like Carlos Valle than a war veteran like my uncle. You know what that makes you?"

M. Hamilton waved me off like he would a buzzing fly.

"An asshole," I said. A fair assessment.

"Hey, kid," I heard the detective say, but the door was swinging behind me already, my aunt and uncle were on the stairs, and we were headed out. If he wanted to detain me for exercising my First Amendment rights, he'd have to chase me or dial down to the front desk. He'd have to explain what I had said and why I had said it, and, if it were to go to court as a charge of some kind, he'd have to prove beyond a reasonable doubt that he wasn't an asshole. I didn't think he had the energy for any of this, and I was right. All this analysis of the situation, however, came after the fact, once I was in the backseat of Tio Luis's Cadillac.

What were the chances that Carlos and his giant friend would be back when the officers pounded on the door of 3C at 3:30 P.M. or so, right before the end of their shift? In fact, now that M. Hamilton had been so publicly, though justly, insulted, what were the chances that the officers would be going back to the apartment at all? Everyone knows when the shifts change; all good street dealers and prostitutes must pay attention to the shift changes, I reasoned. This was their bread and butter.

Tio Luis's plan, now that we couldn't expect the help of the NYPD, was to drive Titi Clarita home, come back to Carlos's neighborhood, and wait for the shift to end. Some time after that, he expected Carlos would figure the coast was clear, and come waltzing back. Sounded good though I would have liked to have known more precisely *when* Carlos would be arriving. I slept the half-hour ride back into the Bronx.

Carlos had plans too. His plans included using the house key Jasmine had been given when she turned thirteen. He took a Nintendo, a color TV, a VCR, and a CD player. He also made himself a sandwich and left the fixings on the kitchen counter. The gun cabinet, where Tio Luis kept his rifles and shotguns and for which Jasmine did not have the combination, had been dragged across nice parquet floors Tio Luis had put in and shellacked himself, scratching into it deeply. It weighed a ton and would not have opened with a sledgehammer, so it was left behind, blocking the bathroom. This made things worse since Titi Clarita could have used the toilet bowl to throw up in and was instead forced to use the kitchen sink, an offense to her housekeeping sensibilities.

In the bathroom, on the mirror, "STUPID SON OF A BICH" was scrawled in lipstick—Titi Clarita's Chanel.

She tried to clean up, but it was too much for her. She started sobbing though she had no tears. Every part of her body shook with grief. She had to lie down. Tio Luis went for a rum bottle, found it had been taken, and gave me money to get another. I went as fast as I could.

By the time I came back, there was a squad car in front of the building, and uniformed police officers were taking a statement from Tio Luis and Titi Clarita, who had gotten some of her strength back.

"So you think they used her key?" the officer asked.

"Well, the door's not broken. The lock looks good. Yeah, I think they used her key."

The officer grimaced.

"Are you sure you want to go forward with this?" he asked. "If this is true, then she's an accomplice."

"But she's a minor," Titi Clarita said.

The officer shrugged—the way the law worked was out of his hands; he was just giving them fair warning. Normally, my aunt and uncle would not have thought twice. No way would they have put Jasmine through the system. Few parents would. But there was the temptation that if the police thought she was committing crimes, they might actually find her. Then the system could be dealt with, leniency could be pled, straight A's might be entered into evidence, and they might get their daughter back. Fantasy. The NYPD was hardly going to put much effort into finding a girl who had taken her own Nintendo set.

"I'm sorry, officer," Tio Luis said.

The officer nodded. He knew the equations that had just passed through my uncle's head, the additions and subtractions that had come out to a round zero. He and his partner went out to the front of the house, made a few notes and a radio call, got into their car and drove off.

Back inside, Tio Luis went into Jasmine's bedroom and brought out a notebook. He waved me into the bathroom and asked me to compare the handwriting on the mirror to hers.

"She wouldn't misspell bitch," I said. Titi Clarita was relieved by my assessment, and I was allowed to forget the letter-by-letter comparison.

The rest of the afternoon was spent in removing the old lock and putting in a new one. Tio Luis had done this often before in the different apartments he managed, but this lock gave him some trouble to take out.

"What if she comes back?" Titi Clarita asked. "She won't be able to get in."

Tio Luis seemed troubled by the question.

"She can knock," I said. That settled the issue, though I think my aunt had reservations.

Afternoon

Tio Luis and I were back in Manhattan that afternoon and stayed deep into the night. There was no point. Carlos may have had drug trafficking roots in the neighborhood, but he preferred to stay away. The giant also didn't come back. I tried to gain the confidence of some of the children in the neighborhood. They weren't afraid of Carlos, not yet. But they also had no useful information. As far as they knew, Carlos was as gone as he seemed to my uncle and me. He wasn't hiding, he just wasn't there.

There also wasn't some secondary location he worked from. Not one they knew of at least.

"Carlos ain't that interested in the drugs," one little boy told me. He was eight, he told me, holding up the right number of fingers.

"What's he interested in?" I asked.

"Girls," the boy said. His friends all smiled.

"He has a lot of girlfriends?" I asked.

"Not girlfriends," he said. "Just girls. He brings them in." The boy pointed toward Carlos's building.

"And then what?"

He shrugged.

"Do the girls ever come out?"

"Sure. He takes them places."

"And he brings them back here?"

"Sometimes."

The boy's friends were getting tired of my questions. It was a beautiful afternoon, a shame to waste it talking with an old guy.

"What about the giant he hangs out with?"

"Drugs," the boy said.

"Any name?"

He didn't know.

"How long has he been around this neighborhood?" I asked. The boy shrugged, his head tilting to let me know he had reached the end of his store of knowledge. I gave him a ten dollar bill. He was a smart child, and I might need more answers.

There wasn't much I could do with this information. I couldn't see how it would help to share it with Jasmine's parents. It would add to their anxiety and kill off any remaining hope, but give them nothing they could use to find Jasmine.

Night

Throughout the night, I left the Cadillac to get food or information. Tio Luis went out for the bathroom and to call Titi Clarita. Otherwise, we didn't talk much or listen to the radio. We just sat.

Near midnight, I went out onto the street again.

"I need to stretch a little." Tio Luis nodded, but the raised eyebrows told me that he couldn't conceive of a need that wasn't directly tied to finding his daughter.

I decided on a quick walk. If Carlos came back, I didn't want my uncle alone.

Two blocks from the Cadillac, there were two officers standing side by side, watching the street corner. A half block farther on, the giant from 3C was standing on a corner. He was conducting business as usual. Addicts came up to him while I watched, while the police watched. They shook hands with him and went away happy. It was clear to me, and it must have been as clear to the police, that drug transactions were taking place. For a moment, I wondered if these were dirty cops on the giant's payroll, but that didn't seem likely—if he were paying them, they should be staying off the block altogether. Then I saw two white young men drive onto the street in a red convertible—very suburbs. They slowed the car, clearly looking for someone to come to them and offer something they could use at a party. The giant didn't move an inch; the police officers did. They waved to the driver, bringing the car to a stop. A ten-second talk later and the kids were on their way. If NYPD did nothing for Tio Luis and Titi Clarita, at least they were keeping some parent's child from the wickedness of crack cocaine.

My skin is fair enough that I sometimes pass for white. I figured that if I approached the giant, I had at least two bodyguards who would insure he did nothing to me.

I stand five ten when not slouching and weigh two hundred bulky pounds. The giant was a head taller, and his shoulders were about a foot broader. He was black with long curly hair and a scar that ran a crescent from right beneath his left eye to within an inch of his mouth. He was wearing shorts, a Hawaiian print shirt with only the bottom buttons done up. Under that was a black T-shirt. Muscles grew untrained on his frame.

"What you want, punk?" he asked in a normal speaking voice; he probably wanted to avoid special notice from the officers.

"You know what I want," I said. This seemed like an awful waste of time, posturing like this, but it was a game where I wasn't writing the rules.

"Where's that old man?"

The giant looked up and down the street as though expecting an ambush.

"You tell me where the girl is, and I'll tell you where the old man is."

41

"Forget the girl." He stepped closer to say this.

"Can't do that. She's family."

"Not no more, son."

"Look," I said. I was gesturing, pointing. "I don't want trouble. That old man doesn't want trouble. But there might be trouble if she doesn't come back to us."

"You threatening me?" Good question. I suppose I was. Heat of the moment. He pulled up his shirt a few inches and flashed the butt end of a handgun sticking out of his waistband. "Don't talk," he said.

He meant that I shouldn't threaten if I had nothing to back up my words. A good philosophy for life.

"We need her," I said, and I started walking back the way I had come.

"You know she's a ho, right?"

This turned me back around. I didn't understand what he had said.

"She's a ho now. She's a poor little crack ho. You don't want her back. She's had guys all up in every hole she's got."

The giant was smiling, the crescent smile making it seem like his whole face was enjoying what he had to say. The smile bothered me more than the words, bad as those were. The smile reinforced how out of my control Jasmine's fate was. It told me that I could never hope to protect the ones I love and that the world had no pity. Humanity was not on my side. The thought streaked through my mind that this knowledge was not something that Tio Luis could handle. If he had heard those words and seen that smile, he might have pulled out his handgun and started shooting or done something else stupid. I just walked.

I walked and thought of the smile.

"Officer," I said, as I neared the two patrolmen. "That man has a gun."

I pointed out the giant, making the classic pistol shape with my hand. I wanted him to know why the officers were walking toward him.

The giant, when approached, tossed his hands up in the air as though to complain that he was being unfairly stopped and that he had nothing to hide. As soon as one of the officers was close enough, the giant pushed him on top of his partner and ran. The officers chased him, but I could tell within three steps that the race was over and the giant was going to spend the rest of the night a free man. He moved a lot faster for a man his size than I would have guessed physically possible.

Still, he had pushed an officer, knocking him to the ground. The NYPD was now going to be interested in him. With his bulk, he wasn't likely to stay hidden for too long. I had disrupted his business for the night and if he was caught, he might spend a day or two in jail awaiting his arraignment. I'd made his life difficult. For all that, I still had no idea where Jasmine was or what she was doing. Was she even alive? Was she the crack ho the giant had claimed she was? I had learned nothing new that could help, and I now had a mammoth man with a gun who hated me.

"I saw the giant," I told Tio Luis when I got back to the car.

"Where?" he asked. He was excited by the news, as though seeing the giant meant something.

"Around the corner," I said.

Tio Luis waited for the rest of the story. There wasn't much I had to say.

"I asked where she was. He didn't tell me," I said. "Then I told the police that he had a gun. They went up to him, but he ran."

Tio Luis thought about this for a while. Whatever smile he had ran from his lips. He was pensive for some time, even biting his thumbnail. Finally he spoke.

"Don't involve the police anymore," he said.

I wanted to know what he meant by that. I decided not to ask.

Tio Luis put the car in gear and drove me home.

DAY THREE

Morning

I slept. It had been two days without regular sleep. Twenty-four and jobless, I slept irregular hours, but this was more than I could take. No idea how Tio Luis took it. The sleep was dreamless until morning. Then the sounds of the house awoke me briefly as my mother got ready for work, making her coffee, rushing around to get dressed. When I drifted back to sleep a dream came to me—I was running in a desert, then all of a sudden I was in an apartment building, on the stairs, running up when something caught at one of my legs and started to drag me back down. I kicked at it with my free leg, and I told it, in a calm voice, 'Not yet, not yet.' My mother woke me from the top of the stairs to tell me she was going out. Tio Luis would be over soon. I was sweaty.

I had just made my breakfast, when the Cadillac

sounded its horn outside. I put waffles onto a paper plate and went out.

"What's the plan today?" I asked, shoving half a waffle into my mouth. I knew there was probably no plan besides staking out the neighborhood of Carlos Valle again. I had an idea of my own I wanted to throw out there. I thought there was a chance Tio Luis would take the suggestion.

"We're going to One Hundred Thirty-fifth and Broadway," he said. Just like I thought.

I finished my breakfast before speaking. The streets were not yet congested, the sun was not yet high in the sky. It was a Monday morning, and I knew we were on the road before the rush hour had begun. Getting an early start on the day.

"I was thinking that we might do something a little bit different," I said.

"Me too. What's your plan?"

"How about a private investigator?"

Tio Luis took a quick look at me. I couldn't tell if he thought I was insane.

"What do you mean?" he asked.

"I mean why don't you hire a private detective, give him the information you have, and tell him to bring back Jasmine. At least that way, we have someone else out there looking for her, and we increase our chances of bringing her home. I would say hire a whole team of investigators but that would be expensive." In actuality, I had no idea what the cost of a private investigator would be. I had a feeling, however, that Tio Luis and Titi Clarita were what Puerto Ricans call *guillao*. That is, that they had money that went unflaunted—a stash. I knew for a fact they were willing to part with all of the money they had if it brought them their Jasmine back.

Tio Luis thought about the proposition.

"Good idea," he said. "I know a guy."

The phrase "I know a guy" sounded ominous to me. Was this guy an investigator or a hit man? It's not too hard to know a guy who would be willing to break a leg or two if you lived or worked in some of the neighborhoods Tio Luis has lived and worked in.

"The buildings I work for," he said. "Sometimes people leave without paying rent; we get this guy to find them. Last year, he found a guy who had moved to Wyoming and changed his name. We got our money. I'll talk to him."

Talking to this guy did not involve making a detour from the straight road to Carlos Valle's neighborhood.

As soon as we had parked on Carlos's block, Tio Luis showed me what his new tactic was. He said he had gotten a dream about it the night before, thought about it in the early morning, and put it into action as soon as the shops in his neighborhood had opened. He went to the trunk of the Cadillac and brought out a box holding a ream of paper. He had made flyers.

The flyers advertised a reward for information about Jasmine Ramos, aged thirteen, missing since Friday, thought to be in the neighborhood of City

College. It gave a phone number where information could be left. The reward was five thousand dollars.

The problem with these flyers was the amount of information dedicated to describing Carlos Valle—there was an accurate physical description, then the phrase "Drug Dealer and Child Molester." Then came a line about Carlos's relationship to a giant black man. My first instinct was to warn Tio Luis against posting anything inflammatory and making Carlos angry. I kept quiet. Of course, what he wanted most of all was to draw Carlos out. He wouldn't care if Carlos came after him shooting. He'd take his chances.

We posted the flyers on every street lamp and telephone pole in the area, we went into buildings and handed them out to passersby. We pinched them with the windshield wipers of parked cars. We were done with the ream by ten in the morning, but it was only the first ream. He had two others in the trunk. Titi Clarita, he told me, had a ream of her own that she was putting up around the Skate Key in case Carlos had friends there.

I ran through two rolls of tape putting the flyers up, and as I worked, I wondered about the efficacy of them. After all, a hardened criminal, like Carlos seemed to be, was hardly going to fall for a little name calling, and I didn't think many people would be willing to risk their lives for a few thousand dollars.

"You think this will do any good?" I asked Tio Luis when we had stopped for a soda break.

"Maybe," he said. I had to agree there was always a chance. "Tomorrow, the reward goes up. Twenty thousand."

Afternoon

Hector Sepulveda, the private investigator Tio Luis had worked with before, was a Puerto Rican man in his thirties, tall and thin. He brushed his thinning hair back and wore a gold necklace with a little, carved island of Puerto Rico dangling from it.

He was having lunch in an aluminum take-out dish when we entered his office. He waved us into chairs. The office was on the first floor of a small apartment building, a few steps off street level. The walls were thin—we had to talk over the music playing in a neighbor's apartment.

"Forgive me," he said. "I haven't had breakfast." He speared a forkful of salad and fed it into his mouth, which was already going full strength on a serving of *arroz con gandules*. There were three pork chops in the plate. Another plate, the clear plastic top to the meal, held a dozen sweet plantains.

"*Coje*," he said motioning to the plantains. "Take."

Tio Luis helped himself.

"They gave me too many plantains. There's an extra pork chop in here if you want also."

We waited for him to settle back into his eating regimen before presenting the case to him. I did most of the talking; Tio Luis helped with the plantains and had a piece of the spare pork chop, tearing it off with his fingers.

"So let me get this straight," Hector said, his jaw working at full speed between each word to clear the food from his mouth. "What you really want is your daughter, no?"

"Sure," Tio Luis said.

"So this Carlos guy, if I don't ever see him, that's okay as long as I get her, right?"

"Get her safely," Tio Luis added.

"*Pues, seguro,*" Hector added. "Of course."

"I can pay," Tio Luis said. Hector waved him off.

"We talk about that later. Don't worry. First, we get your daughter."

My uncle pulled out an envelope from a jacket pocket and put it on the desk next to the plantains. Just like the movies. Hector used a pinky to lift the envelope flap and peek in. He nodded. He pushed a business card across the desk. My uncle took it up and inspected it.

"You got one of those mobile phones?" he asked. Hector shrugged and nodded.

"What's your plan?" Tio Luis said. Hector was wiping his hands with a little wet-wipe from the bag his food came in.

"It's best if you don't know everything," Hector said.

Tio Luis accepted this.

So this is how things get done. I don't want to know too much about Tio Luis and his plans for dealing with Carlos. I don't tell him much about the rumors surrounding his daughter and how she is being used. Hector Sepulveda finds out the story from us but doesn't tell us much about how he plans to go about working for us. The police department doesn't want to hear about a missing thirteen-year-old, nor do they suggest we tell them anything official about the break-in at Tio Luis's house. They will care, however, that some giant guy with a gun pushed one of their officers. Everyone tries to do what needs doing with the cards held closely to the vest, with informative bits kept from those who should hear.

What is Hector hiding about his methods? More important, what is Tio Luis keeping from me? Titi Clarita? Jasmine?

The giant's name is Nestor. This comes from the eight-year-old who finds me to say this. He's asked around. Nestor has been in the neighborhood for only a few weeks. He works with Carlos. Maybe works for Carlos.

The eight-year-old has come alone to tell me this.

"Did you have to share the money?" I ask.

He nods.

I give him another ten dollar bill. He smiles and runs off. I will have to double-check his information next time. He might tell me anything for another ten.

Nestor's name is given to Hector. It might help, he says, but probably won't.

* * *

At three in the afternoon, the flyers have an effect. Jasmine calls her mother at home. She says she's fine. Carlos's voice can be heard in the background. "Tell her about the flyers," he says. Titi Clarita says the voice sounds angry, the words are threatening.

"I need you to take down the flyers," Jasmine says. Titi Clarita tells her there are more than a thousand flyers. It would take time. Maybe a whole day. Why do they need to come down? She whispers this last question as though Jasmine is her confederate, her friend in the struggle against the forces of evil represented by Carlos. Jasmine is no friend. She puts the phone down and Titi Clarita hears her asking Carlos why it is important that the flyers get taken down. Carlos grabs the phone.

"Take them down!" He's angry.

The phone slams.

All of this gets reported to Tio Luis, to Hector, to my mother at her job, to me.

It's a good news, bad news situation. Jasmine is still alive and in reasonable health. Able to talk, able to walk. She is, however, in the thrall of Carlos. She will do what he says. And he is a bad man.

"He sounded demon possessed," Titi Clarita says. "Very angry."

"Any hint of where they were?" Hector asked. "Anything in the background?"

"Oh, you mean like in the movies when you can hear a train station being called out by the conductor?" I asked. I was being sarcastic. There is a reason why these things happen in the movies. Because the movies are about fantasy.

"Yeah, like that," Hector said. He was serious.

"The TV was on," Titi Clarita said. "I think there were some commercials."

I see this only as a sign that Carlos didn't want to interrupt his viewing of whatever was on. Hector grills Titi Clarita about which commercials were playing. She can't be sure. Maybe Colgate.

"Anything else?"

"Cars passing."

"Any buses? Sirens?"

"I was trying to listen to Jasmine," Titi Clarita says. She whines this as an apology. Hector doesn't forgive her.

"It is very important," Hector says. "We have to set up a recording device."

At five, Carlos calls. He leaves two messages because Titi Clarita is still in Hector's office and the machine cuts him off in the first go-around.

"Leave me alone," he says. "I haven't done anything to Jasmine. Yet. Nothing that she hasn't liked." He's serious when he says this. "When I do something to her, it'll be in the newspaper." He's bragging. "Anyway, I want all of those flyers down by—"

The machine beeps.

"I want those flyers down by tonight. Don't make me say this again."

Then Carlos calls out for Jasmine.

"Jasmine. You want to leave a message for your parents?"

Nothing is heard, but Carlos gets back on to say that Jasmine doesn't want to talk to them.

When we hear the messages, we spend some time speculating about why Jasmine's voice isn't heard. Is she dead? Is she high? Has she already run away from Carlos, made her way onto a bus or train, in the middle of her passage home?

Hope rises. It wins over Tio Luis and Titi Clarita.

Hector hears the message by six that evening. He plays it over and over, amplifies it. In the background, there is an intercom buzz. Nestor announces himself. It was Jasmine's voice asking, "Who?"

Still alive, still talking, with the freedom to move about an apartment. The hope that arose is not dead or quenched.

And if the flyers with a five-thousand-dollar reward get them this close, Tio Luis cannot wait for the morning when he posts one with a promise of twenty thousand.

There were more than twenty phone calls that Titi Clarita took that day in reference to the flyer. Some were friends and family who hadn't heard of what happened to Jasmine. Some were people who claimed to know everything about it. She took down their information, but none of it seemed even remotely useful. One was a psychic who said she knew nothing about the case, but that she could know something for a fee.

Titi Clarita took these sorts of claims seriously and called this woman back. The psychic's fee covered the effort of opening her mind to the spirit world and talking to the dead.

"Jasmine's not dead," Titi Clarita said.

"Are you sure?" the psychic answered. It wasn't so much a question as a challenge.

"I spoke to her on the phone."

The psychic laughed.

"That's the first sign," she said. Titi Clarita hung up the phone.

Night

At seven that evening, just as we were coming back from Hector's office, the phone rang again. Titi Clarita picked it up. In a minute she was waving at me. I picked up.

It was the eight-year-old. He was speaking low, but I knew his voice.

"That girl on the flyer," he said. "You want to know where she is?"

"Yes."

"If I tell you where she is and you find her, I get the money?"

"Yes."

"Five thousand dollars?" he asked.

"Yes."

"She's in 3C."

"Which building?" I asked.

"The same as always. My building."

"How do you know?"

"I saw Carlos coming up the stairs. Him, the giant, and about three girls. One of them is the girl on the flyer."

He described her. Nothing different than he

could have gotten from the flyer. Said she looked too happy—drugged. He'd seen the look before. They'd come in only fifteen minutes earlier. Already one male customer had gone up and not yet come down. The eight-year-old was sitting near the front door of his apartment on the second floor. He could hear if they came down. He would call back if they left.

Tio Luis and I got into the Cadillac; his face was nearly glowing with determination. It would end tonight.

The plan was thought up while Tio Luis drove to Manhattan. Hector would meet us there. He was licensed to carry a gun. I would go inside and watch the apartment from the stairwell. When we were sure Jasmine was inside, Tio Luis would get out of the Caddy, come up the stairs and the three of us would get into the apartment and get her out.

There were holes in the plan. How would we know whether Jasmine was in the apartment? How would we get in? Was Hector bringing a gun such a good thing? If it was such a good thing, why didn't I have a gun? Guns or not, could we be sure of forcing our way in and out of the apartment? I brought all these things up with Tio Luis as he drove, but he couldn't hear me. He was in a completely different city. A city where he would be able to get his daughter in an hour or so.

I didn't get out of the car when he parked. Hector wasn't there yet, but it wasn't a part of the plan that I wait for Hector. I wanted Tio Luis to do a little more thinking, especially about ways to keep me alive.

"Why don't we try to get the police to find out if Jasmine is in there?" I asked.

Tio Luis shook his head.

"You heard the detective. They don't care what happens to her. We're all she has."

That was a strong argument for trying to do all this on our own. I could imagine M. Hamilton's response to us saying we thought Jasmine was with Carlos in 3C—the same as it had been the first time we told him that.

I waited in the stairway, only a few yards from the door to 3C. Light came from beneath the door; music, conversation, and TV chatter filtered through the walls into the hallway. I tried to think of what I would do if confronted by a gun before Hector got there. I couldn't think of anything to do but turn and run. I tried to refocus. If Jasmine was in the apartment, a word or two in her voice would tell me. In my first five minutes of surveillance work— that's what Hector had called it—the music in 3C was turned up loud and a man passed by me on the stairs, knocked on the door, and was let inside. In the second the door was open, I saw no signs of anyone, certainly no evidence of Jasmine. The man came out less than a minute later. If he did any business in 3C, it wasn't sex. A few minutes later, someone left one of the other apartments on the third floor, and another man went up to 3C—he knocked, went in, came out.

The stairwell had a window out to the street. At

the fifteen-minute mark, I put my head out and craned my neck. I could see Tio Luis's Cadillac, but I couldn't see if he was still in it. Hector and his car were nowhere to be found.

A few more minutes, a few more customers for 3C. One didn't come out right away—a big guy, about five five in height and around the gut. He was wearing overalls with a red bandanna hanging out of the chest pocket. I had been trying to keep track of all those who went in, and this guy was the most distinctive. It took him at least five minutes to come out. He gave me a look as he headed back down the stairs. I returned it with the New Yorker's eternal "What are you looking at?" face. He kept moving. I kept sitting on the steps.

The music from 3C got louder still. I wondered why no one complained. You could call the police anonymously, I thought. Then the door to 3C opened and the music's volume jumped up a notch. I didn't hear the giant step out into the hallway with his gun in hand. I didn't notice him at all, until his shadow hovered over me.

The gun was pointed at my torso. There was no Hector, there was no Tio Luis, no place for me to run, just an angry Nestor with a black shiny gun. I put my hands up. Somewhere in my mind, Nestor would not shoot an unarmed man, not one who was surrendering.

Nestor didn't shoot. He wasn't going to kill me right there. This he told me as he pulled me up to my feet by my hair and forced me into the hallway.

This was the part of the movie where I would have been shouting for the victim to kick and scream rather than go silently into the apartment. It always seems like a good idea, until the bad guy's fingers are laced into your hair and his gun is jammed into the small of your back. At that point, it looked like obeying him was the smartest move. Still didn't think it would help much.

Losing hope is so easy, so painless, in some ways such a relief. As soon as the door was closed behind me, I knew I was going to die. There was no reason for them not to kill me. One shot. Later everyone would tell the police the truth: they had heard nothing.

Carlos was there with a revolver in his hand. Jasmine stood behind him, her face expressionless. Another young woman, a girl really, opened a bedroom door, stuck her head out, looked at me, and went back in again, closing the door behind her. There was a knock at the door. I didn't even think it might be Hector or Tio Luis until after Nestor had looked through the peephole, dug into a back pocket for a tiny plastic bag, opened the door and made a transaction, stuffing a few singles into a back pocket. He changed gun hands to do this. Apparently, killing me was no interruption to their business. When I turned back from watching the deal, Carlos was saying something to me.

"Turn down the music," I shouted.

Instead, he took a step closer.

"I said for you to leave me alone," he shouted into my ear.

The thought occurred to me that this was the best time to struggle for the gun and save my life. It was just a thought though.

"I can't do that," I told him. "Family."

He nodded like he understood my predicament, but apparently he didn't. He turned half away from me, then swung with full force, mashing the gun into my face. You wouldn't think it, but getting hit with a gun is much more painful than a normal punch. With that one swing, I thought every bone in my face had not just broken, but exploded. I tried to swing out an arm to defend myself, but I found that I was already on my hands and knees. Carlos gave me a kick to the head that gave me no extra pain; it just disoriented me. When I opened my eyes again, I was looking up at the ceiling. There were a couple more kicks that I tried to block, my arms getting nowhere near where I needed them. For a moment, Carlos stopped. He paced; I watched him from my side. Then he came at me with a few more kicks to the gut. I was curled up by then, and I thought to myself that as long as he didn't use that gun, I would survive. Apparently, Carlos thought the same thing. He stooped to slap the top of my head with the gun. That was even more painful than the first hit; the pain blotted out my vision and my sense of self. He could have kicked me all he liked as long as he didn't touch the top of my head. I felt the scalp in that area, felt the warmth of my own blood, brought my fingers in front of my eyes, felt a pain in my arm and when I checked again, I was being kicked by the tiny feet of my cousin.

Her face was fury. I tried to say something to her. I don't know what actually came out. She concentrated her kicks on my face, as though she were trying to erase me. I remembered what Tio Luis had said just a couple of days earlier.

"Do this for me. Do this for her. Help her. She's only thirteen. Only a baby. My sweet baby."

There I was on the ground, and there she was standing above me, being held back by her pimp-lover, her crack-daddy, her rapist, her abductor, her whatever-the-hell he was. I was covering up strategic spots and she was kicking me with the heel of her sneaker—thank God it was a sneaker—imprinting her shoe size on my face and arms, on my thighs until her master-man dragged her out of the apartment and there was quiet in the room. Then I got up and looked around. There was only a sad old dude sitting on a beanbag, drooling a smile at me. I dusted myself off a little though it was outrageous for me to do it—I knew I was a mess and dust was the least of my troubles. I limped out and down the stairs thinking about what my uncle had said.

"Baby, my ass," I thought as I hit the street. They drove past as I got my bearings. No furious peeling out, just a black Camaro with the windows rolled up trapping the A/C, loud rap music seeping out, my little cousin yelling at me from the backseat, two middle fingers representing all that I could not hear.

* * *

On the street, several people had congregated to discuss what had happened. They stopped talking when I approached. They looked away. I started to think of what I must look like. Let alone the blood, the bruises, the torn clothes, and the footprints all over me. I looked like trouble—like someone who would be asking for help or looking for revenge.

I limped toward where Tio Luis had been sitting in his Cadillac. He and the car were gone. There was blood on the sidewalk. I checked to make sure it wasn't coming from me. It wasn't.

The eight-year-old came up beside me. He was the only one who would.

"Did you see it?" he asked. I realized he was standing in what was now a blindspot—my left side. I turned to him.

"What happened to you?" he asked.

"Carlos," I said. "What happened here?"

"The old dude and Robertito got into it."

"Robertito?"

"Fat boy in overalls." The eight-year-old spread his arms to the approximate width of the guy who had passed me twice on the stairs. Not just a customer but an employee of Carlos and Nestor, LLC.

"Robertito pulled out a sawed-off, the old guy pulled out a handgun." He was smiling. As far as he was concerned, he'd just watched the best bit of the movie without having to fast forward through any mushy parts.

"What happened to them?" I asked.

"Robertito fired twice, but the old dude got him

in the leg." He put a hand over his own hip to show where.

"And then?"

"Robertito went this way, and the old guy went that way." He pointed in opposite directions.

"How long ago?"

He shrugged.

The blood started about ten feet from where the car had been parked. Robertito had walked up to Tio Luis, pulled out the sawed-off shotgun, and fired. Twice. There was a good chance Tio Luis was dead behind the wheel of his car. I was limping and half blind. There was no sign of Hector. The police apparently had not heard the shots. No one had called them, and no one was likely to.

"Was the old guy hurt bad?" I asked.

Another shrug.

"How about the other guy?"

A nod.

I pulled out a twenty dollar bill; there was blood on it.

"You got a clean one?" the eight-year-old asked.

I didn't think so. He took it and ran off.

Standing on the sidewalk, adding to a puddle of blood, the only thing that came to my mind was to follow the trail of blood Robertito left. It didn't occur to me that he might have reloaded his shotgun.

The blood drips ended at the top of a set of steps leading down off the street to a basement door.

Robertito was dead, faceup. He had slid down about five steps; his left leg was stuck between the wall and the pole that held up the handrail. His eyes were open, the wound at his hip was coupled with one in his upper right arm; the butt of the shotgun was still in his hand.

At the corner, fifty feet away, three or four guys were drinking and joking. If they had seen someone Robertito's size stumble, fall, and die, they were certainly calm about it. For half a minute, my attention was divided between Robertito—could I be sure he was as dead as he looked?—and the group. They paid me no mind. A joke brought a loud laugh, and I made up my mind to move.

The nearest pay phone was busy, the next two didn't work. Tio Luis pulled up alongside me as I limped to the next one.

"Get in."

I did as told. It was a few minutes before I took a look at my uncle. He was bleeding from scratches on his face. There was window glass shattered on his lap, on the floor of the car, even on my seat.

"Your face is bleeding," I said.

"What?"

"Your face," I said. He looked at me, and I motioned.

"That's not the worst part," he told me. "Besides, you should look at your face."

The worst wound Tio Luis suffered was a grazed scalp. Had the pellet traveled a half-inch lower, it would have lodged in his brain.

"He was shooting like he's seen too many Clint

Eastwood movies," Tio Luis said. "From the hip. You get no control that way. Your aim angles up."

I told him I remembered that lesson from the time he took me hunting. He seemed a little nervous and after all we had survived, I didn't want him crashing into the back of a garbage truck.

He pulled the car into the driveway of his house, got out, and I helped him clear space in the garage so he could park it out of sight. I noticed there were two holes in the roof of the car. The pellets had punched through from inside and landed who knows where.

"That fat guy who shot you is dead," I told him as we went up the front steps of the house. He stopped for a moment. He was thinking.

"You sure about that?" he asked.

"I saw him myself. He was on some stairs. Eyes open. Ugly."

"They're always ugly," Tio Luis said. "This guy wasn't so great to begin with."

"What are we going to do?" I asked. Tio Luis had his hand on the doorknob.

"About what?" he said. His face revealed no concern.

"About the dead guy."

"He's not my son," Tio Luis said. I filed into the house behind him. I reminded myself that I wasn't his son either.

We took turns washing up in the bathroom. Tio Luis went in first, avoiding his wife. I got the full force of her attention. She had to touch everything that hurt including a nose I was pretty sure was broken and the cut at the top of my head.

When I got into the bathroom, I wet my hands and passed them over my face, getting off some of the dried blood before taking a good look in the mirror. There was no angle from which I didn't look beaten. My left eye was nearly shut, my right eye was raccooning, I had a cut on the ridge of my nose, and bruising on my jawline. My left cheek had the light imprint of a sneaker tread on it. Under my shirt there were more bruises than I could count. There were knots of purple forming over two ribs. I was sure they were cracked.

After I had cleaned up, I stood in front of the mirror and stared at myself. Under other circumstances, normal ones, I would have been in the emergency room of a hospital waiting for my turn to see a doctor and maybe get an X-ray. Tio Luis would have insisted on it. He would not return his sister's son to her in such bad condition. These conditions were not normal. Tio Luis didn't bat an eyelash at seeing me. And there was no thought of a doctor. Nor was there a hint that he might report his shoot-out with Robertito to the police. As plain as it was that the shooting had been in self-defense, the investigation, the questions would only slow him down.

Tio Luis got me out of my thoughts with a double knock on the bathroom door.

"You almost ready in there?" he asked.

"For what?"

"To go back out," he said. I could hardly believe my ears. Shot at, beaten, but he was up for more.

"I think they broke my nose," I said through the door. Clearly, he had to see that we were done for the night.

"When your nose is broken, you know it."

"Okay, then, I know they broke my nose. And two ribs."

Tio Luis was silent a moment. Maybe he saw reason. If he did, he waved it good-bye.

"You'll heal," he said softly. He wasn't joking, or chiding me. He was pleading. He was begging me to put my pain aside and think of him instead.

"Five minutes?" I asked.

"Oh sure, sure," he answered, and he walked away from the door.

Five minutes later, we were in Titi Clarita's Toyota Corolla. Newer than the Cadillac by ten years and smaller by about as many feet. Tio Luis hated to drive it, thought of it as a Matchbox car, but the Cadillac had bullet holes in the driver's side door and the roof, a cracked windshield, and a missing driver's side window.

"Why was the window up," I asked. It was a hot summer night, and Tio Luis had driven over with the window completely down, his arm dangling out.

"I saw that punk coming at me. He was staring me down. I started to roll it up in case he was planning to do something like reach in or stab me. I didn't see the shotgun until he was ten feet away. He swung it out from behind him. I dove for the floor of the car."

I have no experience in these things, nothing more than what I see in the movies, but he sounded to me like he was rehearsing.

"When I heard the two rounds go off, I waited a second, then popped my head back up."

He gave me a look as he drove. I think he was waiting for me to confirm his story.

"Anyway, when I looked he was gone. I put the car in gear and went around the block a few times."

"Looking for him?"

"Looking for you."

"So when did you—?"

"What?"

"When did you shoot him?"

Tio Luis was silent for a while. Understandable. There are times to be silent, times to be very careful with one's words.

"I never shot him," Tio Luis said. He looked straight ahead. "Here." We were at a red light. He reached down and pulled a revolver from an ankle holster. And handed it to me.

"What do I want this for?"

"I never shot him."

I looked at the gun. It had six bullets. I smelled the barrel like cops do on TV. I couldn't make out anything. I guess it would have smelled like gunpowder if it had been fired. But he could have cleaned it. We passed a patrol car as I was looking the gun over, but they didn't notice me or my uncle when he reached across and put his hand over the gun, pushing it gently toward my lap and out of sight. I guess gangsters don't drive Corollas.

Tio Luis headed back to Upper Manhattan. We did a few turns in the area where Carlos lives, saw nothing useful. Then we both went up to his apartment. There was no noise at all coming from inside. We waited a few minutes. A skinny guy, dope fiend of some kind, came up the stairs. We went over to one of the other doors, he knocked for Carlos, but there was no answer. The guy left.

"Let's follow him," Tio Luis said.

Going down the stairs behind the drug addict, I tried to think of a logical argument why we should just go home instead of following a crackhead. Couldn't come up with anything Tio Luis would listen to.

We followed the addict on foot for three blocks. He went to a playground near the college and bought what he had to buy from some guy who wasn't Carlos or the giant.

"I was hoping," Tio Luis said. He was hoping Carlos had some backup location nearby and that a loyal customer would lead us there.

We sat in the car half an hour, nothing said. Then Tio Luis dropped me off at home.

DAY FOUR

Morning

I curled up under a blanket and was still curled up nine hours later. Sun was shining in my face, but it was my mother who woke me up.

"I'm leaving," she called down the stairs to me. "Tio Luis is coming over soon."

Bad nightmare: Tio Luis coming over every morning for the rest of my life so he can take me out to get beaten.

I crawled out of bed. I couldn't remember my legs being kicked or stomped, but they were covered with bruises. There wasn't a part of me that wasn't marked. There wasn't a part of me that didn't feel like it either. I passed my hand through my hair but found the cut in my scalp on the ridge of a knot and closed my eyes from the pain. It had scabbed over. I yawned, and that highlighted the pain in my ribs. Brushing my teeth was hard: my right arm didn't want to go as high as I needed it to. Putting on my jeans took five minutes, and I didn't know how I was going to get my socks on. My rugby shirt slipped on pretty easily. I went up to mom's kitchen and put waffles in the toaster. If Tio Luis was on his way, he wasn't coming over to take me to a diner or McDonald's.

I plated the waffles, poured on the syrup. The phone rang.

"Get out of the house." It was Tio Luis.

"What?"

"Get out of the house. Now. Hurry."

"What are you talking about?"

There was a banging on the door. I told Tio Luis to hold on a minute.

I went to the door, nervous. If the giant was out there, I could be in big trouble. I certainly wasn't up to fighting him. I wasn't even up to running away. Apparently, I even walked too slowly; the person who banged on the door banged again.

My mother's front door doesn't have a peephole. Instead, we go to the foyer window if we want a look at who's at the door. I looked. Two trench coats. Detectives. Not as bad as having the giant on the doorstep, but if Tio Luis was warning me about them, it was bad. One of them saw me. He tapped his partner's arm and he turned around. Detective M. Hamilton. Something had made him take a trip from Upper Manhattan to my door in the Bronx.

"Open up," I heard. I wanted to run back to the phone to hang up on Tio Luis. I wanted to get my waffles in case there was going to be a trip to a station house. One of the detectives flashed his badge at me. I opened the window.

"Yeah?" I asked. I knew what they wanted. There was a fat dead guy with a shotgun lying on some steps. It was about time someone got around to asking about him.

"We need to talk to you," M. Hamilton said.

"Go ahead."

"Can we come in?" This came from the other detective, a younger man.

"The house is a mess," I said. Not true. My mother would have been offended.

The trick to dealing with police who knock at the door without a warrant is to not feel embarrassed or afraid. Sounds easy.

M. Hamilton waited a moment. There was someone coming down the block, a woman from a few doors down. He timed it just right.

"We need to talk to you about a murder." The neighbor lady looked up at me in the window. I waved.

"Who'd you kill?" I asked.

"You some kind of wise guy?" M. Hamilton said.

I shut the window. If he had enough evidence for a warrant, it would be in his hands and a uniformed officer would be breaking down my door. M. Hamilton banged again.

"Don't make us come back with a warrant," he yelled through the door.

I said nothing. The phone in the kitchen had a recording playing asking me to please hang up. I did.

Hamilton and his partner waited on the doorstep a moment. Then they got back into their "unmarked" car, a large, dark Ford that screamed "Police!" They sat a while, then pulled away. I called Tio Luis's house as soon as their car started moving. Titi Clarita answered.

"Where's Tio Luis?" I asked.

"Where do you think?"

"In jail?"

"Upper Manhattan. More flyers. He left as soon as he heard the detectives were at your mother's house."

I was quiet for a second. I had no idea what Tio Luis had told his wife or what she suspected. I didn't want to say anything about the fat guy, Robertito, if the police hadn't said anything to her.

"What did they want?" I asked.

"They found a body," she said and sniffled.

"A man?" I asked.

"Yes," she answered. The relief in her voice traveled clearly through the phone line.

What was it about New York that chewed people up and usually just swallowed them? Jasmine had disappeared from a public place crammed with teens and responsible adults and not even the police cared. I had almost literally gotten the shit kicked out of me in an apartment building full of people and no one heard or cared. Tio Luis had been shot, Robertito had been shot and walked off to die in the open air of the city, and no one cared. My Aunt Clarita had just told me about a murdered man and her voice told me it was good news to her ears since it wasn't Jasmine the police had asked her about. This was a woman who was usually so sweet that some of my other cousins and I parodied her and how she cared about everyone, everything, even pigeons. *Pobrecitos* she called them—"poor little ones."

When she told me the police wanted to talk to Luis about a dead man, I had thought of Robertito. With her next words, she said it was a black man and that she couldn't see what it had to do with Uncle Luis or me. Robertito was not at all dark skinned, so there couldn't have been a mistake. I figured Uncle Luis hadn't told her anything about the giant.

"What did they say?" I asked.

"Nothing," she answered. "They wanted to talk to Luis, not me."

"And what did you tell them?"

"Nothing, I said Luis wasn't home. I told that Hamilton that he should know where Luis was. I asked him where Jasmine was. What was he doing to get her back? I said he should have helped us and maybe we'd be able to help him."

I imagined she had gone into hysterics accusing the detective, and he probably gave up trying to talk to her. Not a tactic I could use, but useful.

I wanted to get more information out of her, like why M. Hamilton came to my door if he should have gotten the clue that Tio Luis would be staking out Carlos Valle, but I figured I didn't have that kind of time, and she didn't have that kind of information. M. Hamilton would be back at my door; he'd have a warrant if he really wanted to talk with me. With a dead guy, no, two dead guys on the street, chances were good that he had just moved the car around the corner until someone delivered a warrant to him. He'd watch the front door and maybe someone was already watching the back door. Once I was on the street, I was fair game. They could brace me and ask me questions and there wouldn't be all that much I could do about it. It's not like you can push past a homicide detective. But first, he'd have to catch me.

Adrenaline works wonders for the broken body. Once I knew M. Hamilton wanted to talk to me about a murder case, it didn't take much imagination to see myself behind bars for the rest of my life. Really, how hard would it be to convict a young Puerto Rican who looked like stepped-on shit?

I went back down to my basement apartment, got out the fifty dollars I kept tucked in a book for emergencies, debated whether I should take the carpet cutter I had used in my struggle with linoleum a few months back, decided against it in case M. Hamilton did catch up with me, and went out the back door in a hurry, the two waffles in my hand. No limp, no gimp, I felt ready for a hundred-yard dash.

There was no need. I went over the short fence at the back of the yard, crossed through Mrs. Busoni's yard, down a driveway she shared with her next-door neighbor, and out onto the street. This left me a couple blocks from the nearest train station, a #6 train not headed anywhere near Carlos Valle.

The plan was simple. Go as far as a token would take me and spend the morning there. Call Titi Clarita after a while and see if M. Hamilton ever came back.

I was just about to take my first step onto the stairs leading up to the elevated station when a hand clamped onto my shoulder. As alert and awake as I felt, as pain-free as I was at the moment, I still had a whole side of the world that I couldn't see—the left. I spun around half from the surprise and because I wanted to see the person grabbing hold of me, half because the hand on my shoulder had a firm hold and wanted me to turn.

"Come on," Tio Luis said. "We can't waste time like this."

I breathed a "Shit" of disbelief. Seeing Tio Luis was only a shade better than running into M. Hamilton and, when I thought about it, not at all better than seeing Carlos Valle himself because I had no doubt Tio Luis only wanted to take me to see Carlos anyway.

"What?" Tio Luis asked. The shotgun blast going off so near his head the night before hadn't done much for his hearing.

I shook my head to let him know he could ignore my comment, but he didn't see me. He was already leading me to his Corolla.

Back to Manhattan. A stop at the detective's office, but Hector wasn't there. Back into the car. I felt like a fugitive, though as far as I knew there wasn't any warrant out for either of us. Yet.

I wanted to ask Tio Luis what the hell he was doing. He had entered into the full *Death Wish* vigilante thing, getting into shoot-outs, getting me roughed up, getting drug dealers angry at us, and getting nowhere closer to getting Jasmine home. And maybe she didn't even want to be home, not yet, maybe not ever. But then those aren't the kinds of questions I had been raised to ask of my uncle. Besides, I knew what he was doing. He was doing the most he could do to bring Jasmine out of the lion's den and back to safety. If a few lions died along the way, it didn't matter.

"What do you know about how Nestor died?" I asked. That seemed safe to ask.

"Who's Nestor?"

"Big black guy with a gun," I said.

"Oh, him. I don't know nothing about it," Tio Luis answered. "All I heard was that detective wanted to talk to me about some black guy that got killed in Manhattan. Vague." Tio Luis waved a hand in the air as a symbol of vagueness. He was right. With two thousand plus people being murdered in New York each year for the last few, M. Hamilton would have to do a little better at describing the circumstances if he wanted any information.

"Did you go back to Manhattan after you dropped me off?" I asked. I figured that if he did, then there was a good chance Tio Luis had rung up another bad guy. Eventually he'd kill Carlos too by process of elimination.

"Nah," Tio Luis said. "I slept a few hours."

"And then?"

"Then I went to Manhattan, yes. Listen, why are you questioning me?" He took a look at me as he pulled to a stop at a red light. I craned to stare back at him with my good eye.

"You look worse now than last night," he said as the light turned.

Tio Luis found a parking space a block from Carlos's building.

"There goes your little *chota*," he said. My snitch. I looked up to see the little boy I'd been getting information from. He was sitting on the curb fifty yards ahead of us next to a fire hydrant. His arms were crossed over his bare chest and he wore shorts and Velcro laced rubber sandals though it was cool out; the buildings would keep the sun from hitting the street for a little while longer. He was waiting for someone to open the hydrant, a couple of other kids were with him.

I got out of the car.

"Where you going?" Tio Luis asked. I kept walking.

The boy looked up at me and frowned. He got up and met me halfway.

"You looked like you got whupped," were his first words.

"You should see the other guy."

"I seen the other guy. He looks like he got some exercise."

If it hadn't been for the pain it would cause me, I

would have laughed. I liked this kid. He was smart. Smarter than me or Tio Luis or M. Hamilton or Carlos or Nestor. He wasn't in trouble, and he wasn't looking for it.

"Where's my money?" he asked. A sensible question.

"What money?"

"Five thousand," he said. It was a whisper. He knew enough not to blurt out a number like that where bigger kids might overhear him.

"You have to read the flyer again, little man. It says, 'For information that leads to the capture of Carlos Valle or the return of Jasmine Ramos.' We haven't caught him yet."

His shoulders slumped, he sucked his teeth, and rolled his eyes.

"I'm never gonna get paid if you keep getting beat," he said. Clearly he knew when he had backed the wrong horse.

"What happened to Nestor?" I asked.

"Nestor?" I had clearly asked the wrong question. "Nothing happened to him. Why?"

"I heard he was killed last night."

Little man just smiled at me like my idiocy was something he was putting up with out of a strained sense of charity.

"That big dude's fine. I saw him come out of the building a little while ago. He went that way," he pointed down the street past Tio Luis in his car.

There was no point asking if he was sure. Nestor was not easily confused with anyone else. The police can lie to trip people up. They probably really wanted to hear about a roly-poly Puerto Rican with a bandana and overalls.

"What about Robertito?" I asked. I was digging into my pocket for some money.

"What about him?" Little man asked.

"What's the word on him?"

"Nothing that I heard," he said.

It seemed absolutely impossible that a guy weighing three hundred pounds and who was clutching a sawed-off shotgun could be lying on some steps a half dozen feet away from the sidewalk in one of the busiest neighborhoods in the world and no one had seen or smelled anything. But that was New York, a giant mouth that just ate and ate.

I handed over a folded twenty, no blood this time, and started to turn away.

"Just some bum dude got killed last night, over by the bank," Little man said. "I heard they took out his eyes right there on the street."

Coincidence? I think not. I hurried back to the car as though being on the sidewalk might cause my eyes to be plucked out. I hoped that telling Tio Luis about this might make him see the error of his ways. And drive me home.

"What'd he say?" Tio Luis asked.

"It wasn't Nestor that got killed last night," I answered. I paused to give him time to show interest.

"Too bad," he shrugged. I tried again.

"Remember that panhandler that helped us out the other night? Out in front of the bank?"

"Panhandler? Oh, the bum. Yeah, yeah."

"Somebody took his eyes out last night."

Tio Luis shook his head slowly at the news. That's it. No other reaction. I made one last try.

"Look, these guys are willing to kill—"

"Me too," Tio Luis interrupted me. He looked out the driver's side window, sat up, and popped out of the car. His hand went to his waistband at the small of his back. I craned around to see what the commotion was about. Then I jumped out of the car too.

There was Nestor, as big as life or bigger, walking down the center of the street with a monkey wrench in his hand. It was two feet long, but his size made it look like a swizzle stick if a swizzle stick could mash your head in.

I put my right hand to the small of my back too. There was nothing there, but Nestor didn't know that, and he didn't have to know.

"Peace, my brothers," he said. He made a peace sign with his index and middle fingers. The smile on his face was large and showed his teeth. He had on shades, shorts, and a shirt that was open almost to the navel. If he was carrying a gun, it was creatively hidden. He shouldered the wrench and walked past us to the fire hydrant, Tio Luis kept his eyes glued to Nestor. I used my one good eye to scan the block. Carlos might not be that far away.

Nestor opened the hydrant for the kids, making it gush halfway across the street. They were happy.

He walked back toward us, still smiling.

"Look, you guys got heart, but get the hell out of

here. Carlos and that chick ain't even gonna be here until tonight. Go home."

"Where's my daughter?" Tio Luis asked. Nestor gave a short laugh. The joke was standing right in front of him.

"That bitch's on a corner in Brooklyn by now. Believe me. Carlos won't be around until tonight. This morning I got a business to run and if you guys mess that up for me, I'm gonna get angry with y'all. That ain't good."

The two men stood staring each other down for half a minute. It felt a lot longer. New York is a pretty easy town to be anonymous in but a show-down between a crazy guy with a gun and a mutant with a wrench might draw attention.

"I gotta get my daughter back," Tio Luis said.

"You do what you gotta do old man. Right now, I gotta take this wrench back to the guy who lent it to me." Nestor took two or three ambling steps past my uncle. Tio Luis didn't move, as if he was frozen for a moment. Then he pulled the gun out from his waistband. It was a big-ass gun. He took three steps to catch up with Nestor and smacked the back of his head with the barrel of the gun. The kids playing at the hydrant couldn't hear the crack, but it sounded like a home run to me. I moved around to Tio Luis's side. Nestor had fallen to all fours, but he wasn't out. Tio Luis took care of that. With another two steps, he was on the man, smacked the back of his head four or five more times and flattened him. I just stood there. I couldn't think of what to do. Tio Luis had this fight pretty much won, and he had the gun. Nestor didn't even have the wrench anymore; Tio Luis had kicked it a few feet away.

"Help me out here," my uncle said. He had put his gun away and was trying to lift Nestor by the right arm.

"What are we doing?" I asked. It was both a general question about long-range strategy and a specific one about what we would do if we could get Nestor off the asphalt, which was a long shot.

Tio Luis used one hand to open the rear driver's side passenger door. The plan then was to give Nestor a ride in the same car as us. Frankly, I would have preferred putting him in a taxi.

We stuffed Nestor onto the backseat floor of the Corolla. He was drooling blood.

"What are we doing?" I asked again. I was in the front passenger seat again, Tio Luis in the driver's seat.

"Don't worry," he said. "Open the glove compartment."

I did as I was told and there was a revolver in a little black leather waistband clip holster sitting on top of the insurance papers and the envelope with the car owner's manual.

"Take it. Now, turn around a little in your seat until you can see him, and keep that thing pointed at him. It's very simple. If he moves, squeeze the trigger."

Since a soon-to-be-awake and pissed-off Nestor was in the back and the car was already moving, I did as I was told. Tio Luis caught green lights for a long while. Had the car stopped or gone slower, I would have jumped out.

The first thing Nestor did on waking up was vomit. I felt like doing the same, but at least I'd had waffles for breakfast. Nestor clearly had Cheetos. He tried to move his arms, but they wouldn't do what he wanted. They weren't tied, which would have made me feel a little less queasy; they just wouldn't respond to whatever commands his brain was giving. Probably his brain's fault.

He mumbled something a few times as we crossed back into the Bronx. A quick glance told me we were headed to the area of Yankee Stadium, but I didn't know why. Tio Luis and I lived miles from there.

Nestor's mumbling got loud, but not clear. The day was warming up and I didn't want to roll up the windows if it could be avoided. Funny how my priorities had changed. I had an angry giant at gunpoint trolling around the Bronx and I was worried about the fact that I hadn't put on deodorant that morning.

"What are you saying?" I asked him.

Nestor mumbled more. It sounded like "Y'all's in deep shit." I agreed with the sentiment, but I hoped he was in deeper than we were.

The neighborhood around Yankee Stadium is not the best. There's a giant courthouse dominating the hill to the northeast of the stadium, some small stores under the elevated #4 train tracks, some low rent apartment buildings. Tio Luis knew the neighborhood well. He still managed a couple of buildings in the area. South of the stadium, under the tracks, there were garages both abandoned and still working. He drove to one of the abandoned ones, got out, unlocked the roll-up garage gate and drove us all through.

Nestor had vomited again. When Tio Luis had finished closing up the gate behind us, I helped him drag Nestor out of the car by his feet. He tried kicking, but the struggle was weak. The back of his head hit the concrete floor of what had been a three-car garage with a hydraulic lift in one of the bays and an A-frame pulley system for removing engines and transmissions in another.

Our prisoner rolled on the ground, trying to get off his back. His coordination was improving. I looked at Tio Luis. We both knew that in another minute or two, Nestor would be able to stand. Tio Luis went to his trunk and brought out a roll of duct tape.

There wasn't much trouble taping Nestor's feet together. He had been wearing flip-flops, but Tio Luis took them off and handed them to me.

"Take his boots," he said. For a moment, I thought Tio Luis was suffering through some Vietnam-era flashback, but he smiled up at me.

When Tio Luis tried to wrap Nestor's wrists together, the giant awakened a bit more and tried to take a swing. He missed and got Tio Luis upset. He wound up tying Nestor's hands to his sides, the tape going all the way around the man.

"I'm going to kill you!" Nestor shouted. Tio Luis shrugged.

"Maybe. Let me tell you something. In a few minutes, I have to leave to keep looking for my daughter. If you give me some good information, when I leave here you'll still be alive. If you don't give me what I need . . ." Tio Luis finished the sentence with a wave of his gun hand as though to say that what would happen was out of his ability to control or predict.

"Now. Where's my daughter?"

Tio Luis pressed the barrel of his gun deep into Nestor's right shoulder muscle.

"Go to hell," Nestor said. His face had the look of grumpiness on it of a child awakened too early.

Tio Luis was angry. He looked at me.

"That wasn't a smart thing to say," he said.

"Wait!" The shout came from me. It was one thing to beat a man, but shooting him was risking killing him. Nestor looked at each of us in turn. He might have considered that we were just playing a little good cop/bad cop with him, but it would have been a stupid idea. We weren't cops and Tio Luis was long past playing.

"Wait for what?" Tio Luis asked. I didn't really have an answer for him. I stood speechless. My uncle turned his attention back on Nestor; he pressed the gun barrel even deeper into Nestor's shoulder and used his free hand to shield his face as though he was expecting a big splash of blood. I'd never shot anyone; maybe there was going to be a splash. I took a step back.

Nestor guessed correctly.

"Hold up, hold up," he said. Tio Luis took his shield hand down. "I can give you some addresses, but I can't guarantee anything." Nestor's voice had lost some of its gangsta slur. He sounded almost refined.

"I can't tell you where Carlos is exactly at this moment, and I haven't seen the girl since last night. Maybe she's with him, maybe she's not. See what I'm saying?"

Tio Luis thought this sounded reasonable. So did I. Nestor gave him three addresses and two other general neighborhoods where Carlos might be. Nestor said he last saw him late the night before. Jasmine, he swore, he had last seen in a brownstone in Greenwich Village. What she was doing there, who owned the building, whether she was still there, he had no idea.

Tio Luis was satisfied.

"We're leaving now. You get out of all that tape as best you can. If I see you again, and your information is good, I'll give you ten thousand dollars. If I see you again and your information is bad, you better shoot first."

"Nigga, if I see you I'ma bust a cap in yo ass either way," was Nestor's answer. The refined speech was gone; angry gangsta tough guy was back.

We got into the car and left Nestor on the floor of the garage to figure out his way out of the tape. It was a couple of blocks before I remembered to return the handgun to the glove compartment. That was when I noticed I still had Nestor's sandals. I held them up for Tio Luis to see. I thought he might go back and hand them over, but he smiled at me.

"Nice move," he said.

"Do you remember the party last year?" Tio Luis asked me. We were driving down the FDR Drive. "Her first communion."

"Yeah, sure," I said.

Jasmine had been beautiful in white, complete with white gloves and a tiara, and she didn't change after church. She went through the hours of the whole party in her dress. She was a princess, and stayed that way the whole day long. She had sung a song to entertain her guests and late in the day she had gotten her father to dance with her. He had dropped a couple thousand dollars on the party, and I knew he was planning to do a lot more at her *quinceañera*—her fifteenth birthday. And I knew that no man was more ready to celebrate his daughter's graduation and wedding and the birth of his daughter's first child than Uncle Luis. I looked at him and thought of this and I knew that he was ready to wreck his fortunes to bring her home safely. He would kill if need be and happily die if that's what it took—and he was about the most dangerous man in the world to anyone who stood in his way.

"That was a good party," he said. I agreed with him.

We drove on in silence for a moment, and he changed lanes to move faster.

"What happened to her?" he asked. He wanted to know how she had changed from that angel to a girl who would leave with a full-grown man and do all she had done in the last few months.

"I don't know," I said, and I would have given any amount of money to have a better answer for him.

The house in the Village wasn't a brownstone, just red brick. Very nice with window boxes of bright flowers that had just been watered as had the sidewalk out in front. There was tree shade and the area was cool. Tio Luis parked a half block past the address because it was the closest he could get. The roadway was narrow; double parking here would have blocked traffic. We walked back. There weren't many people—it was a respectable neighborhood and the respectable people were all already off to work. A man in leather sandals and dungaree cutoffs looked at us over his sunglasses as he passed.

"You don't have sunglasses, do you?" I asked my uncle. My swollen shut eye wasn't good for getting people to help us. No difference; he wasn't carrying shades.

The misconception is that everyone who owns a house in the Village has got to be loaded. There's a reason for people thinking this. The housing market is tight. If you want to buy in the Village now, you've got to have a lot of money, but in truth it's hard to tell who in the village has money and who doesn't. Some people bought their houses in the sixties for the rough equivalent of a dozen boxtops and some loose change. Others paid millions.

The people we were going to see were in the latter category. The maid answering the door made this much pretty clear. She was straight off the boat Irish from the sound of her "Good morning." She had on black slacks, a gray top, and I wouldn't have guessed she was the help except for the little bowtie and the name embroidered on the shirt that marked her as working for da man.

I stayed a step back and tried to look down the street so she had a look at my better side. This was also the only way I could see her.

"And who are you?" she asked.

"Luis Ramos," my uncle said with the confidence that everyone had to at least have heard of Luis. "We're here to see Mr. Ellis." That name was all Nestor had told us about who was in the house; he wasn't sure if it was the owner's name or just someone Carlos had been talking to.

He handed her a business card—the property management company he worked for was always drumming up new business to make up for the business they lost each month. Luis was the only decent manager they had. I know. I was one of their managers for a few months.

Celia looked at the card and at me and thought for a moment. She took the middle road and asked us to wait outside while she announced us to her boss.

"White people," my uncle said when the door

had closed on us. I wasn't sure what he meant. Didn't care either.

The door opened again and Mr. Ellis stood before us. He was tall and thin, maybe fifty years old with fine graying hair that flopped into his eyes.

"Can I help you gentlemen?" His voice was soft but deep.

Tio Luis had the photo of Jasmine out and put it into Mr. Ellis's hands.

"I need to talk to you about her," he said. "She's my daughter."

Mr. Ellis, Thomas, he said, did not hesitate to let us into his home. "She's my daughter," were magic words with him even if nobody else in the big city had cared for them.

The inside of his home was even cooler than it had been on the street. The curtains were partly drawn so that the living room he showed us into was dark enough that he felt he had to turn on a light. The room was only sparsely furnished, but I imagined that if everything in it was real, there was a hundred thousand dollars worth of antiques and paintings around us.

"Sit," he said, but every seat had the uncomfortable appearance of being museum quality to me, and Tio Luis was in too big of a hurry to rest. He pointed to the picture in Mr. Ellis's hand.

"We were told she was here last night," Tio Luis said.

Mr. Ellis took a close look.

"I wasn't here last night." He handed the photo

back to my uncle. I was thinking it was a lie. After all, how else would Nestor know about him and the house? But Mr. Ellis drew himself up and folded his hands in front of him.

"My son was in charge of the house yesterday. He might know something."

Ellis left the room for a few minutes. I looked around. There was a lot to admire though it was all lost on Tio Luis; he just stood looking at the spot where Ellis had been.

Daniel Ellis was led into the room by his father. Ellis senior had him by the elbow. Junior was about my age, tall, thin, and with floppy hair like his father. He was glassy eyed and came in on his own cloud of marijuana stink. The connection to Nestor and Carlos became clear.

Junior smiled to my uncle. He was about to reach to shake my hand, but his father caught him up sharp by the elbow he hadn't let go. I wondered who was being protected by not letting him touch us.

"Have you seen this girl?" Mr. Ellis asked; he pointed to the photo Tio Luis held up. Junior squinted to make sure of what he saw.

"Oh yeah," he said. "She was the one who—" The smile that had been plastered on his face dried up. I thought I saw that Mr. Ellis had given his elbow a little squeeze. No point in letting Daniel say something embarrassing, something that would insult a desperate father.

"Did you have any conversation with her?" Tio Luis asked.

"Conversation?" Junior asked back. His smile

returned, broader, like a grin. Clearly, conversation had been the last thing on his mind the night before.

"And do you know when she left?" Tio Luis asked.

"Oh yeah. She was here. Had herself a good time, a couple of drinks. She left early though, with that guy ... uh ... Carlos, I think. They were cool. She was—" Junior wanted to talk about Jasmine. The smile spread on his face again. Tio Luis interrupted him.

"She's thirteen," he said.

Junior's mouth hung open, and his eyes focused on my uncle. Mr. Ellis let go of his elbow and gave him a hard slap to the back of the head that sounded like a coconut hitting concrete. He hit his son again and grabbed his elbow again. He gave the arm a shake. I noticed that Mr. Ellis's hitting hand had a graduation ring on it.

"Where did they go?" Mr. Ellis asked his son. The words came out from between clenched teeth. Junior cringed a little.

"I don't know where they went from here. That Carlos guy said Brooklyn, but I didn't get an address. I was busy, you know, not really thinking."

Junior looked to my uncle for understanding. I think he was trying to say that he was busy with Jasmine, maybe snorting coke, maybe taking her clothes off, maybe doing other things, certainly not paying attention. Apparently his father understood the same thing from what the guy said. He slapped the back of his head again.

Tio Luis didn't have any other questions really. He asked Junior how his daughter had looked—was she in good health. I thought he might have gone so far as to ask if Jasmine had been happy, but he didn't. Junior sure, sured him on all of this. A minute or two later we were back on the street.

Brooklyn is huge. It holds roughly the population of Chicago. We had an address in Brooklyn, but neither Tio Luis nor myself were too familiar with the borough. I was pretty sure the address Nestor had given us was in a neighborhood called Sunset Park. Thank God it wasn't in Queens.

It took longer to find a decent parking space than it did to cross over from lower Manhattan. We stopped about two blocks from the address and since we had to pass a McDonald's on the way, we made a quick stop, Tio Luis shaking off any idea of buying something for himself. I ate as we walked.

The building was a squat apartment building with four floors and four apartments each. There was a super's apartment in the basement. Tio Luis thought it would be wise to check in there first, but there was no one home. We checked the intercom panel at the front door, but there were few names and none on the third floor, which is where we were headed. I was about to press a random button to be buzzed in past the security door, but Tio Luis gave the door handle a pull and the door swung open.

The stairs to the building went straight up the middle with a skylight at the center. That was the only illumination and it wasn't enough. The walls inside were covered with graffiti, and the stairwell had a strong smell and it wasn't just urine. Wherever the superintendent had gone to, it looked like it was a one-way trip taken long ago. On the second floor, two of the apartment doors had eviction notices on them and another was padlocked from the outside. The last door had graffiti scrawled on it—part of a larger mural taken up mostly by the T&A of several cartoon girls with not much clothes on.

The third floor had loud music bouncing off the corridor halls. A homeless-smelling dude passed us on his way down the stairs. He was humming to the music; whatever he had come for, he had gotten. One of the doors was covered with sheet metal painted brown and bolted on. This was covered in a steel mesh that would have made it just a little more difficult for the police to batter it down. By the time they got through, whatever needed flushing would be well on its way to the East River. Tio Luis headed straight for it. It would have been my choice too.

We should have figured something out when the music got way louder as we approached the door. We should have known we were being watched and waited for. It didn't dawn on us until Tio Luis banged on the door. Through the music there was a faint sound, metallic; I thought it was the door's lock being undone. It turned out to be a shotgun shell being racked into the firing chamber.

I stood to the right of the door while my uncle banged. When he heard the sound, he took a step toward me; it looked to me like he wanted to be ready when the door opened, ready to push in or maybe hold his gun up to whoever's head. His right hand reached around to the small of his back. I rolled my eyes.

The blast came through the door and the metal that protected it, punched a smaller hole than I would have thought. One of the pellets caught Tio Luis in the left love handle, another pellet dug into his forearm, the rest of the pellets made a splatter on the wall across from the door. Without having thought of it, I was crouching in the hallway. Tio Luis was standing. He had twirled around on one foot in pain from the shot. He raised his gun at the door and lowered it. The second blast didn't catch either one of us at all, but I flattened onto the floor nevertheless. Tio Luis was still standing, crouching a little on the left side of the door as though he were waiting to pounce. He was closer to the stairs than I was; I would have needed to cross in front of the door to get out of the building. When the third and fourth shells were blasted through the door, I flinched each time, but I couldn't get any lower. The noise of the shots was not at all covered over by the music as far as I could tell. Tio Luis just crouched. I knew he had seen far worse in Vietnam, but I couldn't help wishing he'd throw himself on the floor or retreat back down the stairs that he stood so close to.

Another blast came through the wall, then another. There were two other blasts, but I didn't see where they went.

"Son of a bitch!" my uncle yelled out. He ran for the steps and went down as fast as he could.

I was still on my stomach. It seemed safer than running past the doorway, but then with Tio Luis headed God knows where, and me with no gun, I decided to risk it. Tio Luis was at the second floor door with the padlock on the outside, kicking it. The padlock would not have stopped him, but there was a police lock on the inside; on the other side a heavy metal bar would be angled into a plate on the floor, barricading the apartment.

"Police lock," I shouted. I was overheated from nearly having a hole punched into me. I was trying to get Tio Luis to see that his kicks would have no effect. He did. He pulled out his gun, aimed it at the lock, shouted out "Fire in the hole!" and pulled the trigger a mess of times. I felt sorry for the lock.

The next kick brought the door open. Tio Luis headed straight across a kitchen to a window with a fire escape. He looked up.

"*Caramba!*" he yelled, then he went out onto the fire escape and headed up. I followed him.

So this was combat. Every thought told me to get away from the gunfire, but it wasn't thought that drove me. Fear was a big part. If there was a guy out there with a gun who wanted to kill me, I wanted Tio Luis and his gun nearby. Blood was another factor. Tio Luis was my family, and I would have gone with him anywhere. Hadn't I already gone with him to a bunch of places I didn't want to go? The rooftop of this building was just another place I would have stayed away from on my own, but was rushing toward because of my uncle. Partly I wanted to prove my courage if only to myself and even if it cost me everything. It's one thing to die—everybody does that—but it's another thing and a horrible one to die a coward, abandoning a blood relative and giving in to nerves.

Tio Luis was over the top of the ladder and onto the rooftop first. I was just a step behind him. When I caught up, he was scanning the rooftop from where he stood, but he saw nothing. It was as if the guy who had done the shooting had become a ghost and disappeared. Rude.

We stood on the rooftop, forty-five feet above Brooklyn, and scanned the sidewalks below us for anyone who might be running. Or carrying a shotgun. Whoever it was could have crossed over to several other rooftops and gone down a fire escape or maybe found his way through a roof door. Either way, he wasn't showing himself.

"Did you get a good look at him?" I asked.

"I didn't see a damn thing," Tio Luis said. "Just his sneakers. And he was wearing jeans." Not much for an all-points-bulletin.

He had taken out a handkerchief and tied it around the wound in his arm. The pellet had gone through as cleanly as one could hope, but there was a lot of blood. I pointed out the hole in his side; he shrugged and pulled his pants up an inch higher so that his waistband covered it.

"Are we going to the hospital?" I asked, but I knew the answer would be no. He thought he'd done a good enough job of patching himself up. He didn't bother to answer me.

I was no longer surprised by anything Tio Luis might do to get Jasmine back, so I wasn't surprised when he went back down the fire escape, climbed in through the window of the formerly padlocked apartment, recovered five shell casings from the hallway, checked his magazine to be sure it was only five that he needed, and went back up to the apartment where it had all started. I stayed close to him all the way.

One of the shotgun blasts had ruined the lock on the door, and it opened with a push.

Tio Luis looked at me before going in.

"Get your gun out," he said.

"I don't have a gun."

"The revolver."

"That's in the glove compartment," I said. He looked me over from head to toe and shook his head.

Inside, there was nothing. A sofa that used to be white, a glass top coffee table, a small television sitting on a milk crate. In the kitchen there was an empty pizza box and an empty two-liter Coke. Other than this, the walls were bare, the refrigerator empty, the closets empty. The place echoed. That reminded me of the blaring music. The boom box had been kicked over near the front door and was mercifully off now. The whole building seemed quiet, and it scared me.

"Shouldn't we be getting out of here?" I said after a few moments in the apartment. Tio Luis was staring at the sofa, and I knew what he was thinking. Jasmine had been in that same room only hours earlier, sitting on that sofa. He wanted to know who she had sat with and what they had done. A half minute more of staring and he was ready to go.

Afternoon

The next few hours included a trip to the pharmacy where I went in for rubbing alcohol, cotton balls, and gauze. Even though Tio Luis had been shot twice now in two days, I was the one who looked like I needed the supplies.

We also ate at another McDonald's. Panic made me hungry.

And Tio Luis called Titi Clarita. Absolutely no news except that M. Hamilton had been back and had even hassled my mom at work. He was also deeply disappointed I hadn't made myself available for an interview. That's it—"deeply disappointed." Titi Clarita quoted him. Apparently, there still wasn't a warrant in place.

Hector, the private investigator who had, so far as I could see, done nothing to earn a fee yet, had also called but he hadn't left a message with my aunt. Tio Luis called him back at his office from a pay phone right outside the McDonald's. The conversation was only three minutes long. Tio Luis pulled out the list of addresses Nestor had told us about that morning, checked it over, then folded it back into his pocket. He uh-uhed the rest of the time.

There was only one piece of information I was truly concerned about. I wanted to know what the police had to say about Robertito's body being on some steps only fifty steps from Carlos's apartment building. As soon as Tio Luis hung up, I asked him.

"Anything about Robertito?" I said. He turned to me. There were tears in his eyes.

"Who?" he asked.

"The fat guy."

He shook his head and got into the driver's seat of the Corolla. He was slumped. Defeated maybe.

"What's the matter?" I asked. It was a stupid question of course. It had been days since he'd seen his daughter and not a single good thing had happened in all that time.

"He said that guy pimps girls out," he said, the words coming out slowly, getting stuck in his throat.

"Carlos?"

He nodded yes. There wasn't much to say to that. I wanted to tell him that Jasmine was a strong girl, that she would resist, fight, but none of that was true. She was thirteen and if Carlos or any other man wanted her to do something, she'd have to do it. I wanted to tell him that there would be justice for Carlos; he'd be punished, jailed, but none of that was useful even if it might be true. If he could get his daughter back intact, Carlos could go free for all Tio Luis cared. I tried to be practical.

"Do you want to try to get the police involved?" I asked.

Tio Luis wiped tears away with his bare hand and rubbed his face as though he was tying to wake

himself. I suppose he was. He stared at the dashboard for a moment before answering.

"After the last address. If we don't get anything
there, strike three. I'll talk to that guy, the one who's
looking for us. That should make him happy."

I figured it would. The one bright spot of the
day: making M. Hamilton happy.

The last address on our list was in Bay Ridge. I
only knew the neighborhood because just about
everything was marked with it—the pizzeria, the
car dealerships, the library.

We pulled up in front of the house we wanted
and knocked. There wasn't any sound from inside
for a minute, but Tio Luis was not about to give up
that easily. At least no one had shot at us yet. He
knocked again and a few minutes later an angry little boy opened up. I figured him to be about ten or
a little more, Vietnamese maybe. He had on gym
shorts, a T-shirt that had said something but was
faded now, and bare feet. I could see that the TV
was on behind him. We'd knocked while he was in
the middle of some car racing video game.

"What?"

Tio Luis had the picture of Jasmine out, but he
didn't hand it to the boy.

"Is your mother home?" he asked.

"Who wants to know?"

"Luis Ramos," my uncle said, but this kid hadn't
asked in order to get an answer; he wanted us to
take a hint and go away.

"My mom's not here. She'll be back soon," the

boy said. He started to close the door, but Tio Luis put his hand on it to stop him. The kid looked frightened for a second but went back to surly when my uncle handed him the photo.

"Have you seen her?" he asked. The boy gave the picture a hard look, but came up empty.

"Never," he said handing back the picture.

We sat in the car a few moments trying to piece things together. At least, that's what I was doing. I can't vouch for my uncle. He was crying again.

"What do you think about that?" I asked him. I wanted him to focus. I was deadly tired and not sure I was thinking straight.

"About what?" my uncle asked.

"We got an address from Nestor, who hasn't lied to us yet. The address was confirmed by Hector. Yet, there's just a kid there. What did Nestor say about this place? Why did he give us this address?"

Tio Luis went through the things Nestor had said once he had decided to be cooperative. There wasn't much information attached to any of the addresses he had given us. Were all of them places Carlos frequented. Nothing much more. The Village house was different because Nestor claimed to have seen Carlos and Jasmine there the night before.

"Maybe we should wait for the mother to come back," Tio Luis said. He didn't have any other leads. The next move would have been to talk to the police, though I suspected he might swing by the apartment building on 135th street before reaching out to M. Hamilton.

"Maybe you can call Hector back and see how he came up with this address."

Tio Luis thought that would be a good idea—any information being better than nothing—but Hector wasn't in his office. We waited and drove around the neighborhood a little as though maybe out of the millions of people in Brooklyn, we'd be lucky enough to find Carlos and Jasmine walking around in broad daylight.

When he was tired of hoping, Tio Luis drove us back to Manhattan.

We knocked on Carlos's door, but no one answered. My little snitch let me know that he hadn't seen Nestor or Carlos or Jasmine all day.

Tio Luis received this information calmly. I was worried about him. As far as I could see, for all the work we had done that day, the shooting, the blood he had lost, the kidnapping of Nestor, the hundred miles driven, knocking on strange doors, all of it was only getting us further from finding Jasmine. Was my uncle's calm a sign that he was losing hope? If it were, that might be the first sane reaction he had exhibited so far. *And it might kill him*, I thought.

"You want to try calling that private eye again?" I asked.

He was silent a moment before shaking his head.

"You want to try and find Nestor?" Another pause, another head shake.

"Maybe that Ellis kid knows a little more than he—"

"I just want her back," Tio Luis said. It was a moan.

"We'll get her back," I promised. He didn't even bother to throw a glance in my direction. He put the car in gear and headed home as the sunlight was beginning to fade. It was as though he hadn't heard me at all.

Night

By the time Tio Luis had driven into the garage of his home, fatigue had soaked into our bones. If Tio Luis had lost his desire to continue searching that night, I didn't have any spare desire of my own to lend him. We were like travelers on a tundra, lost and weak—it was easier to fall asleep and let life slip away than to continue the struggle. Only it was Jasmine's life that was slipping between all the fingers that tried to hold her, pull her back to normalcy and away from evil and harm.

As soon as we walked through the door, Titi Clarita motioned to Tio Luis frantically. She was on the phone, and she wanted him beside her.

"Jasmine?" my uncle asked. She nodded. They shared the receiver.

"Where are you, baby?" my aunt was asking. Tio Luis echoed her in everything.

"It doesn't matter," he said after a short pause. "I don't care about Carlos. I don't care about him at all. He can go . . . he can do whatever he wants. No police. Just tell me where you are. I'll come get you. No, no. You don't have to call me back. Tell me where you are and I'll—"

Jasmine had hung up. She wanted to come home, she said. She was worried about Carlos. Afraid of what might happen to him, afraid of what he might do. She had done bad things, she said. Terrible things, but Titi Clarita had forgiven her, sending absolution through the phone lines no questions asked.

She would call again. Carlos was coming. He already knew she was planning to go back home, but he was upset, nervous. He had allowed the call but wanted it to be brief. Jasmine had already put him off a couple of times when Tio Luis and I entered. She had said the word *Papi* on her end of the line, and this made Carlos all the more jittery. She didn't know exactly where she was; she'd find out and call back. *Click*. The whole call had been maybe five minutes long.

My mother was there at the dining room table. The four of us sat some minutes going over the conversation. There was no bad news in it. The bad things she had done, whatever they were, they were things other people had done in the past and would do in the future and all those people had survived just as Jasmine had. She was young—she could recover and thrive. Her life was ahead of her—I added that to the conversation.

My mother floated the idea of a quick move to Puerto Rico, a house in the mountains, a little farm life to forget everything, to heal everything. Tio Luis said such a move was the easiest thing in the world, should have been done long ago. He smiled and wiped tears from his eyes, and called Titi Clarita a fool for crying. He clamped his hand onto my shoulder. We would be ready when Jasmine's call came; we'd go out, get her into the car, and bring her home. As for Carlos, *"No me importa ni una mierda lo que le pasa a ese hijo'su mai. Que le parte un rayo."* Carlos could go to hell.

Our ten-minute wait became twenty minutes. The sun lowered on the horizon. The phone rang, finally. Tio Luis picked up.

"Who?" he said. It clearly wasn't Jasmine and he wasn't happy. "Ah, Detective Hamilton. We don't need you anymore. We're waiting for a call from Jasmine." He hung up. I imagined M. Hamilton on the other end with his mouth open waiting for a chance to speak.

"What if we missed her call because of that *pendejo?*" Titi Clarita asked.

I pointed out that the call had taken less than ten seconds. And Carlos seemed willing to let her call, so she could try again if she needed. That calmed my aunt some, but she kept watch on the phone as though warding off any more stupid callers with the evil eye.

The half hour passed without a call back from Jasmine. There weren't too many nice scenarios for the cause of the delay. Maybe they were working out the details of her release like the police did in hostage situations. Unsaid was that maybe they had fought and maybe Carlos had won. Or maybe she had changed her mind. Or maybe she had been conning them, fooling them, playing with their emotions.

Another ten minutes, and I reminded my aunt and uncle that Jasmine hadn't said *when* she would be calling back. Maybe not until late that night. Possibly not until the next morning. They didn't like this idea, but there were other scenarios, the unsaid ones, that they liked even less. This could be lived with. And they knew she was well since she had sounded in good health though, both agreed, there was sadness in her voice.

At forty-five minutes of waiting, the doorbell rang and Tio Luis and Titi Clarita looked at each other with wide eyes. There was one scenario that hadn't even occurred to them—maybe Carlos had tired of Jasmine and put her in a cab without giving her the chance to make another call. They rushed to the door.

"Hamilton?" my uncle said. It was a growl. My aunt rolled her eyes, flopped her arms to her sides, and went back to her seat at the dining room table. I took her place at Tio Luis's side at the door. The detective was on the top step. His partner from earlier that day was standing at the bottom of the stairs, one foot on the sidewalk, one on a step.

"I need to talk to the both of you," Hamilton said.

"So talk." My uncle crossed his arms. The bandage on his left forearm showed. It needed changing.

"Can we talk somewhere in private?" Hamilton motioned for my uncle to come outside with him. The air of the night was finally beginning to cool. In a half hour more it would be night.

109

"I'm not going outside, and you're not coming in here, so say what you have to say." I'm not sure my uncle knew his rights, but he knew what he wanted.

For the first time, I saw that M. Hamilton looked a little distressed, nervous. He'd been running around a lot the last couple of days—not as much as we had, but a lot—and it showed in the lines of his face.

"It's about Nestor Jordan, the guy you complained about a couple of days ago."

"What's he saying?" Tio Luis asked. "I didn't touch him."

I knew from Hamilton's face that Nestor hadn't said anything. With his next words he confirmed what I was thinking. NYPD doesn't knock on your door just for general updates. Nestor was dead.

"A pair of bullets to the back of the head," M. Hamilton said. He searched Tio Luis's face for a reaction, didn't get much. "We fished him out of the East River about an hour ago."

For the next fifteen minutes, M. Hamilton had us repeat what we had done that day, working us backward from that afternoon to the morning. In our version, there was a lot of driving around, a lot of waiting for nothing, nothing at all really that might concern the police—no kidnapping, no torture, no shooting or rooftop chases. Tio Luis never uncrossed his arms.

I had the impression M. Hamilton didn't really think we had anything to do with Nestor dying. He would check out the whole story, he told us. Then he invited us to the station house to put the whole thing on record.

"I'll go over with my lawyer once I have my daughter. Remember? The one you didn't want to bother looking for."

"I'm sorry about that Mr. Ramos, but please do remember that your daughter, thankfully, is alive. Nestor Jordan is dead."

"That's somebody else's problem," Tio Luis said.

M. Hamilton shrugged and shook his head. If he was going to wait for Tio Luis and Titi Clarita to care about somebody other than Jasmine, he should have brought along a lawn chair.

He left us a business card and said he was pretty sure he'd have more to talk to us about before very long.

"Don't be in a hurry," Tio Luis said. He shut the door on M. Hamilton with his mouth frozen open about to say something.

The detectives spent a few minutes sitting out front in their car. Tio Luis didn't give Hamilton another thought—out of sight, out of mind. I watched from a window until they drove away.

At the dining room table, an hour passed, then two hours.

"Maybe we should go to Manhattan," Tio Luis said. He was looking at me.

"Well," I started. "She said she didn't know where she was."

I was beginning to doubt Jasmine's sincerity. I hadn't heard her voice. Maybe I wouldn't have been able to tell even if I had. If she had wanted Tio Luis to leave her and Carlos alone, then she had gotten what she wanted. Tio Luis was sitting still for the first time in days.

It was getting close to midnight when there was a knock at the door. We were all still at the dining room table. The phone hadn't bothered to ring. Tio Luis was wearing a bald spot into his scalp, scratching from worry and restlessness. A pot of coffee had been made and we were all drinking. There were crackers and *queso blanco*. And M. Hamilton at the door again.

"What?" my uncle asked. He crossed his arms again. Again, my aunt had rolled her eyes and flopped her arms and gone back to her seat. The detective was as insignificant to her as a mosquito. Even less than a mosquito—she would have gotten up to kill a mosquito.

"I just wanted to know if Jasmine was back home."

"No," my uncle said. He was about to slam the door again, but Hamilton stuck his nose in a little farther, looked past Tio Luis. From where he was he could see the dining room, my aunt, my mother.

"Has she called?"

"Earlier this evening," my uncle said. I could tell he was getting upset.

"About when was that?" M. Hamilton asked.

"Look. Hamilton. You want to help find her, I'm all for it. In fact, if the entire NYPD wants to help now, great, we'll get to work, but I already told you who has her. If you want to find my daughter, talk to Carlos Valle. *Ese titere* has my daughter, my Jasmine. Talk to him."

"He doesn't have her anymore," Hamilton said. "I went to talk to him. He's dead."

Tio Luis was taken aback by the news. To prove it, he uncrossed his arms.

"What?" he asked, though he had heard every word.

"We found this in his neck," Hamilton said. He pulled a clear plastic evidence bag from an inner pocket of his trench coat. It was a blood-covered Swiss Army knife, unfolded. It was Jasmine's.

Tio Luis himself had given Jasmine the knife when she started junior high school. The trip to school everyday included a walk and a subway ride. Officials at her school would have frowned at her bringing a knife to school, but Tio Luis had instructed her: "Never ever take it out unless you really need to." No doubt Carlos had done something to make her feel she really needed to. He had earned the honor of first use.

M. Hamilton and his partner sat with us all in the living room. The dining room was reserved for guests. The detective explained how it was that Jasmine had gone from being a person of no concern to the NYPD to being a "person of interest." The assumption, and it was a good one, was that Jasmine had killed Carlos—one swift jab and Carlos was stuck like a pig. A minute later, maybe as Jasmine was making her way out onto the street, Carlos was dead. No more Carlos.

"Now," M. Hamilton said. "There is a chance this was self-defense. I'm willing to believe that. But she has to turn herself in so we can talk about this. If she continues to run, it's going to get harder to believe that she didn't just do it out of cold blood, you understand?"

Tio Luis understood. He understood so well that his daughter was being accused of being a cold-blooded murderer, he almost got out of his seat to show M. Hamilton a fistful of understanding. Titi Clarita was sitting next to him with her arm entwined with his, and she anchored him to the sofa.

"But he's a drug dealer," Tio Luis said when he'd calmed. "He has a gun. Of course it was self-defense."

"If she even did it at all," I said. I was speaking to Tio Luis. I didn't want him giving up on his hand before it was fully played out.

"That's right," Tio Luis said. "She may not have done anything at all."

It was M. Hamilton's turn to roll his eyes.

"Look. You can live in a fantasy world if you want, but this is her knife and I'm pretty sure her fingerprints are in that blood. This is as serious as things get, people, and the self-defense thing may not really work for her so well. Carlos was naked and in bed and we didn't find any gun in the apartment. Believe me, we looked."

He stared at each of us in turn. He wanted things to look as dark as possible, to force Tio Luis and Titi Clarita into confiding. He was wasting his time, of course. If they'd had any idea where she was, they'd have gone to get her. I don't know what kind of parents M. Hamilton was used to dealing with, but these ones hadn't held back anything at all in their attempts to find their daughter. I knew firsthand, Tio Luis would be happy to make any sacrifice, including my life, to get back Jasmine.

There was a chance, Hamilton had told us, that the be-on-the-lookout notice for Jasmine might say she was to be considered armed and dangerous. He was trying to apply even more pressure, scare them into talking. The fact that he couldn't tell my aunt and uncle were clueless made me doubt his abilities.

"But you have her knife . . ." Titi Clarita pointed out.

"But if you say Carlos had a gun, someone has it now," M. Hamilton said. His partner nodded. He looked to be about forty years old, but I assumed he was new to the job. Either that or slow-witted.

Within a minute of M. Hamilton and Co. leaving, Tio Luis was holding his face, sobbing into his hands. Titi Clarita was sobbing too, patting his back trying to comfort him. My mother was hugging her brother trying to lend whatever support she could to help him stand up to this latest wave of disaster and survive.

Tio Luis hit his head with his hands as though he were punishing himself. He kept repeating the word *no* and I knew what he meant. Jasmine should not have done what she did. Killing Carlos was his job, not hers. He had failed her.

I stayed in my seat and tried to think of anything I had seen or heard in the last few days that might help me figure out where Jasmine had gone to after finishing off Carlos, but whether it was my tired brain or the crying going on inside the house, it was hard to pull two thoughts together. This much I knew: Carlos and Nestor were the only direct links to Jasmine's whereabouts, and they were both toes up in the morgue. Ellis senior and junior didn't seem like good candidates to have useful information. Somebody in Brooklyn had tried to kill me and Tio Luis, but we didn't have a name or a face to go along with the shotgun blasts. There was a private house, also in Brooklyn, that somehow didn't fit in with anything else. And the private investigator, Hector. He had been a complete waste of time and money so far. I wanted to find out his home number and give him a call. Instead, I fell asleep in my chair, my mouth open and my head tilted back. I dreamed of phone calls that made no sense and had nothing to do with anything. Not long enough later, my uncle shook me awake.

"Let's go," he said. "Jasmine called."

His ragged face was smiling.

DAY FIVE

Early Morning

There was no point asking any questions before Tio Luis and I were in the car and the car was on its way. That was three-thirty in the morning. At that hour, even the city that never sleeps was pretty quiet. I was near exhaustion.

"What'd she say?" I asked.

"She said she was at the Pelham Parkway train station, near the Skate Key place. I told her to stay right there."

No exhaustion for Tio Luis. For him, rest was just a few more stoplights away. He was smiling. He had forgiven the world. Titi Clarita hadn't come along because she wasn't dressed right for an appearance in public and nobody wanted to wait even an extra couple of minutes. I wanted to ask why I was along for the ride—I could have used more than a couple hours of sleep even though my neck was stiff. I kept the question to myself. It would feel good to see Jasmine back safe. Sleep and a hot meal would feel good too.

"Did she say anything else?" I asked.

The smile slid off of Tio Luis's face.

"She said she didn't kill that guy. I asked her. When she left, he was fine. She wasn't even there when it happened." He smiled again.

I didn't point out that if she left before he died and Carlos was killed four or five hours earlier, then she had some hours to explain. Where had she been? With whom? Doing what? But she wasn't my daughter and Tio Luis certainly didn't care.

The Pelham Parkway train station is large and elevated but uncomplicated. There are two stairways up to the token booth and turnstiles, two platforms—one headed downtown, the other up. I found out what I was needed for as soon as Tio Luis parked. I was supposed to use my young legs, climb the stairs, and bring back Jasmine.

I'm not one for trusting gut feelings, but my gut was telling me I wouldn't find her at the top of the stairs or anywhere in the train station. It couldn't be that easy after the past four days. It wasn't.

The only person in the train station at all was the token booth clerk sitting behind bulletproof glass, reading a newspaper from the day before.

"Have you seen a young girl here in the past ten to fifteen minutes? She would have used the pay phone." The phone was only a few feet from the token booth. If she had been there, he would have seen her.

The clerk took off his glasses to look at me, and

I could tell the debate in his mind was between lying to me and telling the truth. The truth won out with a sigh. With my face looking as beat as it did, he probably figured I was prone to violence. He used the microphone inside the booth to talk to me.

"She left a few minutes ago, like two minutes after she hung up. She must have heard something, because she was waiting quietly. Then all of a sudden she ran out that way." He pointed to the same set of stairs I had used to come up.

"Was there anyone else around?" I asked. I would need the full story for Uncle Luis or I had no doubt I'd be making the trip back up.

"Not that I can remember. She was the only one to get off that train. She went straight for the phone, made her call and I just told you the rest."

I didn't know what else to ask. I wanted to find out if she looked well or frightened while she was standing there, but I didn't think that kind of question would get me very far. I went back down.

"What happened?" Tio Luis asked as I took my seat. He sounded angry and his anger was directed at me.

I told him what I knew.

"This is bullshit," my uncle said after I had explained it all. We had missed her by minutes. She had gone off maybe because someone had called to her, maybe because she got tired of waiting, maybe because she was scared.

"This is bullshit," Tio Luis said again. I agreed with him.

Our strategy was to drive the road back home as slowly as we could, trying to find her. It wasn't much of a plan, and it wasn't much of a drive. Not only did we not see Jasmine, we didn't see anyone at all in the fifteen minutes it took to get to Tio Luis's house. I was sent inside to make sure that Jasmine hadn't gotten in or called again, but she hadn't.

"We just missed her," I explained. "I don't know what happened; she wasn't there." Titi Clarita's last nerve broke and I left her distraught in my mother's arms.

"Did she cry?" Tio Luis asked as he put the car in gear.

"A little," I said.

We drove the route again. This time we noticed one person on the street in a short skirt, walking fast with arms crossed against the chill of night.

"Is that her?" Tio Luis asked. He had me call out though this person was a foot taller than Jasmine and three shades darker.

"Jasmine," I called as the car slowed.

"I can be anyone you want," the man said coming over. Tio Luis stepped on the gas. The drag queen laughed and kept walking.

Back to the train station and a jog up the stairs. I walked over to the token booth, but the clerk inside was already shaking his head no. He turned on his microphone to let me know she hadn't been back.

Tio Luis drove up and down several blocks, drove past the Skate Key, drove to the apartment building where Jasmine's friend lived and where I had dodged the "yo" man. The entire building was dark as was that whole street. It was past four in the morning. Soon enough there would be activity. We stopped at a pay phone and I called my aunt's house. My mother picked up. There was no news at all. Titi Clarita was sleeping—my mother had given her a tall glass of brandy.

I got back in the car. My face must have said a lot. Tio Luis had no questions for me. I fell asleep on the drive to Manhattan.

When I woke up, it was because Tio Luis had slammed shut the driver's side door and was nestling back into his seat. We were out in front of Carlos's building. It was still dark out, but the sun was announcing itself with light shades of purple on the bit of horizon visible through the canyon of buildings I sat among.

"Anything?" I asked. I couldn't even imagine what Tio Luis had hoped to find. We were miles from where Jasmine had last been seen. Carlos was dead, Nestor was dead, and none of that was likely to change.

"Big blood stain on the bed, but there wasn't anything else in the apartment," he said.

"What do you mean?"

He shrugged. We were headed out of the neighborhood.

"Nothing," he said. "I mean there was no furniture, no nothing. You were in there. What kind of furniture did they have?"

All I could remember was the dirty, drooling guy

121

on a beanbag. I was pretty much concentrating on the guns when I was there. Beanbag and a boombox.

"Nope." Tio Luis shook his head. We got onto the FDR headed south. "Maybe the neighbors took that stuff."

"The police should have put up some of that yellow tape—DO NOT CROSS," I pointed out.

"They did," my uncle answered. I wanted to tell him that disturbing the crime scene might slow down the police investigation into the death of Carlos Valle, that he might have incriminated himself, but I didn't see how any of that would matter to him, so I shut my mouth.

In the Village again. Dawn. We waited and watched. Tio Luis did anyway. The Ellis household slept. So did I. The sun was just up when Tio Luis nudged me awake. I felt refreshed for several seconds until I saw that Ellis junior had just come down the stairs of the red brick house. He seemed happy, and I knew Tio Luis was just about to ruin that for him. I felt sorry for him a little. More sorry for myself really.

"Go talk to him," my uncle said.

"About what?"

"How does he know Carlos? Did Carlos come to the party with anybody else? Things like that." My uncle's tone told me he was undecided whether I was truly dense or just pretending. I got out of the car and jogged up to Ellis junior.

"Hey," I said, coming alongside him.

He was startled and raised a hand to bite a fingernail, cringing a little. I wondered if he was already high. If he wasn't, he was probably out headed to fix that problem. I noticed his nails had a little rim of black along the cuticles. Probably nail polish he'd thought better of and removed. The thought passed through my mind that Ellis junior was likely to make a lot of decisions on the spur of the moment and regret them later. When he recognized me he relaxed, but just a little.

"Hey," he said back. He kept walking and I stayed with him.

"My uncle had a couple more questions. I was wondering if I could bother you for a minute."

"Sure," he said, but he didn't stop moving.

I asked how he knew Carlos. He said he didn't really. He had gone to Columbia University, met Carlos at a party there a couple of years earlier. Now, every once in a while, if he was having friends over, he'd give Carlos a call and Carlos would come over and bring a few things.

"Mostly weed," Junior said, eyeing me as though I might be recording the conversation or interested in what he snorted or injected or drank or anything. I smiled a knowing smile. The secret was between us.

"Maybe something a little stronger sometimes?" I asked.

"Maybe."

"And girls?" I asked.

"Just whoever he was with. You know. He wasn't a pimp or anything."

I guessed girls were a different phone call the party planner had to make.

"Did any of your friends at the party know Carlos better?" We were headed for the Jefferson Market library on Tenth Street. It was a pretty building, formerly a court, but it was surrounded at that hour by guys who all seemed to be waiting for a fix of some kind.

Junior took a while in answering. He seemed to be giving it real thought, but he might have been pretending or giving thought to how to get rid of me.

"No, not really. I think I was the only one who knew him."

"Anybody take any interest in Jasmine?" I asked.

"Who?" I stared at him. "Oh, the girl. Well, a couple of guys . . . uh . . . liked her, you know, talked to her and shit, but . . . Look, why are you hassling?"

"She's missing," I said. He nodded, remembering. He shook his head and seemed to forget about me. He eyed someone. Probably a dealer. In a few more steps we'd be among the crowd at the library, then he'd lose what little interest he had in anything I had to say.

"And these guys that were talking to Jasmine. . . . Who were they?" I tried to make that as innocent as possible, and Junior paused in his walk a moment and seemed to be searching his memory. Then he figured out what I wanted and started walking again.

"Not cool," he said. "Not cool at all. I'm not your snitch. Never will be. Look, your little sister—"

"Cousin."

"Whatever. She had a few beers, took a toke or

two, talked to some guys—she was into it. All of it. Her and Carlos? They left together, happy as can be. She didn't do anything she didn't want to do. Nothing happened to her that she didn't want. You get what I'm saying?"

He didn't wait for my answer. He jogged away, shook hands with a couple of homeless-looking guys in front of the library, and I was a fading memory.

"Anything?" my uncle asked me back in the car. I wanted to be able to say yes. Junior was hiding something, but I had a good idea what it was and telling Tio Luis that this rich drug addict had slept with his daughter wasn't something I was ready to do. I didn't think I ever would be.

Next stop, Brooklyn. Tio Luis drove past the apartment building in Sunset Park where he had shot the door lock to death. Two squad cars and a Crime Scene Unit truck sat outside. Probably the building super had come back and found two of his doors shot to crap and decided to report it so that the cost of replacing them wouldn't be taken out of his salary by whoever owned the building.

One of the Crime Scene techs was walking into the building with what looked like a handyman's kit. He was just starting the job of processing the shooting. That might take a while.

Next stop, breakfast. There were a lot of cars on the street by this hour. We ate more McDonald's food. There wasn't much conversation. I knew we were headed to Bay Ridge next and another knock on the Vietnamese door. Tio Luis ate his breakfast in a few bites and nursed a coffee. I took my time. I wasn't feeling any pain though I still looked like a beaten man. I had no energy. Putting one foot in front of the other was becoming difficult. I needed sleep. Sleep and a real meal.

Tio Luis called home from a pay phone. It took two seconds for me to figure out that Jasmine wasn't home. That's how long it took for Tio Luis to start wiping away tears.

I didn't ask him about the call. Had there been good news, we would have turned the car in the direction of the Bronx and gone home.

The Bay Ridge house was quiet. We got parking right out in front, blocking their driveway. We both went up a set of five steps to the front door and Tio Luis knocked. The same little boy from the day before in the same clothes answered. He looked at us and turned his head to yell into the house. It sounded like "Ma!" at a very high pitch. I must have heard wrong because a man came to the door. He looked Vietnamese or at least South East Asian. Or at least Asian anyway. Thirtyish.

"What you want?" he asked. He didn't at all seem happy to see us. He also didn't seem interested in an answer. He slammed the door as soon as he had asked.

Tio Luis banged on the door with his fist. Feet shuffled on tile inside. Somebody spoke angrily in a language I didn't get. My uncle pounded on the door again. It opened.

This time the man was accompanied by a woman. She said something to my uncle in Vietnamese and pushed him. Tio Luis stood his ground and since nobody was even bothering to acknowledge my presence, so did I. The man behind her also said something in Vietnamese; both were angry. The lady pushed my uncle again and he took a stutter step back. His left foot went back, didn't find any more landing, and he fell off the stairs, his back hitting the walkway pavement. I took two steps down to get to his side, but then headed back toward the door to give that lady a taste of her own medicine. She shut the door in my face.

Because of the war, my uncle knew a little Vietnamese. While he brushed himself off, I asked if he understood any of what she'd been yelling.

"Yeah, some," he said. "Nothing nice."

Afternoon

I slept on the ride back to the Bronx. We didn't head back to Tio Luis's house because that would have been too easy. Instead we went to the apartment building in the Morris Park area, where Jasmine's friend Clarissa, lived. Yo-man was stepping out of the building as Tio Luis and I were going up the stairs. He didn't recognize me from the kick to the groin. Very politely he held the door for us a second as we got in.

I didn't keep close enough tabs on my cousin to know how close she was to Clarissa. I doubted my uncle had any clear idea. We were here to ask simple questions, he told me on the stairs headed to the apartment. Had Carlos gone to the Skate Key with anyone else that night? Were there any friends Jasmine might hide out with if she felt she needed to hide? Had she heard from Jasmine in the last few days at all?

Tio Luis knocked on the door and I stayed off to the side. Anyone looking through the peephole would have gotten a look at Tio Luis smoothing back his hair instead of at my bruised face. The mother who had shooed me away the first night answered. Tio Luis had his photo of Jasmine ready.

They spoke in Spanish for a few minutes. With strained tact, she explained to him that her daughter had already said all she knew and that they could not and would not allow her to get mixed up in anything like this. From what she could gather Carlos Valle was a drug dealer and a dangerous man, and it was her job as a mother to protect her daughter from him.

"He's not dangerous any more," Tio Luis said. "He's dead."

"Dead?"

"Someone stabbed him."

"Mister, that doesn't make things better. That makes things worse. Murder? My daughter has nothing to say. Don't bother us again."

The door shut. Not a slam, but definite.

"We going home?" I asked in the car. He looked at me like I was crazy.

"We still got one or two more people to talk to."

* * *

One of the people Tio Luis had in mind was the man he had on retainer, Hector the detective. So far as I could tell, Hector had been unable to dig up a single piece of information of value or interest. How much that was going to cost Tio Luis didn't bother me much. I knew it didn't bother Tio Luis at all. One good tip was all it would take.

Instead, I started to wonder if Hector was somehow part of the problem, not just a waste. What if Hector had spoken with Carlos on the phone or in person and had taken a bribe, promising to. . . . That's where the idea ended, but it was a strong idea. Paranoia.

Hector was in his office, eating. Again. The fact that he was stuffing his face made it easier to believe he was on our side. Our side would be the one with the food addict who couldn't find anything if it wasn't on a plate in front of him. I sat and admired his ability to pack away huge portions without gaining weight.

"I was just about to call you," he lied. My suspicions dried up. Even if he were working against us, we didn't really have anything to fear. Sadly, neither did Carlos if this detective was on our side.

"You got news?" my uncle asked.

"No, not really. Just to get an update and let you know what I've been doing so that we don't duplicate our work." He popped a *toston* into his mouth and offered us some from another aluminum plate. It was too early for heavy food even for Tio Luis.

Hector's report took a few minutes. He used his

right pinky to turn pages in a small notepad, all his other fingers being greasier. He had spoken to twenty people, mostly from Carlos's neighborhood. He rattled off some names as though we might care more about who they were rather than what they had to say. We didn't. No difference. He had no leads. Some of the people he had spoken to said that Carlos had shown up alone the night before. Others said he came with a couple of others. Possibly Jasmine. Hard to say. Then it was my uncle's turn.

Tio Luis outlined everything we had done the night before, the phone calls, the missed connection in the train station, the drive to the Village and to Brooklyn. My uncle asked Hector to find out what the deal was with the house in Bay Ridge.

"And check into the Ellis people, and the apartment in Sunset Park. Police were all over that this morning."

"It's morning now," said Sherlock Holmes.

"Early this morning," my uncle clarified. Hector nodded his head and took a bite from a piece of steak, holding the meat with his fingers though he had a plastic fork in his hand.

"You want me to talk to this Clarissa girl?" Hector asked.

"Her mother won't let you."

"I've got ways," Hector said. He raised his eyebrows as though he was surprised he had said something that sounded like confidence. I must have raised my eyebrows too. He looked at me a moment then continued with the food.

"Well, if you can talk to her, great."

Back on the street as we headed for the car, I asked my uncle what kind of faith he had in Hector.

"If you're going to pay someone, shouldn't you get someone more aggressive?" I asked.

Tio Luis was not about to cut and run from someone he'd just hired. He wasn't like that.

"I don't need aggressive, I need intelligent," was the answer. It didn't satisfy me, but it was all I was going to get and it wasn't my money.

It was back to Manhattan for the second person he wanted to talk to. My snitch. Little Man and his whole family were either not at home or very, very quiet.

"They not home," another little kid told me. He had opened the door to his apartment a crack when he heard me knocking in the hallway.

"Where'd they go?" I asked. This kid was about ten, barefoot and wearing shorts, no top. It wasn't that hot out yet, but the afternoon temperatures were supposed to soar to near a hundred and he seemed to be prepared to beat the heat. I stepped over to his door.

"You'll give me money too?" he asked.

I reached for my pocket; it was becoming second nature, giving children money for their thoughts. I pulled out a five and handed it to him without showing anything else of the wad Tio Luis had supplied me with.

"That's it?" the boy said. He sucked his teeth and let the bill go limp in his hand. I didn't move for a second. It wasn't a negotiating technique on my part. I wasn't sure how to react to infant greed.

"Anyway. Mo and his family went to the beach."

"Mo?" I asked.

"Another five dollars and I'll tell you what it stand for," he said. He was smiling like he had me over a barrel.

"Maurice?" I guessed. He lost his smile and shut the door.

When I told Tio Luis the boy was at the beach, he could hardly believe his ears.

"Well, it's good weather for it," I said. I didn't say that I wouldn't mind being on the way to the beach myself.

"Yeah, but . . ." He didn't say that Little Man, Mo, was needed. He had work to do, information to provide. We needed him. At least my uncle thought so. I couldn't even imagine what Mo could say that would help us any.

It was lunchtime, and we headed back to the Bronx.

Titi Clarita can cook. So can my mom, but Titi Clarita has both boiled cooking down to a science and elevated it to an art, and when she puts a plate in front of you, you eat and it doesn't matter if you've eaten already or what that food may be doing to your waist or your arteries, you are never sorry. For once in the days that we'd been searching for Jasmine, Titi Clarita had food waiting for us. Her nervous energy finally and finely focused into something to help the cause. Puerto Rican style.

Yellow rice, red beans, a steak so soft it fell apart at a touch, fried *platano,* and a *rellenos de papa,* and there was more. I knew. I could smell *mofongo al pilon.* I could smell *alcapurria.* Was that *pasteles* I smelled? Not possible. They take a long time and a lot of effort and she would have started us off with them if she had any. I sat and ate while Tio Luis and Titi Clarita talked about the lack of progress. When they tossed me a question or comment, I got by with nodding. If Jasmine or even Jesus Christ had walked through the door, I wouldn't have been able to do any better for them than wave with my fork hand.

At the end of firsts, there were seconds. I went into the kitchen to get my own. There wasn't just *alcapurria.* There was a mountain of the stuff, there was a pyramid of *rellenos,* there was a bowl of the garlicy mix for more *mofongo*; it was like she was planning to open a shop for all this Puerto Rican food. Hundreds had told her to do exactly that. She could have made a fortune. I piled my plate high and went back out to the dinning room table.

"Do you like it?" Titi Clarita asked. Her look my way was so sad it nearly stopped me from eating. She looked so tired, so worn, so beaten by the last few days, it was hard for me not to cry. She had been so happy. And she would be again, I told myself.

"We *will* bring her back home," I said to her. "This *will* come to an end." She smiled as though she knew better.

An hour after eating, an hour into a nap, M. Hamilton shook me awake. I took a quick look around to make sure I was in Tio Luis's house still. Tio Luis was being led out the front door in handcuffs. He was telling Titi Clarita something in Spanish about getting their lawyer. She was crying but listening. I looked up at Hamilton.

"You can come quietly, or we can put cuffs on you," he said. "I brought along an extra pair."

Tio Luis and I rode in the backseat of separate cars. He went in a squad car, I went with M. Hamilton. He didn't have his partner along with him.

"What's the charge?" I asked as soon as we were under way.

"You're not being charged with anything . . . yet," he said. He gave me a glance in the rearview mirror, and I supposed it was meant to be meaningful. I didn't get anything out of it. This was the detective I had called an asshole in front of all his little detective buddies at the precinct. I didn't think this was going to go well for me.

I was quiet for most of the ride and M. Hamilton seemed to like it this way. Toward the end of the ride, I spoke up.

"Why no handcuffs for me?"

"Do you want them?"

"I just want to know."

"You're not under arrest. That can change. Right now, I just need to get some straight answers from you. Your uncle is a different story."

"What's the charge on him?" I asked. He seemed chatty.

"That is between him and the district attorney." Not as chatty as I had hoped.

At the precinct, I was shown to a room with a blank wall. I assumed this was an interrogation room. It had a big mirror that I'm sure allowed interested parties to watch me squirm. There was also a table, a couple of chairs, and no way out except the door I'd come in through. Just like in the movies.

"What's this about?" I asked when I'd taken my seat. Hamilton put up an index finger to let me know I should wait.

"In a minute," he said. "I need to get a notepad."

A half hour later, he was back, with a folder, a notepad, and a pen. I assumed that the long wait was tactical, but I was too tired to care really. He sat across from me and looked at me for a full minute before talking. I assumed that pause was also tactical, but I remained calm. I had decided on the car ride that I would remain calm even if they placed me under arrest, even if I had to stay the night. I couldn't be in any real trouble though maybe Tio Luis was. After all, I hadn't shot anyone.

"You're in real trouble," M. Hamilton started. He was fixing me with a deadeye stare, intentionally keeping up a poker face. First sign that he had nothing.

"Should I get a lawyer?" I asked. Hamilton shifted in his seat. Five words from me and he was already squirming. It couldn't be that easy.

"You're not under arrest. If you want a lawyer, I'd need to arrest you first. Do you want that on your record?" he asked. He must have assumed I'd never seen a cop show on TV. I shrugged.

"It could go either way with me," I said.

"Yeah, I guess it could," he said mostly to himself. He opened his folder and took out a photo.

"Do you recognize this man?"

It was a photo of Robertito, dead. He didn't look too good. Pale. Thinner than I had imagined.

"Looks Puerto Rican," I said. Hamilton didn't fill the silence, so I did. "We kind of all look alike."

Hamilton smiled at that. It looked like a real smile, too.

"His body was found near the place you and your uncle say that Carlos Valle held your cousin. Near the place Carlos was found murdered."

He let the words hang in the air, and so did I. He wanted a reaction and I wanted to give him one, but we can't always get what we want. He was giving me information that I could probably get on the six o'clock news or in the paper tomorrow. After a pause, I spoke.

"Looks a little chunky. He have a heart attack?"

"I'm thinking it was the bullets we found in him, but we'll have to wait for the autopsy to be sure. Look, you want to tap dance, I can do this all night, but let me tell you the truth right now. This guy, Roberto Vargas, got shot a couple of days ago near where Carlos was murdered. He worked for Carlos from time to time; we know that. Right now, we're thinking your uncle had something to do with this, and if that's the case, you're probably an accessory. That's a felony, my friend, and you will be prosecuted and do serious jail time. Unless . . . unless you start talking right now."

I shrugged again, and we looked at each other across the table. Plenty of my friends had had run-ins with detectives. There are only two reasons a detective brings someone in—either they have something on you and it's an arrest, or they think they can trick you into saying or doing something for which they can arrest you. They don't just shoot the breeze. If Hamilton had something that concerned me, I figured he'd have put me in handcuffs. After all, he's talking about a murder, and if he thought I was guilty, he wouldn't have let me ride in the car with my hands free.

Hamilton asked me to confirm that I didn't know the guy in the photo. I told him I couldn't possibly be sure. New York is a city with a million Latino males. The neighborhood where the body was found had hundreds of thousands of Latinos.

He asked me to say where I was a couple of nights before. I told him Tio Luis and I had traveled to a lot of places, talked to a lot of people. Half hour of this and he leaves me again, this time for close to an hour. I figured he was probably asking Tio Luis the same questions, making sure our stories matched. They might not, but as long as Tio Luis didn't get too creative, it should be okay, I thought. After all, I knew for a fact that Tio Luis hadn't killed Carlos or Nestor. Robertito I wasn't too sure about, but he had given me an alibi and if he stuck to that story, things would be all right. I'd plead stupid. How did those holes get in the side of my uncle's car? How did Tio Luis get shot? I didn't know about those incidents. Ask Tio Luis, I'd say. I fell asleep waiting.

M. Hamilton returned and it was more timeline stuff, backwards, forwards, and every which way. Where'd I go first, second, fifth, fourth, third? Who did we talk to? What did they say? He never asked why we didn't leave this search for Jasmine up to the police. I didn't think he would.

More alone time, more of the same questions. This was wearing me down though I wouldn't have thought it could. After a while I wanted to tell him something different. Anything to break up the monotony.

Somewhere near dinner time, M. Hamilton opened the conference room door and let me out. Free to go, but stay in the city. He really said that. About time, I was hungry again. I wanted to ask him about Tio Luis, but I figured Tio Luis would have a harder time getting out. I was wrong. My uncle was waiting for me outside the precinct.

We took a cab to my house so I could shower and change. Titi Clarita had made a big dinner and we headed there when I was ready.

Night

I couldn't tell if Tio Luis had heard some good news or lost all hope. He hadn't said much about his experience in the precinct, and when I asked, he had shrugged. There would be time, I figured, to get our heads together and figure out what the police knew, what they didn't, and what they wanted from us. Jasmine was, I knew, still top priority, but there was a shift occurring. He was worrying more about Titi Clarita. Maybe he was regrouping for a bigger effort, maybe he was retreating, counting Jasmine as a loss already. I didn't want to probe. There was a good chance I wouldn't like what I found in his state of mind.

My mother was helping Titi Clarita to serve the food. Tio Luis told a joke. Except for a missing Jasmine, the picture was perfect. It could have been a Christmas dinner or Thanksgiving. The food was good and plentiful. The eating was pretty silent. The mood became sober.

Titi Clarita didn't ask about how things had gone at the precinct, and I didn't bring it up. Soon enough after dinner, the topic of Jasmine came up. She hadn't been forgotten or relegated to the back burner. Whatever their other troubles or mine, Jasmine was the undercurrent of everything. The food, I figured out during a lull, was Jasmine's favorite—*pasteles con carne*. Titi Clarita had probably made up a batch hoping Jasmine would be eating it tonight as her first meal back.

*   *   *

A couple hours after the meal, while we were finishing a plan of attack for the rest of the night—talking to Clarissa, maybe going to see Ellis again—there was a knock on the door, and I went to answer it. Tio Luis and Titi Clarita were holding hands on the sofa; my mother was leaning forward on a loveseat.

It was M. Hamilton's partner. He didn't look happy.

"Mike would have come up personally," he said. "But he . . . he had others things he had to do."

"Mike?" I asked, and I understood just as it was explained.

"Detective Hamilton. Anyway, he needs someone to. . . . We found a body."

What are you supposed to do when you've been looking for someone, and the police tell you they have a body they want you to look at? The instinct is to say, "No, no. I'm looking for a person, not a slab of meat." How do you go in and tell your aunt and uncle that if they want to see their daughter, they need to head to a morgue? With tears in your eyes and the words strangling you in the process of forming and coming out.

Within a very few minutes all of us were ready for the drive over to the morgue. It was part of a large hospital complex not too far away. On a nice day, one could walk there. There was some small argument about whether Titi Clarita should go. Tio Luis wanted to save her the pain of identifying the body. I would have agreed with him if I'd been asked. I wasn't. I didn't see the point of spreading the pain, and I had already accepted the fact that there was going to be pain involved. We weren't going to make the journey just to be shown some-one else's daughter.

All of us wound up going. Tio Luis drove the Corolla, taking his wife and my mother. I rode the short trip with Hamilton's partner. He didn't want to say anything that might upset me, and I didn't want to say anything at all, so it was a quiet trip.

In the corridor leading to the morgue, I volun-teered to be the one to do the identifying. I didn't think Tio Luis or Titi Clarita would accept my of-fer, but they looked at each other as they walked and Tio Luis nodded to me. Hamilton's partner stopped us a few yards from the door in to the morgue. The light in the hallway was yellow and the fluorescents gave off a hum.

"Have a seat," he said. "Please." There were worn plastic chairs. I wondered for a moment how long people had to wait in this hallway and for what reason. And how many used these chairs on an average day. The thought passed through my mind that maybe some of the people who used the chairs would go into the morgue when it was their turn and leave the place happy that the body was not the one they had feared, that it was, in fact, someone else's loved one lying there, getting cold.

Hamilton's partner tapped my arm as my

mother, aunt, and uncle seated themselves, leaning on each other. He led me to the door of the morgue and stopped me there.

"This is bad," he whispered. He looked me in the eyes and nodded to me as though he were answering a question of mine. I nodded back, and he pushed in the door. I followed.

Inside, a jazz set was on a radio playing softly, the light was not as bright as in the hallway, and there was a young black man in a lab coat writing at a small desk off to the right.

"The recent Jane Doe?" he asked the detective. He was answered with a nod. "Good."

He went over to a wall of refrigerated compartments at the far end of the room from me and took hold of the handle. Hamilton's partner motioned for me to lead the way.

"Detective Pearson told you what to expect?" the man in the lab coat asked.

I figured out who Detective Pearson was and nodded. I was instructed to step closer and lab coat man pulled open the compartment. There was a white sheet with something under it. My breathing stopped a moment as lab coat man reached for the sheet. I felt my chest constrict.

The technician pulled back the sheet and there was Jasmine, the lips, the face, the hair, the head. Nothing else. That quickly I lost all the food I had eaten for dinner onto the floor next to the detective. I retched again and again. I tried to walk away, but I felt my legs giving out on me. I couldn't see where I was going, but I was trying to get as far from that nightmare as the room would allow. Even the world wasn't big enough.

"Are you sure it's her?" Detective Pearson asked me. He was stooped low and had an arm around my shoulders. I was on my knees on the floor of the morgue. The technician hadn't put Jasmine away yet. My head was spinning; it was hard to focus on anything in the room including the detective's face even though it was close to me.

"I need you to be sure," he said. "This is very important, and we wouldn't want to bring your aunt and uncle in here if we can avoid it."

I stood up with the detective's arm still on my shoulders. He navigated me around my own vomit and back toward Jasmine. I looked again though it was the last thing I wanted to do. I looked closely because this would be the last time. I wasn't doing this again.

"That's her," I said after a half minute. "She had a birthmark on her cheek, a wine stain." There it was. The loop earrings in the ears had been a gift from my mother for Jasmine's thirteenth birthday a few months earlier. I took a last look. I wanted to see if peace was written onto her face. If the last few days had been bad for me, they had been worse for her, and I hoped to see that her face showed she was finally at rest. I needed keener vision or greater faith. Her face seemed angry to me.

"That's her," I repeated, nodding. I started to step away. The technician closed the compartment.

"Where was she found?" I asked.

Detective Pearson hesitated.

"I think it's best if we just—" he started, but I wasn't half as uninterested as he wanted me to be.

"Where the hell did you find her?" I asked. The words were strained through my teeth. "Where?" I demanded. I wasn't sure Tio Luis could hear me out in the hallway, but I was loud enough.

"Hunt's Point," Detective Pearson said.

"Hunt's Point?"

"There's a transfer station there . . ."

"A garbage dump?"

"Well," he said. I think he wanted to deny that the conditions were as bad as I suggested. He didn't bother.

"When?" I asked. He looked like he wanted to hesitate again. I don't know what my look told him, but he told me what I wanted to know.

"The head was found on the sidewalk outside the transfer station by a sanitation employee at about four this afternoon."

"And the rest of her?"

"Not found yet."

"And what killed her?"

"I can't—"

"Please!" I roared.

"I mean we know it wasn't anything to do with her head, but we need more of the body to know how she died."

"Any suspects?" I asked. Pearson looked to his shoes, then back at me shaking his head.

"We don't have a good suspect pool just yet, but it's early on in the investigation."

I stood in the center of the room with the detective at my side. I was trying to close my eyes without seeing her, but that was no use. I was trying to put together words for Tio Luis and Titi Clarita, but that wasn't working out either. I tried to think of another question for Pearson, but it was no use.

The door of the morgue swung in from the hallway, alerting my family that I was coming. Tio Luis moved forward in his seat, Titi Clarita too. My mother was standing. The looks on the faces of my aunt and uncle were ones of hope ready to be crushed, ready to be uplifted. Tio Luis raised his hands off his lap as though he were waiting to catch something. Expectant. The look on my face told them everything they needed to know.

Tio Luis stood up and covered his face with his hands. Titi Clarita said "Oh no," several times and doubled over in her seat clutching her gut as though someone had kicked her in the stomach. I guess someone had.

My mother patted my aunt on the back and reached out a hand toward her brother at the same time. She would have taken the pain away from both people if that power had been in her hands. Tears streamed freely down her face and off her chin. They did the same for me.

Detective Pearson stayed back some paces. It was the best place for him.

* * *

"You bastards!" my uncle shouted. It was at Pearson. "You didn't care about her! You could have found her on day one! You could have saved her."

"I didn't know about her until just the other day," Pearson answered. He had his hands up in front of him. Tío Luis had made a half-hearted charge at him. I held my uncle back, but it wasn't hard to do—he didn't have much fight in him just then.

"I swear, I didn't even know your daughter's name until the day before yesterday."

"But you didn't *care*!" Tío Luis said. It wasn't so much the detective's efficacy that was on his mind; it was the detective's heart. Did he care? Probably not. Maybe a little more now that Jasmine's death was bound to make the papers. Maybe a little more now that Tío Luis had questioned his humanity.

Tío Luis struggled out of my arms and went back to the plastic chairs. If Titi Clarita tried to make a run at the detective, I wouldn't have stopped her. Her mind wasn't there.

"Can we see her?" she asked. It was a soft voice, shaky.

There would be nothing Detective Pearson could do to stop my aunt from seeing the corpse of her own daughter. There was no mechanism in the law to prevent that. He said nothing to her request. I answered.

"Titi Clarita," I said. "I don't think that would be good until . . . you know . . . the funeral home people have . . . cleaned her up."

She sat back, accepting my words. Tío Luis

leaned forward. He had seen dead bodies before. He sensed my answer was off. He wasn't willing to take my advice.

"What did they do to her?" he said. It came out strong, angry. He stood. "What did they do?"

"We can talk about it later," I said. I was hoping that "later" would turn into never as far as I was concerned. Where was M. Hamilton with the bloody details? Why wasn't he here? He was the one who had refused to help us on the first day. Didn't he want to face the consequences of his racist bullshit? He could have explained to Tio Luis how Jasmine's head had been sliced off her body. Maybe he would have even enjoyed it. One less Puerto Rican. Extra points because she's a young female.

"I want to know now," Tio Luis answered. He was owed that much. Any parent who can't even see his or her child in the morgue, whose child's body was left too mangled for viewing, deserves some explanation. Detective Pearson wasn't stepping forward with anything.

"*Le cortaron la cabeza,*" I whispered. They cut her head off. Simple.

Tio Luis fell back, and the chair caught him. If it hadn't been there, he would have hit the floor hard, but not hard enough. *He needed to be unconscious,* I thought.

The technician came out into the hallway, waved the detective over and said something in his ear. Pearson came back to us.

"We need to move out of this hallway," he said

quietly. He was talking to me mainly, hoping I would corral my family and herd them elsewhere. He was nobody to me. He had no right to talk about "need." He and his partner needed to do their jobs. There was a need.

He looked into my eyes. He looked weak, pleading. I understood him. They were going to be bringing in another body part, an arm or leg or torso, and my aunt and uncle shouldn't be there to see the body bag being wheeled in.

"We should go home," I said. I tried to hurry my aunt and uncle out of their seats. My mother followed my cue and did the same.

"Detective Hamilton and I will . . ." Pearson started. I turned to him and waited for him to finish. He didn't.

"You two will burn in hell maybe?" I asked. I thought there was a good chance of that.

"We'll be by later. Statements."

Is this how police work was supposed to work? Wait until the victim was actually dead, then spring into action? It seemed backward.

I turned away and led Tio Luis. My mother had hold of Titi Clarita. There were reporters waiting at the exit of the hospital with cameras for the newspapers. No TV people. That Jasmine had risen in importance, but not that high, was what first came to mind. Then the photographers got near us. My aunt and uncle didn't seem to care. Why would they? I cared. I kicked out as one photographer got too close. He wanted a photo of my uncle's face, grieving. That photographer just missed getting his camera kicked out of his hands. He sprang up from the crouch he had gotten into and took a stutter step back. He looked angry, but it passed. Others got photos and so did he. I ushered us all into the Toyota, and I drove.

"This won't stand," my uncle said on the drive home. "This won't stand."

I knew what he was talking about. Someone was going to have to pay for this. That was clear.

During the drive, he had asked me how she looked.

"Was she peaceful?" he asked. He was sitting in the passenger seat beside me. Titi Clarita and my mother were in the back. My aunt leaned forward. She wanted at least this much solace. There wasn't anything else to give her at this point. They had already asked if I was sure it was her. I had told them about the wine stain. That sealed it in their minds. I told them about the earrings, too.

"Was she peaceful?"

"Yes," I said. "Like an angel."

Titi Clarita sat back.

"This won't stand," my uncle said.

M. Hamilton and Pearson came over to the house a couple hours later. We had been mostly quiet. There wasn't much to say really. Hamilton stirred things up.

"You stupid bastard," my uncle said. I had opened the door. Hamilton was there. He looked bad. Not as bad as any of us in the house, but tired

at least. He hung his head. My uncle came up behind me when he heard the voice.

"You stupid bastard! You could have done something. She could be alive today. She could have
been home. You stupid bastard. If you think I'm
not going to talk to the press, if you think I'm not
gonna get a lawyer and sue you, the police department, the city, you're wrong. I'll make you wish
you had paid attention to us. Believe me."

My uncle said more, and Hamilton apologized
many times as though anything he had to say
would be of interest to anybody. As though he
could be forgiven. He said something about this not
helping and the killer being out there. My uncle
laughed at that last part.

"You couldn't find my daughter when I gave you
a street address. Now you're going to find her
killer, and you don't even know who he is?" He
laughed again. It was bitter.

I tried to say something constructive.

"I think we need to get a new detective. Someone
who cares about Puerto Rican lives and someone
who's competent."

M. Hamilton didn't know what to say about
that. He stood at the door; he had a notepad in one
hand and a pen in the other and he looked at his
shoes thinking a moment.

"Believe me," he said. "I'd like to hand this case
over to someone else. I don't like dealing with cases
when children are murdered. But I started the work
on this and the department would like me to con-

tinue. Switching detectives is not a good idea. Not in the middle of the investigation."

"Don't worry. We can handle this ourselves," Tio Luis said. He was about to slam the door. Hamilton put a hand on the door to stop it.

"No. You can't. First, I'm assigned to the case, so I'm going to work it. Second, not for nothing, you've been working hard at this for a few days now and you don't have any more idea who killed your daughter than I do. I'm sorry to put it this way, but it's the truth. Now, I'm sorry for your loss, I really am, but I need to know everything you know, everybody you talked to, what was said, if I'm going to have a good chance at catching this guy."

He sounded firm but reasonable. It was the best voice to use at the moment with my uncle.

The interview lasted a little more than an hour. We told him about everything we had tried to get Jasmine back alive. We told him about the reward flyers, we told him about talking to Nestor though in our version, it was a lot friendlier, we told him about Jasmine's phone calls, about missing her at the train station, about talking to Ellis and his son, about Clarissa, about my little snitch, about Hector the private investigator who hadn't gotten very far, about the trips into Brooklyn and the Vietnamese family. Some of this was new to Hamilton, a lot wasn't. He filled several pages from his notepad with a sprawling longhand. In the end, he took down the contact information for all the people we had spoken to.

When he left, it was late, and Tio Luis and Titi Clarita had phone calls to make to let the family know what had happened. We had asked M. Hamilton when the funeral home could get the body. He said, "Not yet." From his hesitation I knew the pieces had not all been found yet. I wondered what was missing, but didn't ask.

I slept that night in my own bed. The sleep was restless. I woke several times, frightened. I had had nightmares, but I couldn't remember even the vaguest outlines of them. It was like my mind was just drifting off into darkness and the very black of it scared me.

DAY SIX

Morning

Who was Jasmine? Why was she important?

Jasmine was family. Does that make sense? Maybe I should say she was young and beautiful, the future ahead of her bright, lit by her intelligence, her smile, her laugh, and the way she held her head high when she walked. Maybe it makes sense if I say she invented her own knock-knock jokes, terrible ones, when she was five or six. She gave in-depth analyses of the movies she saw when she was ten. At twelve, she had a crush on a boy in her class who didn't know she existed, and it hurt her.

She had told me just a week before she went off with Carlos that she wanted to be a lawyer. Some people in this world did bad things to others, and she wanted to help stop that. And if I say that I didn't think that was out of her grasp though no one in her family had ever finished college? It never crossed my mind that she would be unable to achieve her goal if it was still what she wanted when the time came. She wanted to be a lawyer and save the world. Why not?

To frame for you what she was, the height and width and depth of her, is not possible though she was young. To say what she meant is not possible. To say how profoundly her living and leaving life touched and changed the lives of those around her, those who loved her, is not possible. She was loved and now she's missed. The loving was great; the missing is terrible. That may not make sense either. But it's all there is.

In the morning my mother and I went to my aunt and uncle's. There was a lot to do for them. They needed to eat, more phone calls and arrangements had to be made. And they needed consoling. They needed to be told that they had done all they could, that the city swallowed people whole and didn't care, that Jasmine was in a better place.

M. Hamilton came by with Pearson in tow. The anger this caused in Tio Luis was probably therapeutic.

"I wanted to tell you that your daughter's body has been recovered and the cause of death has been determined. The coroner has found that Jasmine died as the result of a homicide—"

Hamilton was reading from his notes at this moment, but Tio Luis couldn't restrain himself.

"*Que pendejo,*" he said. "It took all night to come up with that? A homicide? Get out of my house." Tio Luis had been sitting on the sofa facing the detectives. He sprang up to say all this and pointed at the door he wanted them to leave through. He walked away. Hamilton finished his report to me after a half minute of feeling awkward.

"Well . . . I just wanted to be the one to let your family know that we are working hard on this case; better from me than on the news, you know what I mean?" He paused here like he was waiting for me to acknowledge his too-little, too-late efforts and reward him with a hug or something. I sat.

"Anyway, the cause of death was a single gunshot wound, at close range. The bullet went through her heart. The coroner says death would have been very quick." He put away the notes he was reading from.

"Was she raped?" I asked.

"Well," he said. That's it. He scratched his head. He didn't want to say, but I wanted to hear it from him. I had all day to wait.

"Well, a foreign object was . . . used on her, but we don't know what it was." He cleared his throat. "There was some heavy bruising on the torso, pretty close to the time of her death, so we're thinking that she put up a good fight."

"And where were the other parts found?" I asked. I might as well have all the bad news at once. There was no point of getting the information little by little.

"Ah, well," he referred to his notes again. "The left leg was found in Crotona Park by a park ranger. The right leg was found in front of an abandoned building near West Farms by a drug addict.

The torso with arms was found along a horse trail on Pelham Parkway."

Those were all pretty public places, miles apart. M. Hamilton didn't have anything to say for a few moments. I glanced over at my aunt and uncle. They were watching us, expectant. I didn't think they could hear what we were saying.

"I think it's supposed to be a message," Hamilton said.

"About what?" I asked.

"I think the killer wants to be left alone. I mean, we don't know where he shot her, but we do know that even if he felt he had to move the body, he certainly didn't need to . . . cut her up like that. Even if he thought he did, he definitely didn't have to drive all over the Bronx leaving . . . parts of her everywhere. You see what I mean? I mean, that was a good way to get caught. He wanted the parts found. I think he wanted you and your uncle to . . . stop."

I had to think. I stood up as though that would help. It didn't.

"You mean one of the people we've talked to got scared and did this to stop us?"

"No, no, no. Don't jump to that conclusion. Please don't, I beg of you. I didn't say you had spoken to the killer. Maybe yes, maybe no. What I would say is that the killer knows you've been investigating. Maybe they found out from Carlos. Maybe they found out from Nestor. Maybe it was the flyers. We don't know. But the killer, I'm pretty sure he wanted to send a message. That's all I'm saying."

The detectives left a little while later. They took their condolences with them. We didn't want them.

I put my hand out to stop anyone from asking me any questions about the conversation. There was a thought trying to form in my mind, and I needed a little time and a little quiet to put a few things together.

What the hell kind of message was that? "Leave us alone or we'll kill your daughter," is a message. Killing her, chopping her up, and scattering the pieces—that's not a message, that's murder. If they wanted Tio Luis to stop digging, they needed to kill him, not Jasmine. Or they could have just let Jasmine go.

Besides, if they were trying to scare us off, they'd just given Tio Luis no reason to fear them. They couldn't hurt him more than he already was.

The only reason to use murder as a message is if it is a message about something bigger. But what was bigger? What was so big that murder was just a message in comparison? And why was Jasmine the one who had to die?

I told my aunt and uncle everything. The process was a long one. Each piece of information was gone over and over and over. The location where the parts of Jasmine were found seemed like a puzzle. If they only made some sense together or separately, we could figure out the killer.

We spent time trying to figure out who would want to send a message and why. We tried to calculate exactly how long Jasmine had suffered after the bullet to the heart. Was there significance that it was the heart and not the head? Foreign object? I had to tell them that too. The talk was punctuated by phone calls where all this was repeated or censored depending on who the person on the other end of the line was.

The hours passed, agonizing and slow. We tried to talk about how good that Jasmine had been, but it was hard staying on that track when the calls reminded us that she had been murdered and that murder was not the worst of it.

Afternoon

In the afternoon, Hector the detective stopped by. He was wearing shades and a dark suit with a black shirt underneath. He looked like he'd just stepped out of a gangster film.

He spoke in Spanish, the right language for Puerto Ricans to cry in, and apologized for everything that had happened. He hugged my uncle and gave my aunt a kiss on the cheek. He had a hug for me as well as my mother. He asked to speak to my uncle. My uncle called me over.

Hector pulled an envelope from inside his jacket. It was the retainer my uncle had paid. "Intact" he said. My uncle shook it off.

"I promise results. Satisfaction," Hector said. "I didn't get you shit. You have to take it."

"You're still on the job," Tio Luis said. "I want to know who did this."

Hector had been sitting at the edge of the sofa, my uncle a couple feet away from him. What Tio Luis said froze the detective for a full minute.

"No, no, no, no," he finally said. He had figured things out a few seconds after I did. That seemed to be about our luck with detectives. We drew the slow ones.

"Tu no quieres hacer eso," he said. You don't want to do that. "These people, they're killers. They killed drug dealers, they killed your daughter, they—"

"I want to know who, and I want to know why. That's it."

"Okay, okay, but let the police do that. That's what they do. It'll come out. This will be in the papers. It's already on TV. Believe me. You will find out all of that. You will find out more than you want to know."

Of course, we already knew more than we wanted. It wasn't a question of wanting.

Hector turned to me for common sense. I had to agree with him, but that was something for my own heart. I said something to the effect that Hector was right, and Tio Luis shot me a look. It wasn't a question of right, either.

"I'm not asking you to do anything illegal," Tio Luis said. "I just want the same kind of information I wanted before. That's it."

I knew, of course, that the illegal stuff was something he'd handle himself. Probably with me in the passenger seat.

Hector looked at me again. He threw a glance over at my mother and my aunt at the dining room table, but they weren't a part of this conversation. They hadn't heard all that had been said. They hadn't heard what Tio Luis was whispering now. That's the way he wanted it. Titi Clarita could deny knowing anything about anything except the grief in her heart. Anyway, I didn't for one minute think Titi Clarita would have had a different view of things. If murder had been good enough for Jasmine's end, it was good enough for whoever had killed her.

Hector looked around the room as though he wasn't sure whether he should accept the work Tio Luis had for him or turn my uncle over to the police. He slowly put the envelope back into his jacket pocket as though waiting for someone to stop him.

"Well," he said. "I can start out by seeing what there is to know about Carlos, Nestor, and whoever was employing them. That's a possible angle. Maybe Jasmine heard or saw something and whoever handled Carlos and Nestor thought she'd be a liability. I could see where that leads."

Tio Luis thought that would be a good place to start. He and I would follow up other leads. I had no idea what that meant.

Hector and my uncle shook hands and Tio Luis led the detective to the door. I followed.

"Remember. If you want to call me off, there's

no problem. One phone call. Full refund. *Con confianza.*"

He was about to turn and go when I thought of a question for him.

"That house in Bay Ridge. What's the deal there? How did it come up?"

At first he didn't seem to know what I was talking about.

"Oh, that. I asked around on One Thirty-fifth Street. The people who knew Carlos said it was one of his recent hangouts. Why?"

"Any reason why he'd hang out there?"

"Well. . . . It could be business or pleasure."

"And who said this about him?"

Hector eyed me a moment, then my uncle.

"She's a source. A girl who works the street. Marissa. You can find her on One Hundred Thirty-fifth and Broadway sometimes. She's around. When she's not busy."

That didn't clear up the connection Carlos had to the house in Bay Ridge. Like Hector said, prostitutes could be either business or pleasure for Carlos. The fact that a prostitute knew about this house and had probably been there didn't tell me anything. The neighbors might have more to say. I told my uncle that after the detective had gone. He nodded as he listened, but he had something else in mind.

Tio Luis's eyes were red with red rims and dark bags under them. He hadn't slept much in the past few days and the past few hours had been spent crying and wiping tears. He looked like the dictionary definition of fatigue. Titi Clarita actually seemed to improve as the hours went by. My uncle did not.

In my mind I've kept to myself the idea that with a few hours of sleep, another couple of good meals, and with Jasmine's funeral, Tio Luis would lose interest in revenge. What was the point of it? Jasmine was dead, wouldn't come back, and there probably wasn't a single person to be blamed for it. Whoever had pulled the trigger might have been working for someone else, or had help or people who knew what had been done to her. If we dug deep enough, there was probably a long line of people who deserved a bullet.

Near evening, Tio Luis picked up a phone call from a coroner's office official who said we could arrange to have a funeral home pick up Jasmine's remains for burial. The most surreal phone call, as he explained it later. Like getting a call that your dry cleaning was done, but it was a person they were talking about. Someone you loved.

More phone calls to be made in response to this. I made some of them. The news was deflating. As though there was still a chance while they weren't discussing her burial. Now that this was the case, hope finally died.

Night

Later, after many more phone calls made and received, after a silent dinner, and after plans with a funeral home, my uncle pulled me aside. It was about ten at night.

"I've got to do things," he said. He looked at me for a sign of understanding. The last thing in the world I wanted to do was give him that sign, but I didn't have a choice. I would have to go with him wherever he led. I was family and this was family business. Absolutely necessary to the working of the world. I nodded.

"You see how things are, right?" I knew what he meant there too. We couldn't trust the police to find the responsible parties. What did they care, really? No doubt Jasmine was already a set of numbers on a case file somewhere. If the leads were slow in developing, there would be no media pressure on them. If there were any, they'd say she was a prostitute running with drug dealers and leads were hard to come by in those circles.

"Come on," he said. I followed him out to the car.

We drove to Brooklyn. It was where the most unanswered questions sat waiting for us. At the Sunset Park building, there was TV noise coming from the super's apartment. Tio Luis banged on the door. It was ten-thirty. The super padded up, and we could hear him move a little peephole cover aside.

"What you want?" he asked.

"To talk."

We could hear him sigh. Maybe he thought we were the police. In that neighborhood, and in that building, plainclothes men banging on the door at night were probably not too uncommon. Another hassle.

The door opened. The super was dressed in slippers, shorts, a blue T-shirt, and a revolver.

"What?"

"The shooting on the third floor," my uncle said.

"What about it?"

"Who rented that apartment?"

The super looked like he really wished he had asked to see a badge. If he had, and we didn't produce one, he could have refused to talk to us. He still could, but now that would make him look like a punk trying to weasel his way out of answering a specific question as opposed to a guy who couldn't be bothered with non-police generated questions at all.

"Miguel Aponte. They call him Mickey. Drug dealing son of a bitch."

Tio Luis asked for a description and got a brief one: twenty or so, five-six, one hundred and twenty pounds, a scar running through his left eyebrow, another on his lower lip. He had ears that stuck out from his head—hence, the nickname. He wore braces with rubber bands in his mouth. Always wearing baggy clothes, always carrying something that could kill you.

The super started to close the door.

"Did you tell the police this?" I asked.

"Of course. They should know all about that asshole. Kind of kid that gets to talk to the police a lot."

"Where can we find him?" Tio Luis asked.

"Hell if I know. Damned if I care. And if you guys are looking to kill him, see if he's got any rent money on him. He owed a month. And for the door."

The door closed. Tio Luis stood there looking at it until the noise from the TV grew louder and it was clear the super wasn't interested anymore. He dug into his pocket, pulled out a thick wad of cash, peeled off four fifties and slipped them under the door. The bills were crisp.

"In case we need to ask more questions," he told me as we left.

We drove around to whatever seemed like a good place for a drug dealer to do business—alleyways, park benches, street corners where the stores had rolled down their gates for the night. We parked and watched the transactions of one group for a few minutes. They were doing good business in handshakes that passed along money and drugs. If we had been police officers, there wouldn't have been anything we could do to them. It was obvious they were selling drugs, but there wasn't any probable cause to stop them from shaking hands or refilling their pockets from a worn paper bag they kept in the wheel well of a parked car.

None of the guys in the group had ears sticking out the sides of his head, but Tio Luis asked me to step out and ask for Mickey anyway. I did.

"What you want him for?" I was asked. It took a second to size me up as bad for business.

"I need to talk to him," I said. I tried to sound

tough, but there were five guys and two girls and one of the guys had moved around to someplace behind me, and I knew Tio Luis would come to my rescue just as soon as we had the information we needed.

"He did that to you?" The speaker was a tall thin guy wearing basketball shorts and a jersey with a warm-up jacket on top. He was talking about my face, which still had bruises on it.

"That's between me and him," I said. I thought that sounded appropriately tough. I had on a light jacket and my hand was in my pocket. The guy asking the questions looked from my face to my pocket and lost a smile in the process.

"Look, I don't want no trouble. I haven't seen Mickey in a couple of days. He got into a beef with someone who shot up his door; the police asked around a little. That's it. Ain't seen him since."

"And where would he hang out if he's not in the 'hood?" I asked.

"I don't know," the drug dealer said. He was looking past me. No doubt he had figured out that Tio Luis was guaranteeing my safe return. "Try this place," and he gave me the address of the house in Bay Ridge.

"What goes on there?" I asked.

"Never been," the dealer said with a shrug. He started to walk away and so did all his friends. A squad car was rolling up. I stayed where I was. A uniformed officer squinted at me and the car rolled up a little farther to corner one of the guys who had been at the corner with me.

"Anything?" Tio Luis asked me when I got back in the car.

"Let's go to Bay Ridge," I said.

So everything connects to Bay Ridge and yet, there seems to be an average Vietnamese family living there. They didn't seem to want any trouble, yet they were in the little black book of drug dealers and prostitutes. And children lived there. And it was a nondescript house—redbrick, a few stairs out front, attached on both sides to other houses just the same in a neighborhood that was just a little busy but otherwise residential. No snarling pit bulls, no barbed wire fences, no steel plating on the door. Maybe we had the wrong address, but then, it was the same one everyone gave us.

We parked a few doors down from it. The neighborhood was quiet. Almost everyone was sleeping. In a couple houses, there was the blue flickering light of a TV on in second-floor bedrooms. In the house we wanted, there was nothing on and nobody came out or went in though we stayed until one in the morning.

I knew what the morning had for me. I would be woken up early to help find Mickey or some other hoodlum. As soon as he dropped me off at home, I went to bed.

DAY SEVEN

Morning, Noon, and Night

Nobody came to wake me up early the next day. I woke up an hour before noon, startled; I was so rested, I felt sleepy again. I went up out of the basement apartment to my mom's house. There was a note stuck on the refrigerator door: GET DRESSED AND HEAD OVER TO THE FUNERARIA PEREZ OVER ON TREMONT. Perez was one of several funeral homes where Spanish was spoken fluently. No one wants to have to struggle to be understood when discussing these kinds of arrangements. I had been there several times before. It was nice enough as far as those kinds of places go, but that doesn't say much. Short of hiring a clown, there wasn't much a funeral home could do to rid itself of the cold and oppressive atmosphere it carried.

I ate and hurried.

At the funeral home, there were a couple of other family members outside. It was a workday. There'd be more at night. People would be arriving from Puerto Rico before the day was out. They would visit Tio Luis and Titi Clarita, but they'd stay with my mom or someone else in the family. When it was all just a case of Jasmine running away, when there was every hope she'd come back, these people called often enough to worry my aunt that she might be missing a message from her daughter. Some had come over for short visits to see with their own eyes how things were going, to pat my aunt and uncle on the back and tell them hope was alive and there was no reason to give it up. Now they were here to help them mourn because that was not something that can be done well and properly alone.

I didn't talk much to these people though they were all family too, and I loved them. There were two reasons. First, they hadn't come for me. I was a fellow well-wisher. More importantly, if I started to talk, there was no telling where I would end. Tio Luis and I had already done much that shouldn't be spread too far-and-wide. And last I saw him, he had much more planned. If he still had those thoughts and I still went along to help and if I could find no way to reason Tio Luis back from the edge of the cliff, the fewer people who knew, the better. The only person I could trust myself with in any deep conversation at the moment was my uncle. I wanted to catch a few minutes alone with him. I hoped he had calmed down, changed his mind. I even hoped that if he still planned to get his revenge, he might think it was a good idea to leave me out of it. I'd worry for him from home if he still needed to get himself killed.

I found Tio Luis inside, sitting with and hugging Titi Clarita on the front row bench facing the open casket. My aunt was whimpering to herself as though she were a kicked dog. Tio Luis was passing his hand over her back, murmuring something to her, calming her. He gave me a quick look as I neared. He looked more haggard than the night before. I guessed he hadn't slept at all. Even if he had closed his eyes, he might have had dreams that made him regret it. He'd told me once that coming back from Vietnam had done that to him for a while—given him nightmares. Slept soundly during the war though.

I went up to the casket. I didn't want to, but I felt I owed Jasmine that much. I owed my aunt and uncle too. They needed to see that Jasmine's death could be looked in the face and survived. I wasn't sure I was the one to show them this, but I tried.

Jasmine was not beautiful in her coffin. Anyone who said so must either not have known her well or meant it in comparison to whatever picture of death they had in mind. She wore her white communion dress with the tiara. The dress had a high neck and covered her throat. Her smile seemed fake and strained; it was close mouthed and didn't reach her eyes. Her face didn't seem peaceful to me. It looked tense, but maybe that was just me.

Makeup covered her entire face and her hands. I wanted to put two fingertips to my lips and then to her cheek as a send-off, but I was afraid of smearing the work that had been done on her.

I wanted to think a profound thought at her coffinside, but nothing came to me. My prayer was short. "Take her," I said. "Take her and let her have some rest."

I sat next to Titi Clarita. A few minutes later, my uncle stood and went to Jasmine's side. Whatever fear I had about her makeup was not shared by Tio Luis. He stooped and kissed her. He caressed her face and hair. He held her hand. One of the funeral directors was at the back of the room ready to get the Kleenex if it was needed. I'm sure he would have liked to have told Tio Luis to get his hands off Jasmine, but that would not have been wise.

"Se sabe quien hizo esto?" one of my cousins asked later in the afternoon. Do we know who did this? My cousin, Paco as far as I had ever known—and I'd never heard his real name—was talking to Tio Luis at the front bench just a few feet from where Jasmine lay. I was shocked at the question. Perfectly good question, but not quite right for the inside of a funeral home, I thought.

My uncle got up and walked Paco a few feet away, huddling close with him. They looked alike standing so close. They certainly couldn't deny the DNA connection. I hoped it didn't go beyond appearances. I didn't need two family members driving around New York with guns looking for people to kill.

"The police are following some leads," my uncle said. He was calm, and I thought for a moment his thirst for revenge had died in him. If anything could kill that desire, I figured it might be seeing his daughter laid out as she was. What had violence gotten him so far? What had violence gotten her?

"Because we should do something about the bastard," Paco continued. "I don't care. I'm with you no matter what." Paco was getting a little excited. Tio Luis walked him farther away from Titi Clarita and from the casket. He gave me a look to follow him.

"An eye for an eye, bro," Paco said, and the three of us headed out of the salon and into the foyer of the funeral home.

For a moment I had hope; then I felt guilt. I thought Paco might be able to replace me in my uncle's schemes. If Tio Luis still wanted to do something, he could take my cousin. I could rest, I could heal, I could not be there when the bad things happened. But Paco was drunk.

His eyes rolled a little when he should have held them straight, and his words were a bit slurred. He was gesturing a little more than he normally would have, and the gesture started out at the knees and rolled through his body until they got to his hands and were let out. Tio Luis was humoring him and winking at me.

"The police will do what needs to be done," he said. "For now, all we have to do is cry and bury her."

He didn't mean a word of it, but Paco wasn't seeing clearly enough to figure that out. Not only wasn't he going to be taking my place, he wouldn't even remember this conversation a few hours later when he was sober again.

A little later, my uncle called me to his side.

"Go home and rest," he said. "I'll pick you up tonight."

It was three o'clock and the funeral home closed at nine. I had six hours of waiting ahead of me.

In six hours, so much could be done. One could call the police and say, "My uncle's gone crazy, please take his guns away." They wouldn't do it, of course. Or one could go to Grand Central Station and get a train ticket to somewhere really far away. Stay away a few days and everything will be a lot calmer upon return. Maybe the police would have actually done their job by then, figured out who had pulled the trigger on Jasmine and put them behind bars.

Or I could spend the time trying to figure that bit of information out and turn over the information to the police. If nothing else, they could get to the killer a few steps ahead of my uncle.

None of those possibilities mattered. M. Hamilton and Pearson were pulling up in front of my mother's house as I climbed the steps to the front door. I waited for them there. Getting arrested might be another way out of this and if that's what they were there for, I'd be happy to go.

"We need to talk," Hamilton said, walking toward me. I didn't budge, though he paused a moment two feet in front of me as though waiting for an invitation inside for coffee or something.

"What's your uncle doing?" he said.

"Mourning," I answered.

"I mean long term. What's he planning? What's he thinking?"

"What are you talking about?"

"I just got a call a little while ago. Some private investigator has been upsetting citizens, asking questions like he's part of the investigation into the death of Jasmine Ramos."

"Murder," I corrected him.

"What?"

"Not 'death' like she had a heart attack. It was a murder. Rape and murder and dismemberment and then some sort of message, you said."

Hamilton moved his jaw like he wanted to say something, but kept whatever it was to himself. He seemed flustered rather than apologetic, mad maybe that I was throwing his words back at me.

"Look. This private eye, Hector Sepulveda, he's stepping on toes. He talked to this girl Clarissa and her mom. They called us. He spooked them. We can't have him doing that if we're going to do our job. You people wanted our help, now you've got it—"

"Bullshit," I said.

"What?"

"What is it with you and your hearing today? I said 'bullshit.' We wanted your help when Jasmine was alive. You said you couldn't be bothered. Now it's a front-page case. When you say we got your help, I say bullshit. Too little, too late. Pretty pathetic, I think."

He regrouped himself, reined in whatever it was he wanted to let loose. He had to see I was right.

"Listen, this private eye isn't going to break any new information. Even if he does, he can't make an arrest; I can. But if people don't want to talk to me because he's already been pressing them, my job gets harder, and whoever murdered your cousin walks. You understand that?"

I nodded. I wanted M. Hamilton to find the killer, not Tio Luis. My uncle was going to do something, and only an arrest or a bullet was going to stop him.

M. Hamilton and partner were stepping away, but Hamilton stepped back.

"Listen, if we find this Hector guy, we're going to compel him to report to us, and we're going to tell him to back off. Tell your uncle to do the same. What does he want out of this anyway?"

I told the truth. Not sure why. Didn't seem like a good idea at the time.

"He plans to find out who killed Jasmine. Then he plans to put two bullets in the man's head," I said. I pointed to the spot between my eyes. Hamilton shook his head and waved me off like he thought I was pulling his leg.

"Go to hell, kid," he said. He got back into his car, and he and his partner pulled away.

I walked up the steps to my mom's house. I couldn't believe the incredible bad luck we had in detectives—a private one to scare away the only leads we had, and a police one who couldn't tell trouble if it kicked him in the ass. I had only entered the world of detecting and crime fighting a few days before, but I was already the smartest one in the group. That was distressing.

It was almost eleven when my uncle came over. I had been watching the news. On each local broadcast, Jasmine's story filled a few minutes of airtime. "Bizarre" was a word that came up several times. The field reporters hadn't managed to get a response from my aunt and uncle, but a couple of my cousins spoke on camera. They all attested to the horror of the tragedy and to the beauty Jasmine had been. Detective Pearson had told the camera how hard the NYPD was working to catch the maniac responsible. If anyone had any information, et cetera.

I told my uncle about what Hamilton had said. I suggested he call off Hector. The man hadn't found a solid clue in days' worth of trying. Besides his ability to put away large quantities of Spanish cooking and stay slim, I didn't see much about him that impressed me.

"No, no, no," my uncle said. "This means we're getting somewhere."

I waited for him to make himself clear.

"If Clarissa and her mother are upset, it means they know something. Carlos is dead, Nestor is dead, that fat guy is dead. If Clarissa doesn't want to talk, maybe she knows of someone who's still alive and might do something."

"All she has to know is that those three dudes are dead and so is Jasmine and whoever is out there doing the killing is still free and probably not going to hesitate about killing some more." I hated to burst his bubble, but I'd already gone far with him and now he was jumping to conclusions that didn't quite fit reality.

He shook his head as though my words were just a fly that had landed on his hair, nothing more.

"Nope. Her name has never been mentioned in the papers, in the news, nothing. She has nothing to fear unless she knows another name or two."

That sounded rational, but then we were talking about a preteen and her mother. Jasmine's death was reported everywhere. I said what I thought.

"Good reason for Clarissa to try to keep out of this thing altogether. That's it."

"But we have to talk to her again," he said. "Tomorrow."

We talked for another hour. Clarissa was just one person we had to see the next day. There was the house in Bay Ridge, the search for Mickey the drug dealer, maybe even the Ellis family to bother. It was a big day for investigating tomorrow, my uncle said. He had a smile, weak, but the first one in a long while.

He left the house with the smile on his face still. He had visions of finding the killer and handing out some justice the next day, and that gave him hope.

I didn't have the heart to remind him that his morning would be filled with burying Jasmine.

DAY EIGHT

Mourning

We buried Jasmine. We buried Jasmine. We buried Jasmine, and for the first time, it felt real. I had vomited when I identified her; I had prayed for her coffinside. As I stood with two dozen others near her grave listening to the priest, I felt drained of everything but pain and loss. The cliché was that we should all concentrate on the years Jasmine had lived and loved, the good she had been. But there had been so few years.

Afternoon

It was four in the afternoon and the sun was going down, cooling the city for once, when my uncle finally had a chance to talk to me alone. It was my hope that he had forgotten his scheme, that he would be able to block his ears to the screaming from his heart and let Jasmine rest. I was angry too, pained. I missed her, not as much as he did or as much as he would for a long time probably, but I knew it would pass and that revenge, whether it was busting kneecaps or killing someone, would not be strong enough to overwhelm the pain and dissolve it.

No such luck.

"We have to talk to that girl, Clarissa."

He looked at me as though he were stating the obvious. I wanted to tell him there was no "have to" about it. We could let Clarissa go about her life; we could go about ours. Talking to Clarissa, finding the man who had pulled the trigger was not going to do anything at all. Not even make us feel good, and certainly not take away his pain.

He turned from me and headed out to the car because he knew I would follow. I did.

Tio Luis was not a big drinker. I had always admired that in him. At all the parties and celebrations, he was always sober. Now I wished he could find something to anaesthetize himself besides this mission he had set for himself. Himself and me.

Yo-man was out in front of Clarissa's building, two new friends with him, a forty-ounce bottle of beer being shared among them. He gave me a sharp look as though he was on the edge of recognizing me as Tio Luis and I went up the steps, but he didn't say anything.

Tio Luis knocked on the apartment door and stood up straight, folding his hands in front of him, giving whoever looked through the peephole a clear view of a decent man.

"*Que carajo tu quiere? Yo no puedo hablar contigo,*" Clarissa's mother said. She had opened the door just a crack. The chain was still on.

"Just a few minutes," Tio Luis said. "If you want, I can call you from a pay phone or something, but I need to know more about what happened at the Skate Key."

Clarissa's mom sighed loudly.

"I don't know nothing about what happened there," she said. It was most likely the truth. There was a good chance she'd never been there, herself.

"But if I could just talk to your daughter for a few minutes—"

"Clarissa's not here," the mother said.

"Where is she?" my uncle asked as though it were any of his business.

The door closed. Clearly, Clarissa's mom didn't think Tio Luis had a right to know. My uncle made a fist and touched the door with it. Just a sign of frustration with no heat behind it.

"She's probably at the Skate Key," I said out loud as we walked down the stairs. I wanted to kick myself for saying it as soon as the words were out. There was no reason to give my uncle any more fuel, though it was probably safer to try to find Clarissa than it was to find Mickey the crack dealer.

"You think so?" my uncle asked.

"It's Friday afternoon. That's where she was a week ago." It made sense to me, but Tio Luis had a little trouble seeing the logic of it. A week ago, Jasmine's life had started a short, quick, and violent spiral that ended in death but started at the Skate Key. Why would anyone want to go there? Tio Luis had failed to learn or else forgotten that for a child Clarissa's age, life is long and carefree and nothing bad that happened to someone else has the slightest bearing on what might happen to her.

We drove past the skating rink. Several small bunches of teens were hanging out in front. A security guard in uniform watched them from the door. I spotted Stu leaning against the wall, smoking a cigarette. He was making conversation with a young lady, maybe eighteen, at least half his age. Tio Luis parked.

The security guard from the week before was there and let us pass without paying. We went in and took a quick look around. Not as many people as the last time we'd come in, but then it wasn't fully night yet. There was no sign of Clarissa. I didn't know Jasmine's friends. They all looked like kids to me. Tio Luis tried the photograph on a few clusters of preteens, but it got him nowhere. No one even thought they remembered her.

We talked to the guard who had helped the week before.

"Did you find her?" he asked.

My uncle told him the story, and the guard looked truly shaken by it. It was a grisly story to tell. He had nothing new to tell us however.

Back outside, Stu was grinding out his cigarette.

"You think I should talk to him?" my uncle said.

"You could try," I told him. He did. I let him walk over alone.

Stu smiled, then frowned, then moved in close to listen to what my uncle had to say, then put his hand to his heart several times and patted Tio Luis on the back. A few shakes of his ponytail, a few more hands to his heart, a double-handed hand-shake and the conversation was over.

"Asshole," my uncle said back in the car. I wasn't sure what he was talking about. I waved to Stu as we pulled away. Stu looked at me confused, like he didn't remember who I was but waved back anyway.

The next stop was the Ellis household. Tio Luis thought he might have better luck with this parent than he had had with Clarissa's mom.

The house was as quiet as before though the neighborhood was a little louder. Some people had started their Friday nights a little early and were loudly making their way through the area. The same Irish lady opened the door to us and took a minute to confirm it was okay to let us in. We waited in the same room as before. The senior Ellis came to us.

"I'm sorry for the delay," he said. He seemed to be wiping a smile from his face like someone had told him a joke before he entered the room. "I'm hoping that you've found your daughter."

"She was raped, shot through the heart, and her head was chopped off," my uncle said getting right to the point.

Ellis's smile was off his face completely. He stuttered a little to tell us how sorry he was. Tio Luis waved him off. The words didn't matter. The sentiment didn't either.

"I just need to know who did this. You know what I mean? I need to find the guy who pulled the trigger."

"Surely, the police are doing the best they can," Ellis said.

It sounded reasonable, but it was also a shout across a chasm that Ellis didn't even see. Tio Luis neither for that matter. Ellis expected the police to be there for him, to be on his side, to protect him and his. Tio Luis couldn't even conceive of a police department that worked that way, was motivated that way. He was a working man. The police hadn't done him any good yet. They knocked on his door to give him bad news. The thought never even occurred to him that the police would actually work hard to find Jasmine's killer. They might have been able, but he didn't think they were willing. The fact that M. Hamilton had thrown us out when he could have done some good and was still working the case was just proof that the NYPD didn't care. Ellis would not have understood any of this. To him, the police were public servants who would do what he wanted them to do. Hell, he knew all about servants; he had one at his beck and call in a cute little outfit with a bow tie and everything.

Tio Luis didn't know what to say for a moment, but he found words.

"Well, they might find out who did this, but I want to be sure," he said. "I want to give them every tip, every clue. You know, so they can have a good chance."

Ellis nodded like he understood.

"Well, I think David told you everything he knows. I wasn't here for the party. If you want to leave a phone number, I'll be sure that he contacts you. He has spoken to the police though. I'm not sure what else he can tell you."

"Well, maybe if I spoke to him for a few minutes. . . . Is he in?"

"He's sleeping, right now."

My uncle looked at his watch. It was closing in on six in the evening.

"Is he sick?" Tio Luis asked. Ellis smiled.

"He stays up late many nights. I don't think he got to bed until a few hours ago." He smiled again. I looked around the room to avoid his gaze. It was a pretty room.

"Big party tonight?" Tio Luis asked.

"I wouldn't know," Ellis said. "I don't think so. If I recall, he said he'd be going to a friend's house tonight. Probably late."

"Any chance I could talk to him now?"

Ellis seemed to ponder for a moment but shook his head.

"I'm sorry Mr. Ramos, I truly am, but I can't have David disturbed. You understand don't you? One father to another."

Normally, I would have thought that Tio Luis would be totally unable to sympathize. His daughter had been murdered; Ellis's son was sleeping soundly. "One father to another" was bullshit. But

Tio Luis nodded slowly. He understood. We left after a few more words. Ellis promised to talk with his son. They'd pass on any information, even the smallest detail that came to mind. They would try to arrange a convenient meeting time.

My uncle and I got back in the Toyota and he pulled out. There wasn't much to say. He made a left, then a left, then a left, then a left. As we neared the Ellis household, the door opened and Junior jogged down the steps.

"*Hijo de la gran puta*. I thought so," my uncle said.

He pulled alongside him, but we went unnoticed for fifty yards.

"Get out and get him," Tio Luis said like I was some kind of attack dog. He pulled to a quick stop, and I jumped out.

I was a step from Junior when he finally noticed me. I wondered how he had made it this far in his life in New York if he generally walked around so oblivious to his surroundings. High school must have been a nightmare.

When he saw me, he pushed off from me with his right arm and started running.

"I don't know anything," he shouted over his shoulder. I was willing to give him the benefit of the doubt on that point, but we still needed to talk to him. Tio Luis wasn't going to give up until he had gotten every last piece of information.

I chased Junior for a full block. Running had apparently been his favorite defense strategy and it was a good one. He was quick. I was keeping pace, but just barely. I was hoping Tio Luis would do one of those television police show things where he pulls the car out in front of the suspect. He didn't. The street we were on was a two lane and Tio Luis would have had to have entered the oncoming lane to cut Junior off.

"I don't know anything," Junior kept repeating. My calves started to feel heavy. Picking my feet up was becoming a chore. Video games and Twinkies didn't really prepare me for a live chase. In the back of my mind, I thought this didn't look too good. A Puerto Rican chasing a white kid. Sounded like a good opportunity for some cop to put a bullet in me.

At the next intersection, Junior upended a city garbage can in my path. I tried to kick my front leg out over it, but my leg was too fatigued. Instead, I wound up kicking the can. I landed on the asphalt on my left knee and peeled my palms trying to keep my face from hitting the street. I hit anyway, but not as badly. The knee, however, was a different story. Not a good one. I hadn't broken it, but for a full minute I cradled it and shut my eyes even though I was lying near the middle of a New York City street. Cars drove around me and pedestrians went past. Nobody gave a damn, Tio Luis included. He came to my side as I was getting myself up on one leg, hopping back to the sidewalk.

"I lost him," he said as though I cared at that moment.

"Next time you jump out," I said.

"Who's going to drive?" Tio Luis answered. Too precious.

"Me."

"You don't have a license."

"I don't have a license to carry a gun either."

Tio Luis pretended not to hear me. He helped me to a lamppost where I could rest while he brought the car around.

"He got away?" I asked as we were leaving Manhattan for Brooklyn.

Tio Luis nodded. "But he's a junkie. Easy to find as long as he keeps wanting to get high."

Night

Drug dealers were apparently harder to find.

Mickey wasn't around as far as we could tell. We asked a lot of questions from the car. I wasn't about to get out and walk up to these people without the ability to run from them if I needed to. That was a concession Tio Luis made when I told him I thought I was injured enough for one day and wanted to go home. Most of the people we talked to walked away from us without saying a word. The last time we'd talked to people on those streets, the police had pulled up right after us and swept a few away. That didn't buy us any good will.

The super at Mickey's building wasn't in for us. We heard him plainly enough inside, but a look through the peephole told him we were nobody he wanted to talk to. Not even for good money.

"Bay Ridge," my uncle announced as we eased back into the car.

* * *

We ate in Bay Ridge. Pizza. It was good. The meal was relaxed though we ate in the car. We each had two slices and a Pepsi, and we didn't say a word.

We drove to the Bay Ridge house. Lights were on, but the house and the street were pretty quiet. We sat outside. I unfastened my seat belt. I expected we'd be knocking on the door again like Jehovah's Witnesses bent on revenge. Tio Luis didn't move. He just watched the house.

"Stakeout?" I asked.

"I need to think." These were the most hopeful words I had heard from my uncle in a week. If he needed time to think through what he was doing, he was a step away from figuring out that his efforts were all wasted. That the only outcome of him digging was going to be a bad outcome, that the police, as incompetent or uncaring as he might have thought them, were still the best people to handle this problem. I let him think.

If you're not accustomed to deep thought, it can take a while. I was content to let Tio Luis think for as long as he wanted. The seat in the Toyota was comfortable, and anything was better than me getting beaten up or shot at.

The problem for Tio Luis had to be that there was no good way out of the situation he was in. There were limited options, and limited permutations, but you go over them over and over in the hope that you've missed something. In his case, the end result of anything he might have been thinking had to be the same thing. Nothing he did would bring Jasmine back or make him miss her less or heal the wound in Titi Clarita's heart. A small bit of justice was really all he could hope for. Either doing what he wanted to do brought about justice for Jasmine or it didn't. No other options available.

"Who's that?" my uncle asked. I had begun to doze off. We had parked near the Bay Ridge house at about seven-thirty, and it was still light out. Now it was close to eight, and the light was fading.

I looked where he pointed. I couldn't really make out who it was walking down the sidewalk headed toward us. Tio Luis got out of the car. I squinted to get a better look at whoever it was he was going to harass next. It was a young couple, male and female. The young man had an arm across the shoulders of the girl. She wore a short skirt and a denim jacket. He had big ears that stuck out the side of his head.

I got out of the car as quick as I could. Mickey was reported as dangerous by all who had said anything at all about him. My knee was killing me, but I hoped the few steps to catch up to my uncle would help dull the pain. They didn't. I worried, in those few steps, about what I would do if Mickey started blasting away. Turns out that was a silly, wasted thought.

Tio Luis had his handgun out and pointed at Mickey's head before Mickey even knew there was trouble coming his way. The girl screamed and pulled away from him. If there was shooting coming, she wanted out of the way. Smart girl.

"Yo, yo," Mickey said. Not very eloquent. He put his hands up. It was the best thing for him to do. I didn't think Tio Luis would have too much trouble pulling the trigger if Mickey had tried anything else. As it was, he smacked the boy in the face with the gun and Mickey's knees buckled, leaving him with his back on the sidewalk. The girl kept screaming. I took a step toward her and she stopped, turning her attention to me. Someone stuck their head out of a window.

"Shut the hell up!" was shouted at us all.

Tio Luis kneeled over Mickey, pulled him up off the sidewalk by his shirt front and said something angry to him. I couldn't make out the question or the answer, but whatever Mickey said, it wasn't good enough. Tio Luis slapped him again with the gun, hitting him on the crown of his head.

"Are you going to let him do that?" the girl asked me. She wasn't Clarissa or Jasmine, but she was their age. Naive.

"He's got the gun," I pointed out.

"What about you?" she asked. If I didn't have a gun, she might feel safe about screaming again or clawing at my eyes.

"You want to see it?" I asked. Once again the gun Tio Luis gave me was in the glove compartment.

She crossed her arms.

Tio Luis gave Mickey a couple more smacks, not as hard. Then he got up and got Mickey on his feet, sort of. My uncle had to support most of the guy's weight. Mickey wasn't up to the job of staying up-right. Tio Luis led him to the Toyota and for the second time in a week, we were kidnapping a drug dealer.

"What am I supposed to do?" the girl asked me as I started to walk back to the car.

"Were you going into that house?" I pointed.

"Yes."

"Don't. The last girl who went in didn't do too good."

"It's a party," she said.

"Is that what Mickey told you?"

She nodded.

"Does it look like he's having that much fun? Go home. Believe me, it's the best thing for you."

I got into the Toyota. Tio Luis had already duct taped Mickey's mouth, hands, and feet, taken off his sneakers. I thought of getting out the gun I'd been given and keeping guard while Tio Luis drove, but it was pointless. The boy was unconscious.

Mickey woke up in a different garage from where Nestor had been taken. I had no idea there were so many abandoned garages in the Bronx or that my uncle had the keys to them. This one was more isolated, being near a junkyard on one side and a stretch of the Bruckner Expressway on the other. It had a workbench with a vice attached and a slop sink in a corner. These chilled me.

The boy's face was a bit crusted with drying blood, but you could still see he was angry at his predicament. I wanted to tell him it could get a lot worse, but I kept the sentiment to myself. He started to squirm, and Tio Luis went into the car's glove compartment. He came back with the revolver.

"Listen," he repeated a few times until he had Mickey's full attention. Then he pulled the trigger of the revolver twice. The sound was deafening. My ears whistled and I wished my uncle had given me some sign of what he was going to do. I could have covered my ears.

Mickey screamed through the duct tape that covered his lips. Tio Luis had fired into the cinder block walls at the back of the garage, but that didn't register with Mickey, who probably thought he was being executed.

"Good," Tio Luis said. "Keep screaming." He fired another round into the wall. I covered my ears for that one.

Mickey sobered up and his eyes grew wide. He threw me a glance. I shrugged and he went back to keeping his eyes on Tio Luis. Smart.

"I do this to show you that screaming isn't going to help you. Scream all you want. We're in the middle of nowhere, miles from where I picked you up. It's nighttime, nothing but stray dogs in this area, maybe a homeless guy or two, but believe me, if they knew what I was going to do with you, they wouldn't care, and for five dollars, they'd help me. You understand?"

Mickey understood. He nodded vigorously. Tio Luis pulled the tape off.

"I need you to concentrate," he said. He pulled out Jasmine's picture and held it up for Mickey to see.

"I need to know everything you know about this girl, and if you say you know nothing . . ." Tio Luis cocked the hammer on the revolver and put it to Mickey's right knee. Mickey looked up at me. I put my hands over my ears again and winced waiting for the noise. I wasn't trying to scare him, but it worked.

"I saw her once," he sputtered. "She's the bitch—" Tio Luis dug the gun deep into Mickey's thigh muscle and leaned over to whisper something. "She's the girl, the girl Carlos brought over. She . . . partied with some dudes."

"This was in the Village?"

"The Village? No. Bay Ridge. Right where you got me, man."

"The house that belongs to the Vietnamese people?"

"Chinese. Whatever. It don't belong to them. They just the cover for the place, you understand. Look. They live there, but they clear out for the parties."

"What kind of parties?"

Mickey didn't know how to answer that one. He searched for words. No doubt the parties were fun for everyone except the young girls who attended. Would Tio Luis really want to hear what went on? That's what Mickey was trying to calculate.

"Parties. You know. A little drinking. Some music. Maybe a little weed. No big deal . . ."

"Wrong answer," my uncle said. He dug the gun even deeper into the muscle and shielded his face from whatever backsplash there might be. I took a step back and covered my ears again.

"Okay, okay, okay!" Mickey gave in.

"Sex parties. Old dudes who can't get it up give us a call. We get some young, tight . . . girls for them. They pay. That's it. The rest is real. Music, drinks, dope. I wasn't lying about that."

He probably wasn't.

Tio Luis stood up a moment. Worst fears realized.

"What kind of sex?" he asked. Mickey didn't understand. How many kinds of sex were there?

"What did they do with my daughter?" Tio Luis asked. Mickey thought about his answer a second too long. Tio Luis cocked the gun again and pressed it into Mickey's right eye. If he pulled the trigger, Mickey was dead. The boy got the picture.

"Everything!" he said. "They did everything with her. Back, front, mouth. Everything, man." I could tell he wanted to cry.

"Who?"

"I don't know names!" Mickey said. The gun was being jammed farther into his eye. The little sight at the top of the barrel wasn't visible anymore. "I can describe them!" he said.

Mickey described a dozen men. All of them had had some part of Jasmine that night. There were other girls too. He told us about height and weight, hair color, eye color for a few, clothing. He even compared a few to TV and movie actors. I wrote everything down and even asked a few questions to clarify things like age and any identifying marks.

Had he seen these guys before at other parties? Yes, most of them.

Before he finished talking, he had given us three other addresses throughout New York City, one in Northern New Jersey, and one out on Long Island. He had been to these places. They all did the same kind of thing. Many of the same men, sometimes new ones. No names except the occasional first name—Bill, Jim, names like that. Probably not even real names.

"Who arranged these things?" my uncle asked.

"I don't know. Carlos used to give me a call. This morning I got a call from some other guy. He had my private number, he knew about the parties, he told me to bring a girl just like always. He didn't give me a name."

"How do you get paid?" I asked.

"I get an envelope. Different people bring it. Most of the time, teenagers, kids from the hood. I don't ask who gave them what, they don't tell. The ones I get the money from probably got it from someone else. See what I'm saying? These people— the ones who go to the parties—they're legit. They're straight. They don't want no hassles. They just pay for their fun. See?"

We saw. It was a dirty business. If you paid your way in through a series of middle men, then all you were was a guy having sex with a willing girl. Underaged maybe, but no one could ever prove that you *knew* that. And with enough people between you and the money, no one could prove you paid.

This way, you could do anything you wanted and still be straight, still be legit, still be clean.

Tio Luis gave Mickey a small wad of fifties and told him that someone had murdered Carlos and Nestor and that person was still out there and likely to murder him too. Mickey believed it and wanted nothing more than to get on a bus or train and get out of New York City. That's what he said at least, and Tio Luis believed him.

"If I see you again," my uncle said. "I'll kill you myself. Understand?" Mickey nodded and got out of the car near a subway station that would take him to Grand Central if that's where he really wanted to go.

We drove away before he disappeared into the station. I saw through the side view mirror that he was watching the car go.

We went home to eat something. M. Hamilton was there. He didn't look too happy.

"I think we need to talk," he said. We were on the steps going in. He was on the steps coming out.

"What about?" Tio Luis asked. Cool. Like he hadn't just kidnapped someone and put a gun to his head and then sent that person on a mission to get lost or get killed.

"I thought we had an understanding that you weren't going to go around asking people questions. That you were going to leave that to the professionals. To me. Now I got two complaints. The

De Jesus woman and a . . ." He looked into a small notepad. "Thomas Ellis of Greenwich Village. Look. These people are private citizens. You can't just go hassling them and their kids. Ellis says you chased his son through the streets. You can't do that."

"They know things," Tio Luis said. He was quiet and not looking at the detective. He found a spot on the steps to focus on. I was standing a step or two behind him and kept my eyes on Hamilton.

"I don't care what they know or what you think they know. If you keep sticking your nose into this investigation, I'm going to arrest you and let you and your wife sleep some of this curiosity off."

Tio Luis looked up when his wife was mentioned. Detective Hamilton nodded to him. He knew he had gotten my uncle's attention. He smiled.

"See," he said. "This can get real ugly."

"You think this is worse than your daughter being raped and murdered?" my uncle asked.

"Look." Hamilton let out a sigh and thought a moment before answering. "I know what you went through was a terrible thing, but you have to let me handle this. That's not me asking you, that's me telling you. Right now, I'm telling you, I'm trying to investigate a homicide, and you're getting in my way. I'll arrest you if I have to—obstruction of justice. Leave this alone. In fact . . ." Hamilton was working himself up instead of calming down. "In fact, I can say that you've already made my job a lot more difficult and it might be a while before I can begin to put the pieces together and catch the responsible party. Understand?"

What he was hinting at was that as painful as the past week had been, there might never be official closure. He was trying to blame that on my uncle. Tio Luis nodded and waited for Hamilton to go. Nothing that had been said would change any of the facts or attitudes. I wasn't even sure why Hamilton bothered.

Titi Clarita was distraught. M. Hamilton had come inside and told her much the same stuff he had told my uncle. He made it sound, she told us, like the case was never going to be solved. Like if the killer got away it was their fault. Like, in fact, the killer was most likely going to get away. He had mentioned jail time to her even though she had told the truth when she said she didn't know who her husband was talking to, where he was going.

Tio Luis and I listened and ate the food she put in front of us. It was getting late, past nine o'clock. The night had fully fallen. In the end, my uncle told her everything would be okay. He asked if she wanted to go with my mother to a hotel for a couple days to avoid being prosecuted in case Hamilton felt a need to carry out one of his threats. Titi Clarita felt insulted. It was her daughter too that had been murdered. She wasn't going anywhere.

I wasn't asked whether I wanted to go to a hotel.

It was late when we were ready to go out again. I didn't want to think of banging on doors at ten or eleven at night. That's a good way to have people call the cops on you. Just as we were going, Hector knocked on the door. He wanted to make a report.

"I think I cracked the case for you," he said. There was a small smile on his face. He seemed proud of his results though, of course, even a proud man would have to concede it wouldn't really help Jasmine any.

"I spoke to contacts on the streets. The Village, Brooklyn, all the places we talked about. I got from a bunch of people that Carlos had a boss. Remember that dude you told me about, Mickey? That's the one. If anyone pulled the trigger, it was him."

Tio Luis rubbed his hands through his hair. The convolutions of the case were hurting his head. Mickey? A young man nicknamed after a cartoon mouse? He killed Jasmine? That just didn't fit his view of reality. Mickey was a pawn, not a king.

"I don't think your sources are right. Maybe they're covering for someone."

Hector looked confused.

"I just talked with Mickey a couple of hours ago," my uncle said. "If he killed Jasmine, it was because someone else gave him the orders. No way he's a mastermind of anything."

"You talked with Mickey?" Hector was truly surprised.

"Yep. Beat him, talked to him. Let him go. He gave me some decent leads."

Tio Luis explained all that Mickey had told him—the addresses, the descriptions, the routine and how it all rotated from house to house randomly, even how he got paid and how much. Hector wrote a lot of stuff down, but he shook his head the entire time.

"You want me to check these out?" Hector asked. My uncle thought about it a moment. It was getting late and we were all tired.

"Yeah. Do that. I'll keep going after the old leads."

"I'll get on it first thing in the morning," Hector said. He got up to go, offered his hand to my uncle and then to me. I held on a second.

"Did you manage to track down any information about that house in Bay Ridge?" I asked.

He snapped his fingers loudly in "aw shucks" fashion.

"That one slipped my mind today. I got so caught up in tracking down different leads. City offices are open on Monday though. If we still need it, I'll get that information then."

I nodded, but I wouldn't be holding my breath.

Back in Bay Ridge. Midnight. A party going on inside the Vietnamese house—not very loud— probably loud enough to muffle a cry for help though.

Tio Luis wrote down license plate numbers and looked up at the house from time to time.

I wondered if the young girl from earlier this evening had decided to go home or if she was suffering inside the house, being battered and brutalized and if maybe she too would end up broken into pieces, strewn around the city.

The city as slaughterhouse floor.

DAY NINE

Morning

Tio Luis woke me up the next morning and he seemed happy. That alone should have prepared me for greater trouble, but I was happy in return. I hadn't seen him smile in a while.

He waited for me to dress and come up to my mother's house for breakfast. It was about seven in the morning and I had gotten about six hours of sleep. Compared to so many other mornings recently, this felt good. I was drinking orange juice when he started to spill what it was that made him so upbeat.

"You know that girl, Clarissa?" he asked. "She went missing. I got a call from her mother this morning. She was at the Skate Key yesterday. That guy, the manager, Stu, he told her he never saw Clarissa, but the mother, she's sure that's where the girl went. It's where she went every Friday in the summer." He smiled.

"I don't get it. Why is this good news?"

"The skate ring is the key to everything. The girls, they go missing there. That Stu, he has to know something."

"But what if he was telling Mrs. De Jesus the truth? What if he didn't even see her? What if she didn't go there?"

"You thought yesterday that she went there," my uncle reminded me.

"That was yesterday. She probably did go there, but that doesn't mean that she disappeared from there. In fact, just because she hasn't come home doesn't mean that she was kidnapped or that anything bad happened to her. She might have just decided to have a sleepover with a girlfriend. Or a boyfriend. She might be asleep in some bed, resting right now."

What I was saying made perfect sense to me, but I didn't think Tio Luis was going to listen. This was a man who had turned from a gentle man to one who practically crowed to think that some other girl was suffering the same fate as his murdered daughter. He was seeing that as a silver lining to the cloud of his darkened life.

There was no point in driving to the Skate Key. It didn't open until eleven in the morning. Instead, Tio Luis made a call to Hector that lasted half an hour; then he made a few other calls. I stayed away from him as he spoke. The less I knew, the safer I felt though, of course, it was way too late for that.

* * *

Our first stop was near the City College campus in Upper Manhattan where Carlos had first brought Jasmine. Tio Luis seemed to have a plan. I didn't ask him to share. I hadn't been able to change his mind about a single thing yet.

We looked for someone we had never even thought of contacting yet—Marissa, the prostitute who gave Hector his information. If she knew a little, she might know a lot. I wondered, however, what the chances of finding her were, especially in the early morning hours. I pointed out that problem to Tio Luis, but his madness had a method.

"I won't look for her at this hour, though you never know. . . . I'll ask around if people know where I can find her. The storeowners in the neighborhood usually keep tabs on that kind of stuff. Somebody will know something. And the drug dealers. They would probably know."

The logic was that prostitutes were often drug addicts and addicts had dealers.

There wasn't information to be had about Marissa though Tio Luis flashed around enough fifties to paper a small bathroom. After a couple hours, Tio Luis was depressed again. He slumped behind the wheel of the Toyota. It took a couple minutes for him to regroup and regain his energy. He shook his head as though he were trying to knock bad thoughts out to make room for hope.

"*Tu chota,*" he said. My snitch.

* * *

I should not have been surprised. It should have been no shock. I should have expected that the little boy who had given me so much information, Mo, was being buried that day.

The neighborhood Mo lived in was a tough one. Mo had been tough to match. His toughness was mental more than anything else. After all, he was a child with a child's body still. His murder was a simple case of being in the wrong place at the wrong time. There had been a drive-by shooting: thirteen shell casings had been recovered. Most of the bullets had gone wide of any mark. A tree had been hit twice; the bricks of a low apartment building had absorbed a half-dozen bullets. A parked car had taken a couple of others. Mo had taken one to the head. The drug dealers who seem to have been the target of it all went unscathed. In fact, the police had never even figured out who the target had been. Nobody knew. They only knew that Mo was dead. Random act in a careless city. Kids were out playing in the water from the fire hydrant.

Another coincidence? Like the panhandler who had given us information that first night getting the eyes cut out of his head? I couldn't even think of the formula that would be needed to try and calculate the odds of two people who had helped us getting murdered in so short a time. Even in New York City, this had to be a statistical implausibility.

And then Mo hadn't kept his secret like he was supposed to. The children of the neighborhood knew he was helping us. If the kids knew, who didn't?

I wondered if M. Hamilton knew or cared.

We had lunch early before heading over to the Skate Key. We sat in the car munching and thinking. Who had known about Mo? Who had known about the panhandler? Who had known about Carlos and Nestor? Was Clarissa missing because she had some information that might point out a murderer? Or had she just decided to take the weekend away from her mother?

We had told all or part of Jasmine's story to dozens of people. There were flyers around still offering cash for information. There hadn't been many calls recently, but there were a heck of a lot of people out there with the kind of knowledge that could get people killed.

There was a chance that whoever was killing the people we wanted to talk to was following in our footsteps. Maybe we had never contacted them at all.

Neither of us believed that.

"*Ese maldito* Hamilton. He knows everything." Tio Luis was pretty convinced that the man who had not done enough to save Jasmine had done everything to kill her.

"He didn't know about Mo," I pointed out. "Besides, he's a cop. Cops worry about their pensions. They don't go on killing sprees."

We were heading to the Bronx, back to the Skate Key.

"What about Mickey and his crew? They're drug dealers and pimps. They kidnapped Jasmine. They might have killed her. They have people in that neighborhood. They could know everything," I said.

This made sense to me, but no sense to Tio Luis. After all, if this were true then the person most responsible for Jasmine's death was the one he had given hundreds of dollars to and told to run for his life.

We got to the skating rink a little after it had opened. There were few people there though it was air-conditioned and the temperature outside was beginning to rise into the uncomfortable range.

We asked the security guard, one we didn't know, about seeing Stu.

"He's in a meeting," we were told. It sounded strange for a skating rink manager to be "in a meeting."

We said we'd wait, paid the entrance fee, and took up seats thirty feet from his office door.

It was a half hour before Stu emerged from his office. M. Hamilton and Detective Pearson came out with him as did Clarissa's mother, Mrs. De Jesus. She was wiping tears away. Stu walked Mrs. De Jesus to the front door. Hamilton and Pearson headed straight for us.

"What are you guys doing here? Still bothering honest citizens?"

Like always, M. Hamilton took the lead in speaking. He seemed short of temper.

"Girls are disappearing here pretty regularly, I think," my uncle said.

"Well, I'm looking into this case too," Hamilton said.

"Why? Is this related to Jasmine?"

Hamilton looked like he didn't want to say anything at all and was sorry he had started the conversation.

"The thinking is that it may be. That's a big 'may be.' You understand? Me and Detective Pearson are on this case because it might—might—be related to your daughter's case. It may not be. It might just be that this Clarissa decided to hang out later than usual. It happens. These girls start young and—" Hamilton stopped himself, remembering to whom he was talking. My uncle had crossed his arms and was smiling. He could take whatever Hamilton could dish out. "What I mean is, there may be no case here at all. It's early. Clarissa could be waiting for her mother at home already."

Hamilton surveyed the area and brought his eyes back to my uncle. He leaned in close.

"Go home and grieve, Mr. Ramos. There really is nothing you can accomplish by bothering people like this."

Tio Luis shrugged and sat back down. Hamilton sighed. We'd paid for our tickets, and there was nothing he could do about us sitting there. He had other things to do. He started to walk away; my uncle called him back.

"Hey, Hamilton. Keep me posted on your

progress, okay?" Hamilton waved him off and walked out with Pearson in tow.

We waited a half hour longer, but Stu never returned to his office. We went to the front and asked the guard. Apparently Stu was taking a lunch break though his day had started only a little while earlier. No idea when he'd be back.

Did Stu walk right past us without noticing we were waiting for him? Did M. Hamilton and Co. head straight for us and give us a speech we'd already ignored more than once just to give Stu a chance to get away?

It was easy to become paranoid. Hell, paranoia had set in days ago. But we were going on something more than paranoia. There was a trail of deaths, among them, Jasmine's. That was real. As real as it got.

Afternoon

"Mrs. De Jesus, we want to help you," my uncle said. She had refused to open the door to her apartment. I didn't blame her. We'd brought trouble to people in three out of five New York City boroughs.

"Go away," she told us through the door.

"We want to help. I think I know where your daughter might be, but we have to act fast if we want to . . . help her."

I wasn't sure what Tío Luis meant. We had a range of places Clarissa might be if she had been taken by the same people who took Jasmine. I didn't know how much help we could be, and if Hamilton and Pearson had learned anything at all from their experience looking for Jasmine, then they knew as much as we did and were already searching for her with greater resources at their command than anything we could muster.

Mrs. De Jesus, who had slammed the door on us so many times already, opened it this time. She couldn't resist speaking to my uncle even if he had things to say she didn't want to hear. She let us in.

Her face was splotchy from the sun and the crying she had indulged in was only highlighting the defects. She looked worn already though her daughter hadn't been missing even a full day. The same had happened to Titi Clarita. She had gray hairs now that I could swear I hadn't seen before.

Mrs. De Jesus motioned for us to sit at the dining table, small as it was. She spoke first.

"They told me you would say that. That you would say you could help, that you knew where she was. If you're lying to me . . ." She wiped a tear from each eye, digging deep, creating wrinkles if she didn't have them before.

"What else did they say about us?" Tio Luis asked.

"Please!" Mrs. De Jesus said. "If you have information, give it to me. I'll look for Clarissa myself."

That last word made me look around the room and into the living room. She was a single mother with an only daughter. There were no extended family members in the apartment though it was a

Saturday. There was a plastic picture frame that held about a dozen small snapshots; all of them were of mother and daughter, all smiling, many hugs. Perhaps the two of them were all alone in the city.

"I'll tell you what I know," my uncle said, and he did.

If they wanted my uncle to stop prying, why didn't they just kill him? There were times during those days when I know he would have welcomed death, was probably close to bringing it to himself.

Maybe they had tried. Mickey seemed to have been waiting for us with that shotgun and was eager to punch my uncle's ticket. Tio Luis's love handle wound still seeped blood and something that turned yellowish on his gauze. But maybe that was Mickey's normal method of answering the door when someone he didn't know came knocking.

Robertito had also tried to punch my uncle's ticket. That hadn't done anything but left a scar on my uncle and his car and put Robertito in the grave.

Maybe Tio Luis was just a hard target, hard to kill. Maybe he was lucky.

One thing was for sure. There was still a killer out there, and there was a good chance that he'd come after my uncle again, maybe soon. Maybe Tio Luis's luck would hold for a few more days. Maybe not. That runs out sometimes.

We left Mrs. De Jesus with a 4×6 photo of Clarissa. Tio Luis would show this around. Mrs.

DeJesus was glad to have any help and not particular about how we got her daughter back. My uncle had a new mission to live for.

The first stop was to see Stu at the Skate Key, but it was a wasted effort. He hadn't bothered to come back from his long and early lunch. We spoke to an assistant, a teenager who was in charge of the skating rink until Stu returned. The place was filling up by then, and the teen, pimple faced and with long hair he kept trying to brush out of his eyes, could barely spare us a minute. We were just another problem that would have to wait for Stu's return. We asked a few kids if they'd seen Clarissa, but there was no spark of recognition in any eye.

"Bay Ridge," Tio Luis called out as I buckled my seat belt. He was announcing stops like a bus driver now.

We parked blocking someone's driveway. Tio Luis reached over and opened the glove compartment, handing me the revolver.

"Clip it to your belt, cover it with your shirt. When we get inside, pull it out. Don't aim it at anyone unless they attack you or I tell you to aim it. Got that?" Of course, I got it. I couldn't believe what I was hearing, but I understood it all.

"We're going to invade this house?" I asked on the sidewalk leading to the front steps of the house. I said a quick prayer hoping the family wouldn't be home though I could hear the TV from fifty feet away. They had their front windows open trying to catch a breeze that had stalled out somewhere in the Midwest probably.

Tio Luis ignored me. As we went up the steps, he pulled out his handgun, and carried it behind him. He put a hand up to keep me quiet and to keep me from pulling out the gun he'd given me. He knocked. I hoped whoever was inside would be wise and ignore us. Nobody opens a door to a stranger in this city. Except for the little ten-year-old boy. He opened without bothering to ask who we were. Tio Luis pushed him aside.

Inside, it was actually cooler than I would have imagined. They had the windows open, but the air-conditioning was on as well somewhere. The TV was loud with cartoons. The boy who'd been pushed aside didn't say a word until my uncle was five steps past him and the boy saw the gun in his hand. Then he yelled his head off. I would have done the same.

I clamped a hand over his mouth and shut the front door behind me. The boy squirmed and stomped on my toes. It didn't hurt, but I didn't see how we were going to accomplish anything useful this way. A little girl came running from the TV area. She was maybe five years old. She wanted to see what her brother was hollering about. She gasped, but made no noise.

The parents, mama and papa, came out of whatever room they'd been in and Tio Luis raised his gun to between-the-eyes level.

"Cover me!" he shouted. I gave the boy a little push toward his parents and pulled out the gun he'd given me. I aimed at the father. Both parents already had their hands up.

Tio Luis yelled something in Vietnamese several

times over. I had no idea what he was saying. It got the adults and the ten-year-old to lie on their bellies. He yelled some more, repeating always, and they laced their fingers on the backs of their heads. Those parents must have thought they'd entered a vet's Vietnam flashback nightmare.

"Cover me," Tio Luis said again. I thought I'd been doing a good job of that, but he pointed to the people on the floor, and I noticed I hadn't lowered my aim. The revolver was pointing at the air where the parents had been, not at the ground where they were. I adjusted. Out of the corner of my eye I saw the little girl sit on the ground. She looked worried. I would have loved to explain to her that this was all a bad mistake, apologize, and leave. Then I remembered that if the parents had come out of a room in the house, there might be others in other rooms. For all I knew, Mickey and his shotgun might be behind some door in the place. I wanted to put my back against a wall so no one could sneak up on me.

Tio Luis squatted next to the father. Out came the picture of Clarissa. More Vietnamese, mixed with English now. The father spoke English thankfully. Nothing worse than holding a gun on a family with small kids and not even knowing why or whether you should be pulling the trigger.

"No see her!" the father shouted several times. His wife joined him. Tio Luis gave the man a rap on the knuckles with the barrel of his handgun. It wasn't hard, but he followed this up with some more Vietnamese. His face was a snarl. The father changed his mind.

"Last night," he said. "Yes, last night."

In a couple minutes, the father and mother told us what they knew and swore on the lives of their children that they knew nothing else. They made it a point to have someplace else to be when the parties went on. They didn't want to say where else they went, but Tio Luis got it out of them. An address only a block or two away. A cousin's house. Tio Luis told him that we'd check on that. The father's eyes grew wide; the mother burst out crying. I wanted to cry too. The father kept talking and gave us descriptions of the guys who had been, who were the weekly regulars. Tio Luis wanted names, but the father said he didn't know any, didn't want to know any, rarely got to see more than a few of the people who would arrive before he left. The guy who was always there, every week, who ran things, he didn't know his name, he was white, he looked like other white guys, older, as old as Tio Luis, tall, heavy, but then the father couldn't say how tall or heavy. He was himself a small man, maybe not over five feet.

The little girl crawled from where she was sitting over to her father's side. She pushed Tio Luis's gun hand from the side of her father's face. This was the end of the interview. Tio Luis could not with anger fight the little girl.

My first home invasion had been a success. Except for being terrorized, no one had gotten hurt, and we had come away with more information than we'd gone in with. Of course, the information seemed pretty useless—no names, just a description of a white guy. Also, that Clarissa was involved with the same people that Jasmine had been with and that, as of the night before, she was alive.

We passed a squad car, and I shrank in my seat a little. It struck me that at any moment, a siren might sound behind us, and we'd be pulled over and arrested. The charges against us would be less than murder, but they'd be true.

"They're not going to come," Tio Luis told me. I didn't know where we were headed.

"What?" I asked.

"The police. They're not going to come after us. Those people aren't going to call the police on us."

"What makes you say that?"

"They can barely speak English. They may even be illegals. Anyway, we didn't do anything to them. No evidence."

We continued on for a few minutes. Then a thought hit me. Hard.

"What if they call the guys they're working for?" I asked.

"Oh, they probably won't do even that. I'm betting they live there rent-free just to provide a cover story and keep things hushed up. If they tell whoever owns the place, they'll get kicked out. They know that. The parties will go someplace else each weekend. Believe me, it's in their best interest to keep this quiet."

It made some sense, but there were a lot of ways the news of our little adventure could leak out— children, for instance, are not known to keep secrets well, and the parents may decide they would rather face deportation than have my uncle come back. I couldn't help thinking we had just screwed up big. I was turning all this over when a police siren went on behind us. The squad car had its roof lights flashing as it pulled up behind us and Tio Luis drew to the right side of the road and came to a stop.

Every muscle in my body clenched. I tried to think of what the charge would be against us. We hadn't broken in, but we had certainly brandished. I wondered if I'd have to share a cell with Tio Luis and for how long.

A few minutes later, we were moving again. Tio Luis had gone through a stop sign. The officer who came up to the window asked for the license and registration and came back after doing some sort of check on his computer. Tio Luis had a spotless driving record, so he was warned—told to be careful—and we were free.

I had kept my eyes on the glove compartment door throughout the whole thing and couldn't say whether the officer was white or black if my life depended on it. If he paid me any attention, he might have wondered what I was staring at the glove compartment for. He might have asked to see inside. How would he have felt finding a handgun there?

"Did I ever tell you that I was a POW?" my uncle asked.

I had wanted to say something about our run-in

with the law, but Tio Luis spoke up first and what he said shocked me. He gave me a glance and a smile.

"Three days. I was green as a *platano*. I got separated on patrol, captured. I put my gun down faster than you can say *anda, pa'l carajo*. They knocked out a tooth with a rifle butt and gave me this scar."

He pointed to the right corner of his mouth. There had always been a little spiderweb of light, thin scars there—nothing too traumatic, I thought.

"I got scars on the back of my head too. And one bastard gave me the cut I have on my shoulder." He pointed. I knew the cut he was talking about.

"You know what saved me? Napalm. Thank God for that. Our side dropped some. I was running before the bombs hit the ground, my hands tied behind my back. I found this gigantic tree and huddled at it. That shit was flying everywhere, but it missed me. About a thousand times, it missed me. I don't know what happened to the guys that had been holding me. Dead, I think. But when the planes had finished their run, I came out of my spot and ran for the American side. A few hours later, and I was back."

He was silent a little while, then he smiled.

"Never so happy to see a *gringo* than to see that doctor. A few stitches, a couple of days off my feet, then it was back looking for Victor Charlie."

As he drove I couldn't get out of my head the fact that my uncle's sanity was slowly circling the drain, and I was the unlucky bastard along for the ride. We stopped in front of a *cuchifrito* on Fifth Avenue in Sunset Park. I figured we were in the neighborhood for another try with the street lowlifes or maybe the building super again. Instead, my uncle went in and came out again with Cokes and *empanadillas*. He was quiet while we ate, which was fine by me. I ate slowly and listened to the music that flowed from boomboxes and blasted from the stereo systems cranked to their maximums in the backs of hatchbacks with their rear doors up. Some had bass lines so loud, we felt the vibrations coming up through the floor of the Toyota.

I couldn't tell what Tio Luis was thinking though I took a few quick looks his way. When we were done eating I thought we would be on our way, but instead he sat some more. After a few minutes, he searched his side slowly, lifting his shirt and inspecting the wound in his love handle.

"Popped a couple of stitches," he said. He looked up and down the block. I was about to suggest a trip to the emergency room when he got out of the car. He ducked his head back in.

"There's a pharmacy," he said. Then he walked off in the direction of a big chain store at the end of the block. I watched him. He stopped to talk to several young people, and one store owner sitting outside his store in his T-shirt. He had Clarissa's picture out. A lot of head shakes. More conversation, then he walked on to the pharmacy. Minutes later he was back. The bag he carried was far larger than he needed for a simple roll of gauze and some tape, but that's all he pulled out. He shook me off when I offered to help and worked on himself a short while.

We drove around Sunset Park for another half hour or more, Tio Luis stopping a couple of times to get out and talk to young people, old people, anyone who looked like they might know something about something. None of them knew anything that interested Tio Luis. He parked again to think. I gave him some quiet. Three teen girls walked past us shoulder to shoulder wearing cutoff jeans so short butt cheeks were showing. A minute later a woman in her thirties walked by in the same condition. I wondered if that was a Brooklyn fashion trend. Tio Luis broke his silence.

"This is going to get bad," he said.

"What is?"

"This. This . . . investigation I'm doing here. This is going to get bad."

"We could go home," I said.

I said it too quietly. If I had mustered some conviction, he might have listened to me. Instead, he just stared at me. I felt like he wanted me to do the calculation for myself and see if there was any chance that he was going to drive us both back to the Bronx, both back home. I opened my mouth. I wanted to repeat what I had said, add the conviction now, but it was too late for that. He held my gaze for another few seconds then dropped his eyes to the steering wheel.

"I think I know what happened to her, but I gotta find that out for sure," he said.

"She got shot through the heart, Tio. That's it. Nothing you find out, nothing you do is going to change that. Titi Clarita is already missing a child. If you do something wrong, she'll be missing a husband too."

I was playing on his emotions. He was killing himself over the fact that he had failed to protect Jasmine. There was still his wife to protect. Maybe that would bend his will and give him purpose, I thought. He nodded his head a few times, and I had the feeling that maybe I had been listened to. He put the car in gear and pulled out into traffic.

"I'll have to be very careful," he said.

I gave up and sat back.

We drove to a neighborhood we hadn't tried before. Anything that broke the monotony seemed like a good idea to me. We were on the Grand Concourse in the Bronx. This had once been a desirable neighborhood, mostly Jewish. That was at the time of the Second World War. It had gone downhill a bit, but it was still better than many. The street was long and broad and the apartment buildings lining the street were sand-colored brick mostly and only six or seven stories high. Fifty thousand people lived on a mile stretch, but they were good people mostly—lower middle class, but working.

We parked on one of the side streets and I was ready to get out and stretch my legs, but Tio Luis stopped me.

"Stay with the car. I'll be back in three minutes."

He reached to the backseat and grabbed the pharmacy bag. I asked what he was going to do, but he walked off.

A half block away, he stopped at a pay phone. He fiddled with the paper bag a minute, then made a call. He looked a little heated. His knees bent as though he were begging someone to give him a break. When he was done with the call, he stuffed something into the bag and jogged back to the car. He was looking back over his shoulder part of the way, and I checked the glove compartment to make sure the gun was handy in case it was needed.

"What's happening?" I asked when he got back in.

"Wait," he said. He handed me a handheld tape recorder, one he had just peeled out of its packaging and used on the phone.

"Who did you call?"

"Wait."

I waited. Tio Luis kept his eye on an apartment building door about a hundred feet in front of us. It only took a minute for someone to come out.

Hector Sepulveda, our private eye, looked up and down the block but didn't notice us. He hurried a few yards farther and went around to the driver's side of a big old Caddy and got in.

"Listen to the tape," Tio Luis said. He put the car in drive and pulled out a few seconds after Hector did.

The tape was grainy and had all the street noise of Bronx in the open air, but it was clear enough that Tio Luis was talking to Hector.

"Where are you?" my uncle asked.

"Uh, my office," was the answer.

"Well, I think I got some information you need to hear. Maybe you can help me make sense of a few things."

"Anything you want," Hector answered.

"Yeah, I think I got information about who killed Jasmine and why. I was talking to somebody about this old white dude. I didn't get a name, but I got a pretty good description. I think I know who it is. Anyway, let me come over. I'm about twenty minutes away."

"Sure, sure," Hector said. That was it.

"And you taped this because . . . ?" I asked.

Tio Luis shrugged.

"Caught him in a lie, though."

There had to be something in that. Maybe he was a lowlife taking my uncle's money and doing nothing. He had said on the tape that he was at his office, and I was guessing we had been parked outside his home apartment. We were about ten minutes from his office, and I didn't doubt he would try to beat us there. Even if he got held up in traffic and took longer than the twenty minutes Tio Luis had mentioned, he could say something stupid like, "I had to get a better parking spot for the car," or "I went out for a quick errand."

Sure enough, he drove straight for his office.

We were there in about seven minutes. It was a busy neighborhood and someone had put on salsa music from a boombox that faced the street from a third-story window in the building next to Hector's.

"Follow me in five seconds," my uncle said.

He had hopped out of the car a couple of seconds behind Hector. Hector had gone straight for the door that would lead to his second-floor office. He was carrying his handgun and the recorder. I didn't think this was going to be good. At least, Hector would understand what we were saying.

Tio Luis disappeared into the building about twenty seconds behind Hector. I followed as I was told. There was a little old lady trying to get out of the door with a red pushcart in front of her. I held the door open. She blessed me in Spanish, and I thanked her. It was a human moment, but there was a revolver in my waistband.

I walked up right behind my uncle. Tio Luis was in the hallway; the office door was closed. He had a finger up to his lips to keep me quiet and his ear and the recorder both were pressed up to the door. I crept up slowly and quietly. None of the floorboards betrayed me. I put my ear up against the wood of the door. Hector was animated.

"He said he had a description . . . No, he said it was a white guy . . . He knows . . . I can't . . . I can't . . . I can't because he's my client. There's a link right there . . . I don't care if you don't care . . . I can't do it."

He listened for a minute or more. Then he hung up and mumbled something in Spanish ending with *"¡Ave Maria, que puñeta!"* We could hear the chair in his office squeak as he swiveled in it. That was enough for Tio Luis. He quietly turned off the recorder, put it in his pocket and stepped back. He pulled out his gun and kicked the door open.

There was a little yelling in Spanish and the hint that Hector was going to reach into a desk drawer for his own gun, but that didn't happen. From the door to the desk was only about four steps, and Tio Luis had his gun aimed for Hector's head the whole way. I closed the door behind me, and put my back to it since the lock was useless now.

"What is this? What are you doing?" Hector kept repeating in English and Spanish.

Tio Luis used his free hand to pull out the recorder. He rewound it and played it back from the beginning. The part he recorded through the door was hardly audible even at maximum volume, but certain words and phrases were clear enough. For instance, the whole idea that Tio Luis was a problem that needed to be dealt with. That was clear.

Hector put his hands to his head and ran them through his hair.

"And what do you think this proves?" he asked.

"You're going to tell me who you were talking to. I think that person wants to talk with me anyway. That sounds like the person who asked you to kill my little girl."

"I swear to you on my mother that I didn't kill your daughter," Hector said. Both men were tearing.

"I don't care what you say," Tio Luis answered. "You know who did, and you don't want to tell me."

"You think you're going to do what? Go kill this guy? It's not that easy. Believe me."

"Tell me his name, and I'll walk right out of here."

It sounded like a good deal to me, but I guessed it wasn't going to be quite that easy. It wasn't.

"Go ahead and kill me. If I tell you who's behind this, I'm a dead man anyway. Go ahead. Shoot."

It didn't look like a bluff to me. Hector seemed resigned. Tio Luis was silent a moment, collecting his thoughts. He rewound the tape a little, then a little more. He got to the part where Hector was dialing his phone to call the mystery person. With the volume up, we could hear the phone's tones as he dialed.

"I think I can figure the number out," Tio Luis said. "I'm going to know whether you help me or not."

"Go ahead," Hector said. He motioned to the phone. Tio Luis thought about it a moment. He rewound the recorder a bit and replayed the first three tones. He put the recorder on the desk and was about to pick up the receiver when I cut in front of him to do it myself.

"What?" Tio Luis asked. "You think you know the number?"

"Yep." I hit the redial button. The phone rang twice.

"The Ellis residence," I heard in a woman's voice, clear and Irish.

I hung up the phone without saying anything.

There wasn't anything for me to say. We had our information.

"It was Ellis," I said to my uncle. He seemed to chew things over for a minute. Hector had his hands on his head and kept them there.

"You work for Ellis?" my uncle asked. The news wasn't digesting well.

"I work for whomever I have to," Hector said.

The two men looked at each other as though trying to figure out what to do with each other. I thought for sure this was going to be one of those "let's beat him senseless and take him for a joyride" kinds of things, but it didn't turn out that way.

"You killed my daughter?" Tio Luis asked.

"I swear I never touched her. I never even saw her except in the picture you showed me. All Ellis wants is for me to keep you quiet, keep you out of the way. That's it. You have to stop poking your nose into other people's . . ."

He was going to say "business" but it got stuck in his throat. If the murder of your own daughter isn't your business, nothing in the world is.

"That's it, man. He wants you to leave things alone," Hector finished.

Tio Luis waited a moment, then he put the gun back into his waistband holster.

"I believe you," he said. "I'm going to talk to Ellis. If he's not there, if someone tips him off—it's going to be bad. I know where you live. If you think I won't find you and shoot you, let me know now."

Hector shrugged, his hands still on his head. He

wasn't about to call Tio Luis's bluff. Smart of him. I wouldn't have called it either.

"Now, what happened to your door?" Tio Luis asked.

"Some punk teenagers tried to break in," Hector said without missing a beat.

"Sounds like a good story to me," my uncle said. We left and went back to the car.

"How much did you pay that guy," I asked as we pulled away.

"Five thousand," my uncle said.

"And he stabbed you in the back like this?"

"He'll come in handy."

"When?"

Tio Luis pulled out the tape recorder and told me to rewind a bit.

There was Hector telling us what it was Ellis had hired him for.

"We let Ellis hear this and see what he has to say."

This sounded reasonable, and my uncle's voice was calm, but I wondered how it would play out as we drove out of the Bronx and into Manhattan for what I hoped would be the last time.

Night

If Hector was willing to sell out my uncle after he'd been paid five thousand, what were the chances he wouldn't sell him out again? What chance was there of finding Ellis at home? Or if he was home, what chance was there that he didn't have a gun ready for us as we walked up his front steps? A rich white guy could shoot the two of us as soon as we got in the door and say, "the two leaky Puerto Rican guys with guns tried to force their way in." It would sound right. It would look right. Maybe an investigation would show something of the truth. Later. After our funerals. Maybe the truth would never come out at all. Maybe nobody would even bother to look for it.

These were the kind of thoughts that crowded my brain in the last few miles before the Ellis house. Tio Luis looked pretty much satisfied and kept his eyes on the road. They were tired eyes with bags and red rims, and the road was the same as always, black and uncaring, pitted with wear and narrow.

The neighborhood was calm and quiet as any block in the city ever is. An older man in shorts and shades was walking a tiny dog as we went up the steps of the brownstone. I wanted to say something to Tio Luis, maybe about this being the end of the road, but I kept it to myself. For a man who had buried his daughter, he was intense, focused. I wanted to ask him what kept him going, but I was afraid that pointing out that he had stepped off the cliff long ago might make him look at me and wave and drop down like Wyle E. Coyote used to do and he wouldn't bounce back up from that.

Mr. Ellis senior opened the door for us. He had a smile as though he had just heard something funny, but he lost it at the sight of us.

"Can we have five minutes of your time?" my uncle asked. He had already taken a step closer. Ellis hesitated a moment, put a hand to his throat as though that would help him think, then he stepped aside and let us in without saying anything. He closed the door behind us and we faced him in the foyer of his home.

"Is your maid around?"

"Peggy? No. She just left. How can I—?"

Tio Luis took the handgun from the back of his waistband and aimed it to Ellis's head. The man's eyes just about popped out of his head. He hadn't been tipped off.

"What . . . What . . . What . . ." he said. He licked his lips and touched his throat again.

"I need you to hear something," Tio Luis said. He motioned with the gun for Ellis to lead the way into the drawing room he had met us in once before.

The three of us sat. Tio Luis took a chair about ten feet from Mr. Ellis. I sat close to the door and out of the line of fire in case my uncle felt a sudden urge.

"About forty minutes ago a man named Hector called you. He talked to you about me. He said things, you said things. No difference. I need you to know that I paid Hector. I gave him five thousand dollars and he told me everything."

Mr. Ellis looked nervous when my uncle started talking. I probably did too. But he calmed as the words came out. He interrupted the first moment my uncle paused.

"You got this all wrong," he said. "I wasn't on the phone all day today. Not at all until about five minutes ago. Right before you guys rang the doorbell. I hung up to answer the door." He seemed relieved to have cleared up this confusion, but it wasn't likely that my uncle would just take Ellis's word for any of this.

"Who called you?" Tio Luis asked.

"I don't think that's any of your business," Ellis answered. He sat forward an inch or two. My uncle reached behind himself to get the gun from his waistband.

"I have the gun," Tio Luis said. "I'll judge whether it's my business."

Ellis swallowed hard.

"A man named Peter McElmore. I've know him since college. He's flying in from Chicago late next week. We were just talking about old times."

Tio Luis shrugged. He seemed satisfied.

"Now. You and Hector killed my daughter. You need to pay for that," Tio Luis said. He didn't aim the gun, but I got the idea that move might be coming soon.

"Killed your daughter?" Ellis said. He looked like he'd been accused of eating a booger. "Are you insane? I don't know your daughter. I never even saw her. Why would I kill her?"

Tio Luis shrugged again. This time he raised the gun off his lap.

"All I know is Hector says you did and he has your phone number. Sounds good to me."

"Yes, but you forget that . . ." Ellis started his defense, then stopped. It looked like something was on his mind for a moment, but he dismissed it. He didn't finish his sentence. He looked down to his own lap instead.

"What?" my uncle asked and at that moment, I figured out what Ellis had dismissed.

"What?"

"His son lives here too," I said from behind my uncle. Ellis's eyes darted from left to right and back again as though he were looking for a way out of the mess he was in.

"Damn," he said.

Ellis didn't know where his son was. They hadn't spoken to each other all day though they had spent most of it in the same building together. A slamming door was the only reason Ellis even knew his son was out. No, they hadn't quarreled, they simply hadn't spoken. He couldn't see how Daniel might be involved in a murder. Yes, he did drugs, but he had separate funds and didn't need to resort to any labor or crime to afford his habit.

"Really, he's not that kind of person," Ellis said.

"What? He's not a killer?"

"No. He's not. That would require effort."

"Well, I wish I could take your word for it, but I'm gonna have to talk with your boy," Tio Luis said.

"I don't know where he is."

"Well, I can either wait for him to come home or I can go out and look for him myself." Tio Luis seemed to think about his own words a moment. Ellis didn't say anything and my uncle got up to go. I followed his example.

"I'll call the police the minute you leave this house," Ellis said as we were heading for the room's exit. It didn't seem like the smartest thing to say to two guys with guns who are already making their way out, but I'd spent a week watching a father do some of the least logical things to try to save his child.

Tio Luis stopped and turned back.

"Go ahead. Call them right now if you want. I'll wait." My uncle motioned toward the phone that sat just a few feet from Ellis.

"Do you want privacy?" Tio Luis asked. "We can wait in the next room." He said this all in a soft voice. It sounded like my uncle had just that moment grown tired of fighting—like he was giving up the revenge business. Ellis still didn't move.

"Me and my nephew here will sit outside for ten minutes. Call the police. Go ahead. Tell them a Puerto Rican guy with a gun is sitting on your stoop."

I couldn't tell if this was some sort of game of chicken, but we sat out there a total of fifteen minutes. We watched the pedestrians and the cars go by. Every few minutes, from behind a curtain, Ellis took a look at us sitting on his front steps. No police came. Ellis looked out again as we were standing to go. Tio Luis shrugged at him and we left.

"So what's the plan now?" I asked once the car was in motion.

"Huh?" Tio Luis answered.

How hard was it to find a drug addict in New York City? If you weren't particular about which addict, then your chances were good. On some blocks, throw a rock in any direction and you'd probably knock one over. Trying to find a specific junkie in the Village was the problem—like trying to find a specific needle in a haystack of hypodermics.

We went over by Jefferson Market where we'd seen him go once, but he wasn't there at the moment and not a soul wanted to talk to us. If they had souls. I waved cash and Tio Luis waved a gun but that just got us stares. It was like Ellis had called to warn them instead of calling the police. That might have been what happened. Who knows? Trusting addicts to keep a secret wasn't the smartest move, but it seemed to be working. Neither the carrot nor the stick got anything from a single one of them.

We went as far south as Tompkins Square Park. It was nightfall and there were plenty of dealers and users in the area, but no Ellis Junior. Neither was he at Union Square. Tio Luis and I walked miles and went down into the subway stations on the chance he was there, but night was falling and Tio Luis began to see that this was useless. The city was large and there was no end of places an addict with money could go, including out of it. For all we knew, Junior had left his dad's house with a thick stack of cash and gone straight to JFK. He could be thirty thousand feet up and thousands of miles away.

Tio Luis and I got sodas and hot dogs from a vendor who was out late. He seemed at least as tired as we were and put mustard on them without even asking us. We weren't in any mood or condition to argue. We popped open the sodas and found a set of steps to sit on. I wanted to ask, after the first bite and sip, if there was a next step coming. My uncle looked beat, but he'd been coming up with reserves of energy for days now. Looking at him as he hung his head down to drink from his soda, I decided to let it sit until we were done with the food and ready to move on.

"Did you see those drug addicts?" he asked me.

"Sad," I said.

"How many were there?"

"In this city?" I asked. "Thousands."

"No, I mean at that library, Jefferson Market."

"Oh," I said. It seemed like wheels were slowly turning in my uncle's head. "Maybe four or five addicts, about three dealers."

"And how much money did you pull out of your pocket?"

I put my soda on the step and dug into my pocket. At Jefferson Market I had pulled out everything I had. There were four fifties, a twenty, a ten, and three or four singles. I showed him.

"Hmm," my uncle said. I tried to figure out exactly what he was thinking but that got tiring.

"What's the matter?"

"Ever heard of a junkie or a dealer who wouldn't take your money?"

"Well, you had your gun out. Nobody was going to mug me with you right there."

"Not mug you. But they could have said anything and you would have given them the money, right?"

"Yeah, I guess so. But you had the gun. Maybe they got shy."

My uncle looked at me as though I'd grown an extra head.

"Shy? A shy druggie? Never heard of it."

"Maybe they know keeping the secret is worth something to them. Ellis is a millionaire. If they ask him for money for keeping the boy safe, he can give them more than . . ."

Tio Luis was shaking his head.

"Nope." Just that for a minute. "Nope."

"No reason not to lie. They take our money, send us to *las ventas del carajo,* then they get more money from Ellis if that's the plan. Nope."

"Maybe they're friends with Junior. Don't want to rat on him," I said. It sounded stupid coming off my lips.

My uncle gave me a sideways look and a smile.

"A loyal addict?" he said. He was done with his hot dog and chugged the rest of his soda as he stood up. I followed his example.

We went back to the car. He had his energy back and a glint in his eye that reminded me a little of Jack Nicholson in *The Shining*. I didn't bother to ask where we were headed.

Lights were off from top to bottom at the Ellis home as we made our pass. It wasn't late enough for Ellis to have gone to bed, but it was high time for him to have gone to a precinct to report us, so I didn't doubt that he had stepped out. We kept on driving and turned right at the corner. It was then that I was going to ask where we were going, but we made an-other right, then another, and made our way back in front of the Ellis house. Still no lights and I had no clue what my uncle's plan was but to keep circling until something happened. Then it did.

Just as we passed the house a second time, Ellis Junior turned the corner a bit farther down with two friends in tow. They were headed our way. Tio Luis pulled to a stop and put the car in park. He jumped out and was waving his handgun before Ju-nior could react. I jumped out too.

One of the friends said, "Oh shit, bye." And both of them walked off in the direction they had come from. Junior brought his hands up where they could be seen. He had a crack pipe in one of them. Apparently he wasn't too picky what he was using so long as it scrambled his brains.

"Get in the car," my uncle said. Neither Ellis nor I knew who he was speaking to, so we both obeyed.

"Where's your gun?" Tio Luis asked me as I strapped myself in. Ellis Junior was in the back seat, his hands still up. I got the handgun out and pointed it at Junior.

"We're going for a little ride," Tio Luis said at a stoplight. He looked back at Junior through the rearview mirror. "We need to talk."

"I have the right to remain silent," Junior said. My uncle laughed at him.

"I'm not the police, and you're not under arrest."

"Then can I go?"

"Soon," my uncle said.

The way he said this and, in fact, having Junior in the car at all, made me more nervous than I had been in a long while, probably since birth. When we headed for the Bronx, Junior pretty much fell asleep, but I was about ready to throw up. It was one thing to torture a drug dealer in some garage. They weren't the type to report anything to the police. Even if they did, the police wouldn't care. All you had to worry about was the retaliation of one man. With Ellis we had the son of a millionaire and there was no doubt the police would care. Even worse, when the investigation came, we would be guilty.

We passed the exit for any of the garages we had used previously, heading north, and I got the feeling for just a moment that we might be headed upstate to the woods with young Ellis. The scene played out in my mind like a movie. No questions, just a lecture about hurting children, then Ellis is forced to his knees and shot in the head. A shallow grave later, Tio Luis and I are back in the car headed home and, eventually, to the electric chair.

Instead, we got off at the exit that led us to Tio Luis's house. A few minutes later, we were there.

I couldn't see any good in bringing Ellis to Tio Luis's house. He would get to meet Titi Clarita. Maybe that was the strategy—have her sweet-talk information out of him. There wasn't time to ask. Tio Luis drove the car right into the garage, then there was the work of waking Junior and bringing him into the house.

My aunt raised an eyebrow when she saw what the cat had dragged in.

"*¿Un tecato?*" she asked. My uncle nodded to her. It was a junkie all right. To his credit, Junior nodded to her and said, "Thank you for having me," as though he were about to sit down to tea.

In fact, Tio Luis directed him to the dining room table and sat Junior down. He pulled up a chair and asked if he wanted anything to drink. He got a soda served in a glass with ice cubes and a paper towel around it to catch the condensation. If he had been given milk and cookies, I would have been more surprised but not by much. Titi Clarita went back into the kitchen and stood behind the swinging door. I could see the shadow of her feet. She could listen but not watch.

When Junior was settled and had started drinking, Tio Luis pulled his chair a few inches closer to him and I had a vision of that glass of soda being shoved down Junior's throat. It didn't happen. Instead, Tio Luis reached into a pocket and brought out a picture.

"This is a girl named Clarissa," my uncle started. "She went missing a little while ago."

Interrogating a drug addict has to be about the slowest work possible, but when they start to itch they can start to open up. The trick is to play off the period of time when they're clearheaded and anxious to be allowed back on the street where they can shoot up or take a toke or do whatever they do to scratch the itch.

Tio Luis and Ellis went back and forth for an hour before even the least useful piece of information came out. In the hour that followed, there was more information. Then the flow of information became a trickle. The clearheadedness was drying up; the anxiety to get back on the street was taking over. You see, you don't want them so desperate that they'll say anything. What you want is the truth.

"Okay," Tio Luis said. "I need you to answer my questions clearly. You understand? Five blocks from here, there is a park. In that park, I promise you, we can get you anything you want. Crack? Heroin? Marijuana? Anything. You see. In fact, I don't know if you have any money on you, but I will give you enough for a little party, understand?"

My uncle motioned to me, and I snapped to attention and pulled the money out of my pocket.

"See? Just say everything over again."

There really was such a park filled with small businessmen looking to make a buck whether they had to take it from others passing by or sell drugs or guns or the services of the girls always on the benches with them. The promise of this paradise was enough to get Junior to tell us just about everything he knew whether it was relevant or not. In the end, I was asked to walk him over to the park and hand him the money. I did and waited just outside the fence that ringed the park while he made his transaction. If he had run from me then and there,

I would have let him. I certainly wasn't going to follow him in. Even with a gun in my pocket, it wasn't safe for me.

Junior got whatever he wanted and then I walked him to the nearest train station. He had taken a hit of whatever before coming out of the park and was pretty mellow. This sounded like a dangerous thing to me, but if he stuck to showing the small bills, he certainly looked the part of a bum. Three or four dollars seemed to be his bankroll and there would have been no reason to hurt him except for fun.

"Was all that you said for real?"

"Sure thing," he said.

"Why would you say all that?" I asked. He didn't answer.

He had implicated himself and his father and a bunch of others and I figured that any one of them might have taken his nose off with pliers if they knew he was spilling the beans. Certainly, he said enough to get himself serious prison time. What arrogance to think he could say all that and walk away just because he was rich and white.

"That old man can say anything he wants, but no one will believe him. As far as anyone knows, I didn't say anything," Junior pointed out as we entered the subway station. "It's not like he was recording what I said."

Then he slid under the turnstile and went onto the train platform.

The trip to the park and the train station and back had taken the better part of an hour. I got back to my uncle's house as quickly as I could, but it was empty. A peek through the garage window showed me that both cars—the Toyota without bullet holes and the Cadillac with—were gone. From all that Tio Luis had gotten from Junior, I knew there were several people he could want to see. By leaving me behind, I figured he didn't want my help in dealing with these people. That was fine with me, but I wondered where Titi Clarita was going. That little fact gnawed at me as I headed home on foot.

I detoured. Junior had mentioned a guy at the Skate Key—a manager with a ponytail, Stu—and I figured Tio Luis would want to talk to him. I hoped he was headed there. I wanted to catch up to him before he did anything truly stupid like start shooting in a crowded skating rink. It was a twenty-minute walk but by jogging part of the way, I might make it in a little less. I prayed that Stu was off duty.

The streets were empty. On a few of the porches I passed, there were people trying to catch whatever breeze might pass by. I looked at no one.

According to Junior, Stu helped supply young girls for a business that sold them a few hours at a time. Men, and women, he pointed out, paid top dollar for young girls. Thousands he said. Stu was one of many in the supply side of the business. All he did was point out vulnerables to vultures like Carlos and make sure that whoever came looking for the girls or the vultures got some kind of runaround. Stu hadn't molested Jasmine. He probably hadn't even spoken a word to her. He certainly hadn't killed her. Not directly. He was a cog and the machine was vast according to Junior. Still, you dismantle a machine one cog at a time, and I was pretty sure Tio Luis wanted the machine torn to pieces.

By the time I got to the Skate Key, Tio Luis was heading for the Toyota. I shouted his name and jogged up to him. He was smiling a closed lip smile that creeped me out.

"What did you do?" I asked him. I opened the passenger side door and slid in.

"Nothing," he said.

"Stu wasn't there?"

"He was there. We talked. That's all."

"You made a tape right?"

"What of that Ellis boy? Sure."

"And . . . ?"

"And I gave a copy to that *pendejo*, Stu."

I wanted to form a question but couldn't think of what to ask. I tried to remember exactly what Junior had said. It was a lot. I noticed we were headed back to Manhattan.

"And that was it? You didn't threaten him? You didn't beat him up or anything?"

"A little bit," Tio Luis said.

"Of which one? Threatening or beating?"

"Yup," my uncle said.

We went to M. Hamilton's precinct next. It was late and the desk sergeant wasn't too interested in dealing with either one of us. My uncle was patient. I was tired. When the officer finally looked at us and nodded us over, Tio Luis pulled out a cassette and handed it over.

"What's this?"

"Detective Mike Hamilton asked me to stop by; it's evidence in a case he's working."

The officer turned it over in his hands as though he could figure out what was on it by looking. He shrugged and asked for my uncle's name, and my uncle gave it.

"Detective Hamilton won't be here until morning. Is this something he has to know about right away?"

"No, no," my uncle said. He smiled. "It's no emergency. It can wait."

Hamilton and his partner both were mentioned on the tape. They were the muscle of the operation. If you could believe Ellis Junior. If you could believe him, Hamilton had pulled the trigger and cut up the body of Jasmine Ramos.

Back in the Village, a hundred yards from the Ellis home, we waited and waited. Midnight passed us by.

DAY TEN

Morning

Tio Luis nudged me awake. I had been dreaming of running through a forest toward a waterfall. There was a beautiful girl in a white flowing dress. She ran ahead of me, teasing me, but I could never catch her. That didn't make the dream less pleasant. It didn't make the shock of waking at 3:30 in the morning less painful.

My uncle nodded down toward the Ellis home. There was Junior coming down the street with a friend. Junior seemed a hell of a lot higher than when I'd dropped him off at the train station. The friend hadn't caught up yet, but he was nearing the same nirvana Junior had found. Both of them were headed for the Ellis family home, but it looked to me like neither of them could have actually said that was their plan if asked. They were laughing about something. Probably something silly.

I heard a car door open, then another. I kept

watching Ellis and his friend. Then a trenchcoat appeared and another trench coat. They walked up to Ellis Junior. It was Hamilton and Pearson. I thought to myself that this was going to be bad. I was right. Hamilton didn't stop or slow down. In one motion, he pulled his hand out of the trench coat pocket, flicked open a switchblade, and stuck it into Ellis Junior's chest. That looked good enough to kill him, but Hamilton wasn't satisfied so he stuck the boy again and one more time for good measure. Ellis never even raised a hand to defend himself. Easy.

Pearson had his gun drawn for the seconds it took to do this. It was aimed at the friend who had his hands up and had backed himself up against a gate in front of a brownstone. Hamilton approached him slowly, the knife still in his hand. Even from my distance, I could see the friend wanted to cry. I didn't blame him.

I hadn't noticed when Tio Luis put the car in gear. Even when we started moving it was hard to take my eyes off the murderers, the dead body, and the friend who was being handed the switchblade. It seemed to me like the young guy was going to be given the knife and told to run while the hero detectives put a bullet in his back or at the very least made him the number one suspect in the murder. The same thought must have gone through the young guy's mind because he was sobbing and drooling and looked like he was in the middle of a nervous breakdown complete with some psychotic episode.

I didn't notice that Pearson had left the passenger side door wide open until we accelerated into it and sheared it off. The crunch was horrible. The two detectives and the boy all froze for a second. I froze too. Luckily I wasn't driving. Tio Luis shouted something out of the window as we passed the detectives. Hamilton was wide-eyed. Pearson looked angry. The boy took the moment to run as fast as his legs would carry him. I noticed lights go on in a couple of the brownstones on the block as we continued down. I don't know if they were responding to the shouting or the sound of metal on metal that accompanied the door coming off Hamilton's sedan. The detectives were still standing next to Junior's body as Tio Luis rounded the corner.

"What was that about?" I asked. I really wanted to know. For a short while I had thought that maybe Tio Luis was trying to build a case against Detective Hamilton, gathering evidence. Now it just looked like he wanted to stir up trouble, nothing more.

"You got to poke the beehive with a stick if you want all the bees to come out," was Tio Luis's answer.

"What the hell would you want that for?" I asked. Tio Luis gave me a quick look and a smile as he shrugged.

"I want to know everyone who was involved," he said.

"What about finding Clarissa? She's probably still alive somewhere."

The smile left my uncle's face.

"That's coming," he said.

So who else was responsible for Jasmine's death? Carlos, Nestor, Ellis, Hector, Stu, Hamilton and his partner. Without anyone having even suspected it, a whole tribe of people had lined up to take some part in killing her. If only they had revealed themselves early on, she would not have been let out of my uncle's sight.

Where was Clarissa and what would happen to her? How, if he could not save his own daughter, did my uncle think he was going to save someone else's?

Before dawn, we had dropped the Toyota off at a garage in Upper Manhattan. It would be kept off the street, my uncle told me. If the police looked for it, they wouldn't find it. We took the subway into the Bronx and borrowed a car from my cousin Paco who was either very sleepy or still drunk or both. He handed over the keys without any questions at all. If the police found us, it wouldn't be in the car that wrecked Hamilton's ride.

"But anyway, they not gonna look for us," my uncle said.

"What makes you say that?"

"You noticed the car they had in the Village. It wasn't a department car. It wasn't the one those detectives have been using. I think it was something they stole. Probably wiped down. They brought it to do the killing, nothing else. They gonna walk away from it. What they can't do is walk away from the tape."

I wasn't so sure about that. The tape had the voice of a junkie implicating Hamilton and Pearson for a murder. The junkie was dead now. No way to cross-examine him. Even if the district attorney believed what he heard, I didn't think he'd be prosecuting.

"What about Ellis?" I asked.

"What about him?"

"Well, how do you think he's going to feel?"

"What do you mean? He's dead."

"I mean the father."

"Oh, *esta liga'o*. He's mixed up in all this."

"How do you know this?" I asked.

"He gave his son up."

"What?"

"When someone comes into your house and says they want the truth about a murder . . . when someone does what I did, I think the normal reaction is to say anything to take suspicion off your child, no? But I think he put suspicion on the boy."

I wasn't sure I saw Ellis's moment of silence as a finger pointed at his son, but I could see how someone else might read it that way.

"Besides, his son was in my home, relaxed, talking freely, smile on his face, and he said his father was the one running this whole stinking thing. His father made money off my daughter. If the father is crying now . . . *if* the father is crying now, then I'm okay with that. Worse things could happen to him. Worse things should."

We found a parking spot in Alphabet City and listened to the car radio for news of the murder in the village. Details were sketchy about the whole thing. In fact, at first, the police couldn't even identify the victim. Whatever Hamilton and Pearson had done after we left them, I felt pretty sure it hadn't involved calling the murder in or catching the boy who had run away.

A couple of foot patrolmen passed by the car and glanced back at us. My heart nearly stopped. I wondered if the police had pictures of us provided by Hamilton, pictures that weren't being shared with the press. The officers kept walking, and I lost sight of them after a couple of blocks. I turned to Tio Luis, but he, for once, had fallen asleep. He looked peaceful and I hated to wake him, but when I saw the officers coming back around, I didn't feel I had a choice. I gave him a good nudge in the ribs. He woke up and put the car in gear without even looking at me, almost like he forgot he had me in the car. I hoped the feeling would continue.

"Where are we going?"

After eating, there was a trip to a pharmacy. The graze wound in Tio Luis's side continued to seep though, but now it was only after some sharp movement. If he'd give it a rest, it would most likely heal. He went in and it was my turn to fall asleep. It lasted a minute, and I woke up refreshed. That lasted a minute also.

Back in his seat, my uncle checked his wound and put together a gauze bandage for it. He didn't ask me to help. When he was done, he went back into the bag he'd brought out from the store, and got out another tape recorder, some batteries, and a brand-new tape. He put it all together and handed it to me.

"When I tell you to, press play and record at the same time," he told me.

Since I was probably going to have to conceal a weapon, I had a light jacket on just like my uncle to help cover the waistband. Since the temperature was headed for the mid-nineties, we must have looked like heroin addicts hiding our arms. The tape recorder went into an inner pocket.

The drive was short.

No one answered the doorbell at the Ellis home. That was exactly what Tio Luis wanted, and he was ready. He took a couple of wires from his back pocket, knelt in front of the door, and picked the lock. I didn't want to draw attention to us while he did this, but I couldn't help looking around every few seconds hoping no one would see us. The process took several minutes. A lady walking her dog and reading from a section of the *New York Times,* folded and refolded, passed us by without looking up. Tio Luis lost patience with the work, cursing in Spanish under his breath. He started an irritated chant of "Come on, come on" and in a few more seconds the lock obliged him and we were inside.

"When did you learn to pick locks?" I asked when the door was closed behind us.

"Please. I manage a bunch of buildings. I pick locks every week. Tenants forget their keys or need to be evicted."

"Don't you carry keys to the apartments?"

"You know how many tenants change the locks?"

The Ellis house had an alarm system, but the little digital display near the front door said it was unarmed.

"What are we doing here?"

"We're waiting for Ellis," was the answer. I let that hang in the air for a moment hoping my uncle would figure out what I was driving at. He didn't or at least didn't let on that he had.

"And what are you going to do when Ellis comes home?"

"I got some more questions," Tio Luis said. "I think that if I don't come in like this, he won't let me in."

"So you're not going to kill him?"

"Not without some answers first."

I felt my intestines knot themselves. It didn't sound like Tio Luis cared what the answers were—Ellis Senior was going to die, and I was going to be right there to witness it.

"What kind of questions?" I asked. I was hoping they would be the kinds of questions Ellis could get right and live instead of the "Would you like one bullet or two?" kind of question.

"Where's Clarissa?" Tio Luis said. It was a good question. We had moved through the drawing room and into what looked like a study with a wall of books, and a desk with a computer sitting on it. From there we went on to the dining room, very nicely decorated and with a long table and a side-board. Beyond this room was the kitchen.

"And why did Jasmine have to die?"

That was another good question and one I couldn't even begin to answer. Jasmine had been minutes from getting into her father's arms and his car and being driven back home. Minutes. What harm would have come from simply letting her go? Sure she might have told her story to the police, but then, they hadn't cared much when she disap-peared, and it wasn't likely they would take her word against a millionaire like Ellis. Besides, more importantly, Ellis had at least two cops in his back pocket. Had everything just spiraled out of control—escalated? How could a thirteen-year-old barely weighing a hundred pounds do that?

We roamed up to the bedrooms on the second floor. There were four of them. Junior's bedroom was easy to identify—you could literally follow the stink. Whatever the Irish servant did, it obviously didn't involve cleaning that room. With a look in-side, it was clear she wouldn't have been up to the job—nobody would have. The dirty clothes, the dirty magazines, the plates of half-eaten food, even the mattress from off the bed were all on the floor. It was like Junior was a hobo and he had his own private indoor shanty.

Tio Luis stood at the doorway—stepping in was just about impossible without stepping on junk. He looked into the room, and I'm pretty sure he thought of Jasmine and wondered if she had been in that room a few days before. Maybe the decision had been made to kill her there. She had even been killed there. In a pigsty of all places.

Another bedroom was neat as a pin, walls painted a light yellow, windows trimmed in blue. The single bed was made up and a mirror hung on the wall. It barely looked lived in and maybe it belonged to the Irish girl who worked there. Maybe she slept there sometimes like when it snowed hard or if she had to work late. Maybe other things happened in that room, but it didn't look like it.

Downstairs, the front door opened and closed. Ellis Senior was home. He went into the drawing room, and we could hear him pour out a drink for himself. It didn't sound like anyone was with him. We waited. I had no idea what would be our cue. After a first drink, there was second. Then there was a phone call.

"Harry? Hi, Thomas here. Listen. We've run into a little snag here, and I'm thinking we should postpone for a little bit. I don't know what your time frame is . . . uh-huh. Well, I'm thinking we should hold off for a day or two at least, but it would be even better if you could come back in a couple of weeks . . . No, no, don't worry about the airfare. I'll handle that if you can . . . No, I know. I know. Uh-huh. Well, no, don't say that.

Okay, maybe tomorrow. I'll tell you. This new girl, she'll be worth the wait. Hispanic like you want them, cinnamon skin and . . . exactly, a complete cherry. Untouched. No, no. The full fee, but I'll take care of the airfare . . . Oh, just some business I have to take care of. You'll be at the Baltimore tonight? Tenish? Okay, I'll call you then with some details. Bye-bye."

Ellis poured himself a third drink a little while later, and I could have used one too after hearing his side of the phone conversation. I couldn't get out of my mind the image of some old guy named Harry fondling himself on the sheets of the Baltimore Hotel.

Tio Luis had heard every word and recorded it all. The voice had carried well through the otherwise soundless house. The moment we moved, the sound of our steps would carry just as well.

He pulled his gun out of his waistband, motioned for me to do the same and to start recording. When I'd done what he'd asked, he started down the stairs like he owned each one of them.

"Who's there?" Ellis asked. It seemed to me that the answer should have been obvious to him. After he had done what he had done to Jasmine who else should be breaking into his house and coming down the stairs to get him?

Ellis was standing, one hand in his trouser pocket, the other holding a glass of some dark liquor. There was an inch of the liquid.

"How'd you get in here?" Ellis asked.

"Front door," my uncle answered.

When we parked outside, my uncle had told me he knew Ellis would be out because if Hamilton and he were acting like this was a mugging gone bad, the body would need to be identified. Ellis didn't look like a man who had just identified his own son on a morgue table. Maybe the drinks had helped fortify him or maybe the pain hadn't set in yet, but he looked comfortable, rested.

"I need to ask you a few more questions," my uncle said. Ellis took a sip, then put the glass down.

"I have to call the police," Ellis said calmly. "Something about my son's killers threatening me in my own home." He started to move, but Tio Luis pointed the gun at him.

"You going to call Mike Hamilton?" Tio Luis asked. "Did you hear the tape I gave Hamilton? Did he play it for you before he killed your son?"

Ellis didn't seem surprised by my uncle's accusation. He licked his lips slowly like he wanted a taste of the liquor he had been drinking and thought a moment before answering.

"He was a waste," he said.

"What?"

"A waste. I'm not even sure he was my son. Anyway, he was dragging down the finances. Anyway, I'm not sorry."

The words hung there. They didn't implicate Ellis. He wasn't admitting that he had his own son executed to shut him up, but it took my uncle a moment to understand what exactly was being admitted.

"Where is Clarissa?" my uncle asked. "Young

girl, from the Bronx—brown skin, brown hair, brown eyes. Her mother needs her back."

Ellis paused a half second before shrugging to tell us he didn't know.

Tio Luis didn't like that answer. I could tell by the way he worked his jaw that he was angry. After all these days of struggle, of heartache, of skating the edge of sanity, I didn't know if he could take the next few minutes without breaking down completely.

"Can you tell me," my uncle continued. I thought I saw a tear escape his eye, and I slowly moved my hand to the butt-end of the gun in my waistband in case I had to take over and get myself and my uncle out of there.

"Can you tell me why? Why my daughter had to die? Why you couldn't just let her go?"

Now I knew tears had escaped from my uncle. If I hadn't seen them stream down his cheek, I might still have heard them fall to the carpet in the silence of the moments after he asked his question. I felt then that Ellis was a dead man no matter what his answer was.

Ellis took his time. I think he saw in my uncle's tears a weakness he could exploit if he could only say just the right things. I think he felt he could not only walk away from this situation but master it.

"I was ready to let her go. . . . She had given a lot of trouble. You had given a lot of trouble. A lot of father's don't want their daughters back after a day or two. A lot of girls think the whole thing is fun, at least for a while. That guy, Stu, he picked out a rotten one for me."

"So why didn't you let her go?"

"She took something, something that didn't belong to her. Sometimes the girls steal. That happens, but she took the wrong thing. . . . She took a wallet."

My uncle's face showed the strain of disbelief on it. He ran his free hand through his hair. Of all the things Ellis could have said, this was the least expected.

"Money? You killed her for money? I would have sold my house and given you every penny you stupid bastard! I would have given you anything."

"Not money, Mr. . . . Mr. . . ."

"Ramos."

"Right. Not money. The wallet had information. One of my clients. A client who paid me fifteen thousand dollars to . . ." Ellis didn't finish. "To have Jasmine" was probably what he wanted to say, but he was smart enough not to. "Anyway, she took his wallet, his ID, proof of the fact that she and he . . ." Another unfinished sentence. "She wouldn't give it back. Even after she made it all the way to the Bronx and Hamilton found her waiting in a train station, she still wouldn't give it back. He beat her, but she wouldn't say where she had hidden it. He put a gun to her, but she still wouldn't. He tried for hours. Well, you can see. If she wouldn't give back the wallet, she had to be prevented from ever showing it to anyone."

Ellis looked to me as though he wanted confirmation of his logic. I don't know what he saw in my face, but it wasn't approval.

"Business," he said. Then he folded his hands in front of himself.

Tio Luis lowered the angle of the gun, and I didn't know if he was going to pull the trigger or faint. He shook his head as though he could make what Ellis had said fit in his mind if he could only find the right spot for it. It didn't work. He turned to me.

"*Apaguelo,*" he said. Turn it off. It took me a fraction of a second to remember I was carrying a tape recorder. I turned it off without bringing it out, but Ellis's face showed that he knew he'd been recorded.

"Unbelievable," Ellis blurted out. I think he was talking about the fact that he had let himself slip up.

"Put your gun on him," Tio Luis said. I did as I was told. My uncle left the room, and Ellis and I stood there facing each other.

"Is he going to call the police?" Ellis asked.

"I doubt it," I said. I was right. Tio Luis came back with a kitchen knife. A filet knife I'd say.

"Sit," my uncle said. He backed Ellis up toward a leather chair. Ellis reached behind himself to hold on to the armrest as he eased himself to the seat. In that split second, Tio Luis moved the knife with a quick flick across Ellis's left wrist.

"What . . . ?" Ellis assumed he was being murdered and would have liked to have confirmed this, but Tio Luis dropped the knife at the side of Ellis's chair. He pulled his gun out again and aimed it for Ellis's nose, and he shook his head when Ellis made a move to grab his wrist with the uninjured hand.

"Now," my uncle said. He spoke deliberately. "You remember that first question about the girl,

Clarissa? I think you maybe lied to me. I think you know—"

"I don't, I swear it."

"Well, let me say that you need to know if you want me to let you live. You have about three minutes before you start to black out, so talk fast. Where is Clarissa?"

"If I die, you'll never find her," Ellis said.

"Nah. That's not true. If you don't talk, I won't find her no matter what, so I need you to talk. If you don't, I still won't find her, but then, you'll be dead. I'm making a deal. Tell me the truth and you can get an ambulance. Don't tell me, and you die. But hurry up. You're a thin man. Not that much blood."

"You're crazy."

Tio Luis shrugged. The blood was dripping from Ellis's arm at a pretty good clip. I couldn't imagine that he had anywhere near three minutes.

Ellis hesitated. That was beyond my ability to comprehend.

"Hamilton has her," he finally said. "He has her."

"Sounds like a lie to me," Tio Luis said. "Where is Hamilton keeping her? In his locker at the precinct? Come on. Try a little harder . . ."

"No. In his home. He has a house. Hartsdale. There's a basement. When a girl can't be . . . can't be . . . When a girl can't be found a person to buy her with . . . When we can't find a person to buy her, a girl . . . has to go somewhere. Sometimes Hamilton holds on to them. Just for a little while. Like if a father is looking for her . . . Carlos Valle used to . . ."

The anxiety caused by watching his blood drool out of him made Ellis slip up in what he had to say.

"But where does Hamilton live?" Tio Luis asked. He seemed to believe the story.

"Hartsdale."

"Where in Hartsdale?"

Hartsdale was only a few minutes north of the Bronx, but it was a large enough place, crowded with just enough people to make the search for the right house slow.

Slowly, Ellis gave us a street address. My uncle had him repeat it a couple of times to make sure the story didn't change. He quizzed the man for a full minute. Ellis's breath became labored and he struggled to keep focused.

"Please . . . You said you . . . You said . . . You . . ."

"What? What did I say?"

"Ambulance."

"Ambulance? Oh, I get it. I said you could get an ambulance. Well, you're right about that. And the good news is that I do believe you. I'm going to let you get an ambulance." My uncle put the gun back into his waistband. "You can hold your wrist now. I would suggest you raise it above your head so you don't bleed out so much."

Ellis moved his right hand toward his left wrist, but he fumbled as though he could no longer find his own arm.

"Call," Ellis said. It was weak.

"Call? Call who?"

"Ambulance."

"Oh, I never said I would call. I said you could

get one. Go ahead. This is your house. You know where the phone is. We'll just let ourselves out. Oh, by the way. Good luck. Response time in this area is supposed to be pretty good. You still have a chance."

Tio Luis stepped back to my side. We watched Ellis try to get up. Essentially, he slid off the leather chair and onto the carpet.

"Please," Ellis said.

A minute later, after my uncle had checked the knife handle for prints, Ellis stopped moving and we left.

On the drive to Hartsdale, my uncle says, "You know, something like that happened in Vietnam. It was after we had been ambushed and one of our guys died. Grenade. Anyway, a day or two later, we're out in the field again and there are some Special Forces types with us. We catch one of the VC guys alive. That's not an easy thing to do, but we did it. He was wounded. Thigh wound. Lots of blood and it wouldn't stop. The medic put a tourniquet on it. Then the Special Forces guys took over. They loosened the tourniquet and asked him questions. They promised to tighten things up again if he spoke. Otherwise he'd bleed to death in the jungle. Stupid bastard."

"What happened to him?" I asked.

"He bled to death. Never said a word."

We drove on in silence a few minutes before Tio Luis finished his story.

"Thing of it is, we knew. . . . All of us knew he wasn't going to say anything. And we knew, all of us, that even if he did, that tourniquet wasn't going back on. What does that make that? Is that murder?"

How did I feel watching Thomas Ellis fall to the floor next to a puddle of his own blood and breathe out his last breath? Not as bad as I would have thought. Nervous, very nervous. What if the Irish lady walked in? Or, worse yet, what if he simply didn't die? What if Tio Luis helped him back into his seat, thanked Ellis for his answers, and put on a tourniquet?

No. Watching Ellis die wasn't as bad as I would have thought.

Afternoon

There are parts of Hartsdale where the houses cost a lot more money than I would earn in a lifetime, but other parts . . .

The city wasn't so bad, but it was growing, becoming a bit congested, and there was a strip mall not too far away. Working class with maybe a touch of longing for something better.

Hamilton's house was part of that something better the others in Hartsdale were longing for. I didn't know what a detective made in the NYPD, but it looked like all of it went to the house. The edge of his property was lined with large, old trees and with shrubs. Beyond that was a hundred feet of lawn. The drive was red brick and ended in front of a garage with three ports. A Jeep, brand new and black, was parked in front of one of the garage doors. It was sparkling—dripping from a recent hand wash. On the lawn, two little girls played: each was maybe five or six. Too young, I thought, to belong to Hamilton—he looked too haggard. Maybe sin had made him so.

Tio Luis pulled up right behind the Jeep and got out. He had a plan for searching the house. It seemed too easy and we were unprepared. Also, if Hamilton were home at that hour, he might just shoot us. The children watched us closely as we walked up to the front door.

"Mrs. Hamilton?" my uncle asked.

"Yes." The word came out apprehensively. She was young and pretty and didn't know what to make of the two Puerto Ricans on her doorstep. She looked past me quickly to make sure her daughters were okay.

"Your husband called for a free estimate. Exterminating. He said something about roaches."

She looked taken aback. I knew she was going to say that her husband had never said anything to her about roaches, and she did.

"Ah, sometimes husbands don't like to mention it to wives. Some women are scared of the roaches that fly."

"Roaches can fly?" she asked.

"Only the really big ones. Anyway, it doesn't

have to be today. I can come back tomorrow. To-day isn't even a regular workday for me; we were just doing an emergency job in the area . . ." Tio Luis put his hand up to start to wave good-bye and began to turn. I turned and went down the steps.

"No, wait," she said. She didn't like the idea of let-ting us in, but at least we didn't fly. She waved us in.

"He said something about the basement." My uncle was slathering it on now. Mrs. Hamilton was horrified. She was in the basement everyday. That didn't sound promising, but we went downstairs anyway.

The basement was brightly lit. There was no place to hide a girl no matter how small she was. There wasn't even a place for a roach. There was a washer and a dryer, and a play area for the girls; the boiler room was spacious. My stomach sank. If Ellis lied to us about Hamilton keeping Clarissa, Hamilton would know about our visit to his home and there was no doubt he'd find a reason to arrest us—impersonating an exterminator.

"This doesn't look bad at all," Tio Luis said. His face didn't betray anything but tiredness. "You can tell your husband that he doesn't really need a full fumigation. There are no droppings, no remains. Really, if he sees any roaches, a spray can of Black Flag would be good enough."

We were both headed back up the stairs. Getting into the car and the hell out of there seemed like the wisest thing we could do at the moment.

"Wait," Mrs. Hamilton said. "What about Mike's bunker?"

"His what?" my uncle asked.

"He has this work space out in the backyard. It's underground. I call it his bunker, but it might be what he was talking about."

Tio Luis looked at me as though he wanted my opinion, but I couldn't imagine what he wanted it about or why.

Mrs. Hamilton led the way. The backyard was large and at a far corner, there was door at an angle in the ground. It was padlocked shut. Tio Luis asked for the key, but Mrs. Hamilton didn't have one, hadn't thought of it.

"Should I try to call Mike at work?"

"No, no. I can pick it." Tio Luis gave her a story about how a woman had locked herself out of her apartment when a roach had landed in her hair. Mrs. Hamilton took a step back and a quick glance in the air above her and told my uncle to go ahead and do what he had to. His ability to lie was surprising. A minute later, the door was open.

There were steps going down and an upright door at the bottom. There was a bar and a padlock keeping the second door shut. Tio Luis made a joke about Fort Knox and asked what Hamilton kept in there while he started to pick this second lock. Mrs. Hamilton had never been inside the bunker, but she knew the detective kept expensive tools in there—her husband had told her.

The second padlock took a little longer to pick. The two girls had come to stand beside their mother at the top of the stairs. I stood halfway to the bottom.

First there was a smell, then there was a squeal, then Tio Luis backed out of the bunker. The squealing didn't stop. It got louder. I looked up and saw Mrs. Hamilton clutching one of her daughters to herself.

"What is that?" she yelled out over the noise.

I went down to the bottom and looked in. It was dark, but the sun showed me what I didn't want to see—Clarissa De Jesus chained to the cinder block wall, her arms splayed out, her feet together, duct tape over her mouth, a padded strap around her neck to keep her pinned. She was dirty with her own waste and naked.

We watched and listened as Mrs. Hamilton called 911. She was in tears as were her daughters.

"The ambulance is coming for you sweetie. This is almost over and no one is going to hurt you anymore," Tio Luis said. He caressed Clarissa's face, and she seemed to calm a little. She recognized us. He told her that we couldn't stay. That the police would have too many questions for us and we couldn't answer them all just then. She seemed to understand. He told Mrs. Hamilton that we were both illegal immigrants and couldn't risk talking to police. She was so far from being able to comprehend what was going on that I am sure his words were wasted.

When we heard the sirens approaching, we left. From a few yards away, we saw the ambulance enter the Hamilton property. A few seconds behind them came the Hartsdale police. We watched from the car as the ambulance left a little later, and then some time after that a news van approached, then another. Then a crime scene van.

Tio Luis drove to a pay phone and made a call. He was near tears when he hung up and came back to the car.

"The hospital has her," he said. Then he went back to the pay phone. After a minute on the phone, he was squatting and wiping tears away. Mrs. De Jesus would have her daughter back. That was something.

Night

The scandal hit the radio waves and the evening news. We watched the report made from the Hamilton home while eating in a diner in the Bronx. It made us smile like stupid men. The police up in Hartsdale wanted to talk to him as did the police in New York City. His own precinct commander had to go in front of the cameras to say that he didn't know where Hamilton and his partner were. One NYPD detective told the camera that no one should jump to conclusions. He looked into the camera and said, "Who knows? Maybe this was a prank by the girl or some of her friends." When the reporter got back on the screen, she made a point of saying that that explanation seemed "unlikely."

There was nothing at all on the news about Mr. Ellis. I started to wonder if he hadn't faked his death.

* * *

NYPD couldn't find Hamilton throughout the afternoon and into the night, but it took us minutes.

There must have been the thought in his mind that he was just a couple bullets away from erasing his biggest problems—me and my uncle. If we would just disappear, the evidence against him would seem so much weaker—just the word of Clarissa, a hysterical girl who could not have been very good if she was found naked.

We slowed the car down a few blocks from Tio Luis's home. We checked every car to see where he was staking out in wait for us. It turned out he was watching the house from a place fifty yards past my uncle's house. He was alone in the car, leaning his head to be able to watch the house through the side view mirror. Maybe he was tired, but he didn't react as we pulled up alongside him. My uncle honked.

"You looking for me?"

We drove off, and the detective put his car in gear and followed. The chase wasn't always fast, but it was long. We led Hamilton to the West Farms area. There was a big train station there, and a lot of buses making connections, and there was the on-ramp to the highway. Tio Luis pretended to head for the highway, but pulled off onto a side street. It was dark and mostly deserted. The kind of place where the police were sorely needed and would have found a lot to do. Dealers, addicts, whores, and muggers all waiting like Venus flytraps to prey on the stupid.

Tio Luis clicked his seat belt off and pulled up

short; Hamilton just avoided rear-ending us. I didn't know what was supposed to happen next, but Tio Luis bolted from the car. I followed as fast as I could get out of the car. By the time I caught up, Tio Luis had a gun to Hamilton's face, and Hamilton had his hands up. Both men were breathing hard—Tio Luis from rage and Hamilton from fear. They glared at each other. Hamilton spoke first.

"What are you going to do, you stupid moron? You gonna shoot a cop? If you do, there'll be forty thousand cops who'll be—"

Tio Luis gave Hamilton a rap across the teeth with the gun. It wasn't very hard, but the sound of metal on teeth made me cringe. Hamilton looked liked he wanted to cry for a second, but he composed himself.

"Well?" he asked. "What do you want?"

The moment of silence was long. Tio Luis didn't even try to open his mouth. I think he could not have said what he wanted from Hamilton. Or from Ellis or Stu or Hector or anyone else in the world. He wanted his daughter back. He wanted Jasmine. He could forgive everything if she were returned to him.

"Listen," Hamilton said. "Don't be stupid. You can't do anything to me and you know it—"

I cut him off.

"Tell us why you did it. Why did you kill Jasmine?"

Hamilton laughed to himself.

"Listen," he said. "I've heard about your uncle's handiwork."

Tio Luis pulled the recorder out of his pocket. It was already off, but he showed Hamilton. He popped the cassette lid open and dumped the cassette onto the asphalt. Hamilton cleared his throat.

"Put the gun away, and I'll answer your question."

"Put your hands on the wheel and I'll put the gun away," Tio Luis answered. Both men thought a second longer and then each did what the other wanted.

"Jasmine took a wallet," Hamilton started. He went on to explain exactly what Ellis had told us about the client's confidentiality. Jasmine had made herself a liability. So had Tio Luis. From talking with my uncle, Hamilton got the impression that the matter wasn't going to be dropped as soon as Jasmine made it home. Instead, it was like that would just be the beginning of new troubles. If Jasmine had evidence of rape, Tio Luis would see that it went to the police. Worse yet, Tio Luis might hunt down the man Jasmine told him about, the man who had hurt his little girl.

I could see my uncle deflate. His face went slack, his eyes got distant, and I felt like I could read his mind from the tiniest contours of his face. He was buying Hamilton's line. He was thinking it over and finding fault with himself. He was thinking that if he hadn't pushed so hard to get Jasmine back, she might still be alive. He was blaming himself. Blaming himself when the man who pulled the trigger was sitting right in front of him.

"Who is this man? The missing wallet guy? Tell me and I'll leave you alone," my uncle said.

Hamilton rolled his eyes and laughed softly to himself. He seemed to be going over his options. He decided to tell.

"This guy from Chicago. Comes in monthly. Harold Martell. Friend of Ellis's I think. Calls him Harry. Always gets . . . first crack. Anyway, he pays top dollar."

"How much?"

"So that's what this is about." Hamilton nodded as though he understood the universe just then. "Well, if you're going to try anything with him, fine. He's loaded. Pays fifteen K for a night."

"Wow," my uncle said. The words were for himself, but Hamilton heard him.

"It's an expensive habit," the detective said. "Ellis has guys like this coming in every weekend. Four or five of them at a time. Each pays about the same. A lot of money flowing. If I were you, I'd talk to Ellis about some hush money. He might pay. God knows he's got the scratch."

At that moment, a squad car came driving up toward us slowly. It was dark enough that he'd have to get really close to make out our faces, but there was no reason for him not to do exactly that. Before he got in range, he turned on his sirens and lights and drove off at a good clip. Probably someone had gotten shot nearby and whatever business we might be conducting on this side street didn't rate.

"Listen, can I go now?" Hamilton asked. He sounded like a grumpy child to me. Like he was entitled to walk away from all the mess he had created because he had finally told the truth. He was smug, and it ate at me so I did something stupid. I pulled the recorder out of my pocket, held it up for Hamilton to see, and shut it off in front of him. Then I smiled.

"You bastard!" he shouted. He started to reach for his weapon, but Tio Luis was faster. Hamilton put his hands up again.

"Just insurance," I said. "In case you try anything. My uncle is a man of his word."

Even in the darkness of the night, I could tell Hamilton was furious as I put the recorder away.

"You know," he said. "It's really your fault. I don't mean you personally, but your race. You let your girls go out half naked or in tight jeans. You let them have boyfriends. They get knocked up or they go on the job and then you complain to the police. Like we're supposed to teach them how to keep their panties on."

"Watch your mouth," Tio Luis said. We headed back to our car. It should have ended right there, but it didn't.

"I taught her a lesson," Hamilton said. My uncle and I both stopped. "With my nine millimeter. I taught her a lesson."

The foreign object the coroner had mentioned. Tio Luis understood, but it didn't phase him like it might have. He was motionless.

I pulled out the revolver I had in my waistband, took two steps to be at Hamilton's side, and pointed the gun in his face.

"Shut up," I said, and he should have.

His hands were up, but he was smiling. "I think she liked it," he answered.

I don't know if he knew his life was ruined or if maybe he had a death wish. I pulled the trigger three times, missed once, got him in the chest and the throat with the other two shots.

Detective Hamilton didn't die immediately. He died while Tio Luis was stripping him of his guns, his badge, and his wallet. Hamilton was dead already as my uncle undid his seat belt and the belt of his trousers, and opened the detective's pants exposing his privates—pale, shriveled, and uncircumcised—to the night air.

We were five minutes away from where we'd left the detective when I turned to Tio Luis. He looked at me and shrugged. Neither one of us understood what had just happened or what would happen next.

Tio Luis stopped short at a garbage can, went through it and came back to the car with a plastic bag and an old newspaper. Into the bag went the detective's possessions. The newspaper went to me.

"Find a phone number for a reporter or editor or something."

A few minutes later we were on the Grand Concourse heading for Hector's apartment. I had found a general information phone number for the newspaper, but I didn't think there would be anyone there on a Sunday night. Tio Luis came up with a phone number for a local TV news program that was always advertising that they were looking for tips, day or night. He double parked, got out and went to the same pay phone he had used to fool

Hector. He made four or five phone calls. For some he looked bored as if they had put him on hold. For others he was animated, yelling almost. With the last one he was smiling.

"What's so funny?" I asked as he took the driver's seat. As the words came out of my mouth I was sorry I had asked. Tio Luis had gotten a strange sense of humor in the last few days; if he had any more bad news for me, I'd pass out.

"Just talking to your auntie."

"And who else did you talk to?"

"Newspaper, TV, and the hotel."

"What hotel?"

"Baltimore Hotel. You know where 'Harry' Martell is staying."

"What?"

"I had to call twice, but I got his room number. I spoke to him."

"You what?"

"I told him I found his wallet."

"And we're headed there now, right?"

"Sure thing."

What surprised me was that he wasn't ugly or fat or otherwise unattractive. He was handsome, fit, and a millionaire and could have paid full-grown women to be with him and left the little girls alone.

Harold Martell had no reason to hide his identity when in a New York hotel. He was wealthy and unmarried—if he wanted to come to the city, he could. He had made his money in trading commodities and was retired with millions by the age of forty. That was only a couple of years earlier. Since then, he had traveled a great deal. Lots of flights to lots of cities. Yes, lots of young women. Yes, Jasmine too. Yes, he knew they were underage. He liked them when they were just starting to develop. No, he was never violent with them. Never. He knew a dozen guys like Ellis who facilitated these . . . transactions. He knew a dozen places like the one in Bay Ridge. There were dozens of Mike Hamiltons out there.

He told us all of this on his knees in a southern corner of Central Park. He was slobbering and said he was cold though it felt like it was still ninety degrees and there wasn't the smallest breeze.

Tio Luis turned off the recorder a moment and asked Martell to write down the names and addresses of these dozen Ellises and the houses where he'd been and the names of the police who were on the take. Some of the information he wrote out was sketchy, but some was detailed. Then my uncle asked Harry to talk about how Detective Hamilton had been trying to extort money from him and so he had the detective killed. At first Martell burst into tears and said he couldn't do that, but my uncle calmed him down.

"Relax," he said. "None of this will come out unless you try to do something against me."

He turned on the recorder and for the next five minutes Martell spilled his guts about the horrors of Detective Hamilton and how he had Hamilton killed. My uncle put the list of names and addresses in front of him and he read them out, explaining what connection he had to them. That was enough for the recorder.

Tio Luis made Martell touch every item he had taken off of Hamilton, and he made Martell handle the gun I had used. He made him unload and re-load the gun. Fingerprints everywhere.

"Remember, Martell, if you speak to anyone, the tape and the guns and the other stuff, that all goes to the police. Believe me, they won't like you. You understand me?"

Martell understood.

"And one more thing. You are checking out to-night and getting on a plane back to Chicago. Understand? I'm going to drop you off near the hotel and I'm going to watch. If you're not in a cab to LaGuardia in half an hour, I will personally go up to your room and blow your head off. Got it?"

Martell understood that too.

It was that easy. When he wasn't around little girls, Harry Martell wasn't that tough. He wasn't that smart either. Tio Luis dumped the tape and Hamilton's stuff in a mailbox at the corner while Martell was upstairs. We watched him come out with carry-on luggage, and we followed his taxi to the airport from a distance. I got off and watched as he went to the ticket counter. He went through security to his gate. I didn't see him past that point, but I waited a while and he didn't come out again. He was running scared. At eleven, his plane took off.

"Why'd you dump the tape?" I asked. It seemed like that was a mistake. Martell would say he was coerced. Whoever coerced him was the obvious suspect in Hamilton's killing.

"I figured, 'What the hell?' He could talk about how I put a gun to his head, but our voices aren't on the tape. Besides, I have an alibi."

My cousin Paco was with Titi Clarita in a motel in Newark not far from the airport. She had tickets for a flight the next morning headed to Puerto Rico. It couldn't be denied that they needed some rest. The Toyota was there. Paco and I got into his car.

Paco had checked in with my aunt. That was the alibi. The theory was that to most people one Puerto Rican looked like another. If the police came around a day or two later and spoke to the motel manager, maybe to show him a picture of my uncle, the manager would say, "Yes, that man was here at the time Harry Martell says he had a gun to his head and a recorder to his mouth." Certainly the license plate number, the make and the model of the car that the manager took down information for was Tio Luis's.

OTHER DAYS

When I woke the next morning to a ringing phone, it was Tio Luis telling me to turn on the TV. Harry Martell was being led away in handcuffs. He didn't look good. Tired maybe. Monday morning blues.

Detective Pearson was found on his bed, his service gun in his hand, one of the bullets lodged in the back of his skull after having made its way through the roof of his mouth. The stress of the last few days was apparently too much for him. No note. No nothing—just a fat bank account. Fatter than a detective's salary could account for.

A detective came around to ask me some basic questions later that night, but it was too late. Harry Martell looked as guilty as a person could, and the detective didn't really care much about what I had to say about playing video games all night before.

"*Doom*," I told him.

"Isn't that the shooting game where you kill all the monsters?"

"Yeah," I said.

"I was thinking of getting that for one of my nephews."

"Don't bother," I said. "It's not as fun as it sounds."

He thanked me for my time.

It took four days for Ellis's body to be found. It seems like his servant never came. More likely she came back Monday morning and turned right around. Maybe she was in the country illegally and didn't want a hassle with police. Maybe the smell stopped her cold. No difference. Police wanted to talk to her, but the coroner wasted no time in saying grief had killed Ellis. It had forced him to slash his own wrist quick and easy.

The death of one's own child could make you do crazy things.

Tio Luis and Titi Clarita came back to their home after two weeks. They had found a farm on a mountain. Peace and quiet. And maybe it wasn't too late to have another child and be a family. Maybe not too late, but a little too early just then to think about it. Still, the house went up for sale. There was no point to a house if there were no children to fill it.

* * *

How did it feel to be a killer? To erase someone from the universe? To leave a gap in the lives of a wife and children? Not good.

How did it feel to be a killer? To make sure an evil man never committed evil again? To defend myself against a man who most likely would have tried to kill me? Who would have gotten away with killing me? Not bad.

I looked up things in the Bible. They helped. Not the "eye for an eye" part. "Do unto others." I thought about that long and hard. If I turned into a Hamilton or an Ellis or a Martell, how would I want people to treat me? What would I want them to do with me? Wouldn't a bullet in the brain be a relief?

And Jasmine?

And Jasmine? Thirteen and not fully grown yet. Petite. One moment laughing with friends, falling down and getting up at a skating rink, the next moment tortured and murdered. In between, a short humiliation as a crack whore. The last days of her life were the definition of misery, not just for herself, but for those who loved her. Misery and emptiness. She died never knowing how her presence in the world did so much to fill the lives and days of those around her. Her absence leaves voids in so many. And there is the void of the future. She might have been anything, meant anything if only she'd been allowed a little more time.

Yet . . .

Yet, half grown as she was, she was a hero, no? Not like a movie star or a sports legend whose exploits are superficial. Like the ones you read about in high school, like furious Achilles.

Why did she take the wallet? Her father was a soft touch and would have given her anything she wanted. When Ellis and Martell had done what they had done, when Hamilton had done what he had done to her, why not give the wallet up? Why hold on to its location when you've been raped and beaten and the killer's gun is pressed against your chest? There couldn't have been any mercy in Hamilton's eyes that told her a bargain was possible.

The only reason Jasmine had to hold on to the wallet was as proof of what had happened. She wanted to see justice—Justice with a capital *J*. The benefits her sacrifice reaped for the world, no less than the world, were greater than she could have imagined. How many more young girls would have had their lives ruined by Ellis and Hamilton and Martell? How many lives did Jasmine save with the strength of her will? Having known and loved her, having helped her perform this last task of hers, lifts me, cleanses me, makes me better than I ever would have been.

READING GROUP QUESTIONS

1. *The Concrete Maze* is both hardboiled and noir, so it may be seen to fit into a very long and much honored tradition—Chandler and Hammett among the early practitioners and Ken Bruen, James Sallis, and Sara Gran in recent times. How does this book compare to others in the tradition? Are there any elements that don't fit?

2. *The Concrete Maze* can be seen as a "buddy" novel—Marc and Tio Luis are never separated for long in their journey. Tio Luis seems to lead the way while Marc tags along. But is the narrator as passive as he seems to be? Is Tio Luis the driving force?

3. Is justice attained at the end of the novel?

4. On several occasions, Tio Luis refers to his Vietnam experience, but what light do those experi-

ences shed on the ordeal he goes through in the novel?

5. There are several lines of Spanish spoken throughout the novel. Do they add or take away from the experience of reading the book?

6. Are there any heroes in the story?

7. What are some of the social issues brought up throughout the novel?

8. Consider that in the year the novel is set, 1992, New York City averaged more than six murders a day. Having read the novel, does it seem realistic?

9. It might have been possible to write the story in the third person and have Tio Luis do all that he does alone. Why does Marc tell the story?

THE PIPER.

He terrified an entire city. Then he vanished.

No one has heard from him in years.

But now he's back.

And **HE'S KIDNAPPED YOUR SON.**

Turn the page for an advance look at an
exciting new thriller:

PAYING THE PIPER

By

Simon Wood

Coming November 2007

CHAPTER ONE

Scott leaned on his horn and roared through the red light. Six lanes of traffic on Van Ness with the green light on their side lurched forward then slithered to a halt in the same breath. A barrage of blaring car horns trailed after him.

Geary Boulevard rose up on the other side of the intersection. Scott tightened his grip on the wheel and braced for the jarring impact. His Honda sedan bottomed out on the steep incline, but maintained its speed. With the gas pedal floored, the car accelerated and closed in on a slow moving SUV switching lanes. Scott jumped on his horn again. The SUV froze, straddling both lanes to block his path.

"Idiot," he snarled and shouldered his way past the other driver.

Traffic was everywhere, but when wasn't it in San Francisco? He weaved between two cars, jerked out from behind a MUNI bus and still had a stream of vehicles ahead.

His cell phone rang. He snatched it from its holder on the dashboard. "Yes."

"Scott, where are you?" Jane squeezed out between sobs. "You said you'd be here."

Hearing his wife cry split him in two. His own tears welled, but he bottled them for later. He needed to be strong. If he let this overwhelm him, then what good was he to his family?

"I'm nearly there." His hoarse voice cracked in the middle of his short reply.

"Just hurry."

"I am."

He hung up and tossed the phone on the passenger seat next to him.

How could his life have changed so irrevocably? Just twenty minutes ago, he'd been living a normal life. A good life. He was a reporter for the *San Francisco Independent*. He and Jane had a loving marriage—a miracle in this day and age. They owned a house in a good neighborhood in the city, even with its insane real estate prices. It was the perfect place to bring up kids—and they did. They had two great kids.

Had two great kids.

It had only taken a moment to lose one of his children. Some sick freak had snatched him out from under them. How could that happen? He and Jane took every precaution. They'd entrusted their children to a good school—the best they could afford with their two incomes. They'd gone private to prevent this kind of thing from happening. He palmed away the tears clouding his vision and swerved around a UPS truck.

He felt the guilt spreading through him like a virus, attacking his heart and eating away at his spirit. He'd failed his son, Sammy. Abduction was a parent's worst fear, but he hadn't wanted to be one of those parents who saw phantoms on every street corner. Putting bars on the windows and deadbolts on the doors didn't keep them out, it kept you in. But that cavalier attitude had led to this. His worst fears had been realized. Someone had taken his son.

"I'm sorry, Sammy."

A new sensation swept away his guilt. Imagination, strong and invincible, assaulted him. He'd always been able to conjure up images from secondhand accounts. That's what made him such a good reporter. He didn't just relay facts. He told stories—living, breathing stories. He turned readers into eyewitnesses—transporting them to the actual locations, inserting them inside the people present at the celebration or the tragedy. Now that talent turned on him. From the meager facts available, Scott constructed a nightmare. Sammy appeared to him, his smiling face melting into a scream as the abductor dragged him kicking and screaming inside a van. His imagination blinded him with these false, but true, images. The abduction was true, but the events were lies, just images his fear conjured up. He would know nothing until he reached the school. He stabbed down on the gas again and frightened a hybrid hatchback out of his way.

At the cost of a door mirror snapped off against the corner of a Safeway trailer truck, he made it to the school. Half a dozen SFPD cars were staked out in front. Was that all his son warranted—six patrol cars? Not that these cops were any good now. Talk about closing the stable door after the horse had bolted. Where were these bastards when Sammy was being snatched?

He ground to an untidy halt in front of the cop cars and abandoned his Honda in the roadway. Let the city tow it. He spilled out onto the asphalt, gathered himself up and raced towards the school gate. He hadn't gotten ten feet when his cell rang. He darted back and snatched it off the car seat. He hit the green key on the run.

His antics drew the attention of two uniformed officers protecting the school's perimeter. Seeing him charging towards the school gates, they moved as a unit to intercept him.

Scott put the phone to his ear, "I'm here, babe. It's okay. I'm here."

"That's good to know."

The voice on the line chilled him. Instead of his wife's soft tones, he heard a voice that was harsh, blunted by an electronic disguise. The words came out robotic and demonic. Scott recognized the voice, but he hadn't heard it in eight years. The raw adrenaline left him as swiftly as it had come and he ground to a halt with the cops still racing towards him.

"It's been a long time, Scott. I thought I'd reintroduce myself."

"You've got Sammy." It was a statement, not a question.

"Yes."

Scott feared asking the obvious question, but there was no way around it. "What do you want?"

The cops caught up to him. They bombarded him with questions and threats. He ignored them. He listened to the distorted voice on the line until it hung up.

He lowered the phone. A wave of nausea swept over him, taking his legs out from under him. The two cops caught him before he hit the ground.

"He has my son." Misery clung to his words. "The Piper has my son."

"Jesus Christ," one of the cops said.

THE WHITE TOWER

DOROTHY JOHNSTON

It's a mother's nightmare come true. Moira Howley's son, Niall, has been found dead at the base of a communications tower. While the authorities are content to consider it a suicide, Moira won't accept that. She knows only another mother could understand....

Crime consultant Sandra Mahoney is Moira's only hope. While juggling her own daughter, a lover, and an annoying ex-husband, Sandra will travel halfway around the world in search of the truth—a truth hidden by a web of deceit, manipulation...and murder.

ISBN 10: 0-8439-5936-3
ISBN 13: 978-0-8439-5936-9 $6.99 US/$8.99 CAN

GATES OF HADES

GREGG LOOMIS

Jason Peters works for Narcom, a company that handles jobs too dangerous or politically risky for U.S. intelligence agencies. But when his house is attacked and he barely escapes the smok-ing wreckage, he knows this new case is out of the ordinary, even for him.

Jason will travel the globe—from Washington, D.C., to the Dominican Republic, to the volca-noes of Sicily—in a desperate race to uncover the ancient secret that lies at the heart of an unimaginable—and very deadly—plot.

ISBN 10: 0-8439-5894-4
ISBN 13: 978-0-8439-5894-2 $7.99 US/$9.99 CAN